In Darkness Reborn

Alexis Morgan

POCKET STAR BOOKS

New York   London   Toronto   Sydney

Pocket Star Books
A Division of Simon & Schuster, Inc.
1230 Avenue of the Americas, New York, NY 10020

This book is a work of fiction. Names, characters, places, and incidents either are products of the author's imagination or are used fictitiously. Any resemblance to actual events or locales or persons, living or dead, is entirely coincidental.

First Pocket Star Books paperback edition July 2007

POCKET STAR BOOKS and colophon are registered trademarks of Simon & Schuster, Inc.

For information about special discounts for bulk purchases, please contact Simon & Schuster Special Sales at 1-800-456-6798 or business@simonandschuster.com.

Illustration by Craig White; design by Lisa Litwack

Manufactured in the United States of America

10 9 8 7 6 5 4 3 2 1

ISBN-13: 978-1-4165-4658-0
ISBN-10:   1-4165-4658-8

I would like to dedicate this book to my wonderful son-in-law, Jeremiah Brown. Thank you for making my daughter so happy and for being an all-around great guy. Congratulations on finishing your master's degree—we're so proud of you!

Acknowledgments

I would like to thank and acknowledge all of the writers and industry professionals I have met over the course of my career. Your generosity with your time, knowledge, and friendship has made this journey even more special. This business would be pretty lonely without all of you.

In Darkness Reborn

Chapter 1

Get that goddamned freak out of here!"

The injured Paladin could barely speak, but there was no mistaking the venom in his words. Ignoring the tirade, Barak quietly picked up a tray of sterile instruments and put it away. After arranging the equipment exactly the way Dr. Young preferred it, he walked past the man and deliberately made eye contact, taking a warrior's pride in knowing he wasn't the one who'd blinked first.

The patient had been conscious for just over an hour and had been cursing Barak the whole time. Paladins were never easy patients, but having one of their mortal enemies near made them worse. Barak hated the Paladins enough to take pleasure in seeing his enemy chained down while he walked free. Drawing a deep breath, he savored the sweet taste of the man's fury.

When he'd entered this world, he'd fully expected to die at the end of a Paladin's sword. That hadn't happened, leaving him alone in this confusing place. Since he could not defeat his enemy in combat, he would at least irritate them with his continued presence in their midst.

Dr. Laurel Young stood concentrating on the machines that monitored the Paladin's progress. Judging from the frown line between her eyebrows, she wasn't pleased.

Knowing the request that was coming, Barak started for the door.

The guards manning the lobby desk looked up, preventing him from slamming his fist against the wall. Any such action on his part would be reported to Dr. Neal, the local head of Research, who in turn would pass along the information to the Regents. For now, they tolerated Barak's continued existence, as long as he did not become too much of a problem. For Laurel's sake, he behaved most of the time.

It was for Dr. Young's sake that he had walked out of the lab; he owed her that much. Roiling with anger, he decided to work it off in the gym.

He pushed the elevator button, still marveling at the conveniences that humans took for granted. Their casual use of power appalled him at times. They had no idea how blessed they were. Or how wasteful.

When the elevator doors slid open, a pair of the building guards immediately moved to one side of the elevator, as if to make room for him. More likely they were avoiding any possible contact.

He forced a small smile, acknowledging their false courtesy. As they traveled in uncomfortable silence, he wondered if he was wrong to assume everyone had a hidden agenda. Maybe they had problems of their own and meant no slight. But until he better understood these humans and how their minds worked, he could only rely on his instincts, and it was safer to assume they were the enemy than to be stabbed in the back by a false friend.

Several seconds later, he escaped the close confines of the elevator. Pausing outside the locker room, he reached out with his senses to see if anyone was inside. The gods were with him; the whole place was empty. Inside, he stripped down and pulled on the shorts he kept in his assigned locker. After tying back his shoulder-length hair, he entered the gym.

He closed his eyes, searching for the silence deep within to let go of the day's frustrations. Moving slowly at first, he lost himself in the ha'kai, the "death dance" of his people. Through its familiar rhythms, he could almost imagine himself back home. The origin of the dance was lost in antiquity, but those who learned its graceful, lethal maneuvers kept the practice alive in his world. Here, in this land of too much light, it was an unknown art. There was so much confusion in this new life that he drew comfort from bringing this one little part of his world with him. His peace was short-lived as four Paladins came swaggering into the gym. They dropped their weapons cases on the tiled floor and drew their swords.

The closest one groused, "Hell, nobody told me that they let that gray-haired bastard roam free. Hey, Roy, I thought Seattle had a leash law."

Raucous laughter rang out as the biggest one said, "Maybe we should call Animal Control and have them haul it off to the pound with all the other flea-bitten dogs."

Barak finished a last twirl and lunge before acknowledging the intruders' presence. As he picked up a towel and wiped his face, he smiled, relishing the chance to teach them some respect for his kind.

"Better the dogs for company than two-legged cowards. Or do you consider four against one to be honorable?" he sneered.

Their response was immediate and predictable. The biggest one took a step toward Barak. "Listen here, asshole, I wouldn't go around calling other people cowards. The only reason you're still alive is that nitwit Dr. Young took pity and let you hide behind her skirts."

That did it—they'd crossed the line by treating Laurel Young with disrespect. Before, he would have settled for running them in circles without doing any real damage. Now he would demand payment in pain and blood. And if word of their taunts got back to Devlin Bane, they'd be lucky if they lost but one life each.

He calmly crossed the room to the rack of swords

used for practice. After rejecting several, he settled for the one that came closest to the feel of his own, which had been lost to him.

The biggest Paladin stood a few steps ahead of the others, no doubt planning on challenging Barak first.

Barak took a couple of practice swings with the sword before touching the blade to his forehead to signal his readiness to fight. Judging from his opponent's stance, the young fool depended on size rather than skill to win fights. That might work when it came to fists, but he would soon learn the error of his ways.

Barak held his sword at the ready and used his other hand to encourage his opponent to attack. "Shall we dance, Paladin? Have you any skill with that sword, or is it only for decoration?"

Roy's face flushed with anger. "I'm ready whenever you are."

The other Paladins arranged themselves along the wall, calling out their encouragement. "That's it, Roy. Teach him to respect his betters!"

Just as Barak expected, the young Paladin lunged forward, using his weapon with graceless power. If his blow had actually connected, it might well have taken Barak's head off. Roy stumbled past, fighting to regain his balance. It didn't take much longer for Barak to have young Roy pinned against the wall, the point of his sword at the boy's throat. The flash of fear in Roy's eyes was sweet.

"What was that about teaching me respect for my betters?" Barak crowded closer. "I'm listening."

When Roy didn't respond, Barak indulged his anger with a flick of his wrist, slashing a shallow but painful cut down the side of Roy's face. To give the boy credit, he stood his ground, ignoring both the pain and the blood dripping down his cheek.

Barak leaned in close, letting Roy see his full rage. His lips drew back, baring his teeth. "If I ever hear another disrespectful word out of your mouth regarding Dr. Young, I will take great pride in slicing you into tiny little pieces. Then I'll report you to Devlin Bane and Blake Trahern and let them finish the job. Do I make myself clear?"

Roy nodded very slowly. The two scariest Paladins in Seattle, Devlin and his friend Trahern were the stuff of legends. Maybe Roy and his friends hadn't yet heard that Dr. Young and Bane were mates, but it wasn't Barak's job to inform them. It was enough that he defended her honor.

"Get out of here." He'd turned his back to the rest of the pack, saying without words that he considered them to be of no real threat. "And the next time you see me, I suggest you walk away. Better yet, run."

Another voice entered into the conversation. "Is there a problem?"

"Nothing I can't handle." Barak stepped away from Roy and picked up a towel to wipe the tip of his sword. "I was just teaching young Roy here that size doesn't always determine the winner."

Devlin Bane made Roy look a bit on the small side. "Really? I've never found it to be a handicap." He sauntered over to the sword rack and picked one at random, then eyed Roy, obviously taking the younger man's measure. "Let's see, there are two of us and four of you. What do you think, Barak? Would it be unfair odds?"

Barak considered the matter. "Maybe if we promised to use only our weaker hands."

Devlin's grin was pure danger as he switched the sword to his off hand. "I like it."

Barak did the same and moved to stand next to his mortal enemy. "We shouldn't hurt them too badly, though. I don't feel like mopping blood up off the floor."

"Fair enough." Devlin turned to Roy's companions, who looked as if they were about to make a dash for the door. "Come on, gentlemen, pick up your weapons. I've got just enough time to show you how it's done in the real world."

Barak watched their exhausted opponents stumble out of the gym, glad to escape with only their pride bruised. Bane hadn't asked what had caused the initial confrontation, probably assuming Barak's presence alone had been enough to trigger a Paladin's inborn need to fight. Barak didn't tell him any different.

"Were you looking for me?" Barak kept his voice neutral and his eyes focused on his sword.

"Laurel said you were probably up here." Bane returned his borrowed weapon to the rack with more force than was necessary. Clearly his temper still simmered just shy of a full boil.

"She shouldn't send you to check on me." Though it was just like her to do so.

"She worries."

"And you hate that." As a physician and Handler, Laurel Young took a deep personal interest in all her charges, even one who was her lover's lifelong enemy.

Devlin Bane shrugged. "How I feel about it doesn't matter."

Barak understood the Paladin's obvious frustration. People of his own world and the Paldins' world were born to hate each other. Unfortunately, Laurel Young didn't accept the normal way of things. Since Barak and Devlin both cared about her, they were forced to set that hatred aside and find some common ground. Sparring in the gym fit that need. If they couldn't kill each other for real, they could draw satisfaction from pretending to.

"Do you require further practice?" The skirmish with the younger Paladins had wheted Barak's own appetite for violence. Exchanging blows with Bane would help him burn out some of his own temper.

Devlin stood at the weapons rack, picking up swords at random and testing their weight in his hand. "Knives or swords?"

"Swords."

And so the dance began.

In his past life, he and Devlin Bane had been mortal enemies, sworn to kill each other upon sight in the endless war that had been fought as long as memory served. In Barak's youth, he'd sworn the vows of hatred along with all of his generation. Over the years that had followed, their numbers had dwindled as death had claimed many and insanity even more.

When he'd gone looking for answers to the great madness, he'd found nothing but locked doors and accusations of cowardice. He'd argued long and hard that he didn't mind the idea of dying; he'd merely wanted to know the why of it all. Finally, he'd quit asking, quit fighting, quit everything.

Like so many from his world, he'd sought to end his pain with an honorable death at the end of a Paladin's sword. Instead, he'd found and saved a human woman who'd been pursued by one of her own kind, a man who had reeked of cowardice and greed. Laurel Young had offered Barak her healer's touch, then her friendship. To his amazement, even the strongest of the Paladins had been unwilling to refuse her the gift of Barak's life.

But that didn't mean they liked the idea.

With a powerful lunge, Devlin's sword came uncomfortably close to Barak's throat. Barak danced back out of the way and grinned at his opponent. "Is that the best you have to offer?"

"Go to hell." Bane charged again, this time whacking Barak across the back with a blow that would leave bruises.

The pain faded quickly in the triumph of using one of his favorite ha'kai movements to drop Bane to the mat with a satisfying thud, followed by a string of curses after Bane could draw enough breath to speak. Barak offered him a hand up that was rudely ignored. He backed away, giving the Paladin a chance to rejoin the battle.

"You've got to quit," Bane growled.

"Why should I, when I am winning?"

This time it was Barak who hit the floor. Even a practice blade looked sharp when held at his throat. "Not quit this. You've got to quit working with Laurel."

As Bane backed away, Barak wiped blood from his mouth with the back of his hand. He was in no mood to be ordered around by a Paladin, not even one who had stood between Barak and certain death. He slowly climbed to his feet and brought his sword back up into fighting position.

"I won't quit just because you don't want me near your woman." He backed up his vow with a flurry of thrusts that Bane met with a renewed attack of his own.

"I've never liked you being near her, you stupid bastard. That hasn't changed."

"So what has?" Then a sick feeling settled deep

inside him. If the newest members of the Paladins were talking about Laurel, perhaps others were as well.

He stepped back and dropped the point of his sword in surrender. At least Bane was breathing as hard as he was. When it came to fighting the best, a draw was nothing to be ashamed of.

"Does she know that people are talking?" Barak asked. He hoped not, knowing she would feel obligated to rush to his defense. When he'd been wounded and bleeding out his life's blood, it had been one thing. Now that he was whole again, he didn't need her to fight his battles for him.

"She probably suspects, but so far no one has had the balls to say something directly to her." They both knew that Bane would kill anyone who dared to hurt Laurel, and that Barak would help him.

"I will leave immediately." His sword felt twice as heavy as he carried it back to the rack. "It shouldn't take me long to pack."

Bane caught Barak's arm as he headed for the locker room. Barak shook his hand off but waited to see what he had to say.

"She'd only make me drag you right back here, kicking and screaming."

"Make up your mind. First you say that I have to leave; now you're telling me I must stay."

Unless he was mistaken, there was a certain amount of sympathy in Bane's eyes. "I'm working on a plan. The only way she'll let you go is if she believes that you'll be happier with the move."

That was unlikely when Laurel was the only real friend he had, but for her sake he'd be willing to dissemble a bit. Barak nodded slowly. "Tell me about this plan."

"Explain to me again how this came about."

Dr. Laurel Young glared at the two of them with her hands on her hips. Barak drew some comfort from knowing that most of her temper was aimed directly at Devlin, not him. She was right to question her lover's motives in finding Barak a new position within the Regents' organization. As far as she knew, Barak was perfectly content to work in her lab. Now, with no warning at all, Devlin—hardly Barak's biggest fan—was claiming that Barak wanted nothing more out of life than the opportunity to work in the Geology Department.

She rounded on Barak when Devlin started repeating himself. "You've never said anything about this before."

Keeping his eyes firmly on Laurel, Barak did his best to look both innocent and sincere. "I never thought it would be possible. But when we were in St. Louis helping out Trahern, Devlin learned that the study of stone has been a special interest of mine. Until we knew for certain that the transfer would work out, I didn't want to say anything."

Bane didn't know exactly how special that interest really was, and that was a secret Barak planned on taking to his grave.

"If you're sure . . ."

Her easy acceptance of his transfer told him all too clearly how difficult having him around had become for her. He wanted to shake her for not having told him, but that would ruin his and Devlin's carefully laid plan.

"I'm sure, Laurel." He stepped forward to take her hand, ignoring the waves of disapproval coming from Devlin. "I need to feel useful. You have given me time to learn the ways of this world, but my value in the lab is limited. It's time for me to make my own way, and this is how I can best be of service."

She narrowed her eyes. After a long look at her lover, as if to warn him not to say anything, she pulled Barak close for a hug. Barak knew he shouldn't prolong the embrace, but it had been so long since anyone had been willing to hold him. . . .

Rather than test Bane's patience, Barak broke off the hug and put a small distance between himself and Laurel. When he saw the small tear trailing down her cheek, he allowed himself the small privilege of wiping it away with the pad of his thumb.

"There's no call for tears, Laurel. It's not like I'm going far. The Geology Department is located in the Seattle Underground, not far from Devlin's office."

Devlin pushed himself back into the conversation. "Yeah, and let me tell you that we're all thrilled, knowing he'll be so close by. Trahern's already planning a tea party in Barak's honor, and Brenna has him practicing drinking out of tiny cups with his pinky held out."

The image of the cold-eyed Trahern serving tea and scones had Laurel smiling again—no doubt the effect Devlin had been aiming for. Neither he nor Barak could tolerate seeing her unhappy.

"Well, at least you'll be in good company." This time her smile was more genuine. "You know that you'll always be welcome back here with me."

Not if Bane had anything to say about it—but Barak left that unsaid.

"Like hell he's coming here!"

Penn Sebastian gave his shopping basket a shove, sending it careening into the brick wall. The new dent barely showed, and Lacey wondered how much more abuse it could take before her brother had to go scrounging for another one.

"I didn't have any say in the matter, Penn." Hot tempers were the status quo among Paladins, but lately Penn's had been worse than usual. Ever since his sword hand had been badly damaged in a vicious battle, he'd become more and more volatile.

Penn crossed his arms over his chest and blocked her way into the Center. "So why are *you* getting saddled with this low-life Other?"

Though Lacey agreed with Penn, she reined in her own temper. If Penn got busted for fighting one more time, the Regents might confine him to quarters or, worse yet, decide that he was too unstable to continue on as a Paladin. And his kind didn't retire to enjoy their old age: a Paladin either died in combat or he was chained to a steel slab and executed.

"Evidently he wasn't working out in the medical lab. According to Devlin Bane, this Other of his has a special interest in geology. In exchange for major funding increases, my department head agreed to take him on as a lab assistant on a trial basis."

According to her boss, the Other was actually to be treated as an equal by everyone, but she wasn't about to tell Penn that. The whole idea made *her* absolutely furious; she could just imagine how her brother would react.

"Meaning what? That for a few bucks, Bane keeps Barak from sniffing around his girlfriend? Instead, the scum will be hitting on my sister." Penn clearly wasn't going to back down anytime soon.

"It's more than a few bucks, and I can use the help. Toting all that equipment around isn't easy, especially on the steeper slopes." She smiled with a confidence she didn't really feel. "I'll make sure he knows I have a big, bad Paladin for a brother. That should scare him into behaving."

"Not anymore." Penn tried without success to flex his right hand. "I couldn't hold a sword long enough to scare anybody."

The doctors had warned Penn there was no guarantee that he'd ever get full motion back in his hand. An Other had come close to severing Penn's hand completely, and the recovery process had been slow and painful. She couldn't remember the last time Penn had been really happy.

"You're not helpless, Penn. If you were, they wouldn't trust you to guard the Center."

That much was true, but holding a gun or rifle wasn't the same as being able to fight with a sword. Until he could handle a blade, Penn couldn't protect the barrier in the tunnels down below the city and the surrounding area. The desire to serve near the barrier beat strongly in the heart of every Paladin, and Penn could feel the fluctuations in the beautifully colored sheet of energy that separated their world from dark madness on the other side. Until he could do the job he was born to do, Penn would be a miserable man.

"Well, I've got to get inside or I'll be late for work." She would have given her brother a quick hug, but he was in his usual disguise of a derelict living on the streets. If she got too close, some of that grime and stink he worked so hard to perfect would get on her clothes.

He grinned. "What? No sisterly kiss for me before I let you pass? How about a hug?"

She laughed and held up her hands, backing away. "No way, bro. Not unless you're willing to pay my cleaning bill."

"All right, I'll let you get inside." Then he turned serious again. "But if this Barak fellow gives you any trouble at all, I want to be the first to know. Even if

I can't handle a sword, his kind isn't immune to bullets. I'd be glad to remind him of that fact."

"Thanks . . . I think."

After keying in the security code, she stepped into the dim interior of the Center. Leaning against the cool tiled wall, she waited for her pulse to slow down. It was hard enough to deal with her own frustrations without having to take on Penn's as well.

Her boss had warned her not to walk into the meeting with a chip on her shoulder. Somehow she was supposed to hide her feelings from her boss, Devlin Bane, and the Other himself. How could she, when she hated and despised everything about the Others and the havoc they caused whenever the barrier went down?

At least Dr. Louis had given her some warning. He'd called her at home last night to break the news, knowing if he'd waited until she'd reported to work, she would likely have walked right out again. It had taken her a solid hour to unclench her teeth. How was she supposed to work side by side with one of the monsters that had not only killed her brother twice but had nearly crippled him as well?

Was any amount of money worth the constant uproar over a monster in their midst? Why didn't someone just skewer the Other and be done with it? She'd be glad to provide the sword.

Lacey pushed herself away from the wall and started the long walk down to her office, reminding herself each step of the way of all the badly needed equipment this Barak's presence could bring. Though Dr. Louis would hang onto most of the money for his own pet projects, the small fraction he'd promised her would be a welcome addition to her funding.

Once she'd been sure that she could be civil, she had tried without success to call Laurel Young, hoping to talk to her about Barak. She'd email the Handler later to see if she'd be willing to answer a few questions over lunch in the next couple of days.

Until Laurel had forced Devlin Bane to spare Barak's life, she'd been well respected. Now there were grumblings about the Handler, and maybe that was why they'd found a new spot for the Other. The Geology Department was certainly less high profile than the medical branch of Research.

Lacey checked the time. If she hurried, she could record the latest readings from Mount St. Helens before reporting to her boss's office for the official meeting. Focusing on work might keep her calm enough to make it through the day.

On the other hand, maybe she'd do everyone a favor and kill the Other herself.

Chapter 2

$\mathcal{B}$arak watched Bane pace the floor while the nervous gaze of Dr. Louis, the head of the Geology Department, flitted back and forth between the Paladin and Barak.

Which of them worried the elderly professor more? Devlin Bane, the most fearsome of all the Paladins, or Barak himself? Since the professor had never met one of Barak's kind before, he probably expected him to drool and make animal noises. If Barak's existence didn't depend on his continued good behavior, he might have indulged in some theatrics just to see the older man's reaction. Bane might find it amusing.

Or not. The Paladin had gone to great lengths to arrange this meeting; he wouldn't appreciate anything that might jeopardize its success.

Footsteps out in the hallway had all three men watching the door to see if they continued on past, or if the mysterious fourth member of the party had finally arrived. The doorknob began to turn, and Barak leaned back in his chair, doing his best to look disinterested.

Then the door opened. Why hadn't Bane told him that his new coworker wasn't a dusty old geology professor but a beautiful young woman? One with hair the color of the sun and huge blue eyes filled with a fierce intelligence and barely controlled fury. Her rapid pulse thrummed in his ears, and her breath was shallow. Her cheekbones were flushed with color, her passion running high.

After a brief hesitation, he rose to his feet and waited for someone to make introductions. Instead, the human female took matters into her own hands.

She gave Devlin Bane and her boss a curt nod. "Devlin. Dr. Louis."

At first Barak thought she was going to ignore his presence, but once again she surprised him. She closed the distance between them and held out her hand. He was familiar with the custom of shaking hands, but so far none of the other humans had extended that offer to him.

He almost fumbled but managed to fit his hand to hers with some semblance of grace. She tightened her grip briefly as she said, "I'm Lacey Sebastian. *Dr.* Lacy Sebastian."

Her slight emphasis on her title was a clear reminder of who would be in charge. He briefly met her gaze head-on, then looked away before it could be taken as a challenge to her authority. It wasn't in him to be subservient to anyone, but he'd prefer to ease his way with as few complications as possible.

"My name is Barak. Barak q'Young." He nearly smiled when Devlin flinched at his newly acquired last name. Laurel had gifted Barak with use of her surname when he had needed one for all the official papers. It was yet another claim he had on Bane's woman, and the Paladin's displeasure pleased him.

Lacey withdrew her hand and smiled a bit too brightly at her boss. "Sir, shall we get started? The mountain is rumbling again, and I would like to get back to the monitors."

"Yes, of course, Dr. Sebastian." Dr. Louis shuffled the stack of papers in front of him as if searching for the crucial one. Finally, he settled for lacing his fingers together and laying his hands on top of the files. "We all know that Mr., uh, q'Young has agreed to come work in the Geology Department here at the Center."

The man looked as if he'd swallowed something bitter. The woman felt the same way as her boss; she was just better at hiding her feelings. But they were there, running full throttle just under the surface.

Barak studied her profile, liking what he saw. There was strength in that face, and intelligence as well. But it was her energy that drew his eye. His hand still tingled from their brief touch. How much more powerful would it be to hold her in his arms or to taste her lips? Lacey Sebastian had a pool of deep passions she kept carefully hidden, just as the volcanoes she studied kept their true natures blanketed by snow and ice. For the first time, he felt the faint stirrings of real interest in his new job.

"What will my duties be?" He settled back into his chair.

Dr. Louis shuffled his papers again before finally answering. "You'll be working alongside Dr. Sebastian, helping with her studies."

Dr. Sebastian's smile grew more brittle around the edges. "I'm still working on the specifics. I'll have to let you know."

Barak didn't push for a better answer. It didn't take a psychic to know that Dr. Sebastian definitely needed additional time to adjust to the situation that had been thrust upon her. Besides, he was in no mood for a major confrontation, especially with her—unless it involved them getting naked and burning off their anger with some hot, sweaty sex. But the chances of a human female wanting to couple with him, particularly one who knew who and what he was, were pretty slim. He shifted slightly in his chair to hide his physical response to her.

"So everything is settled, and I can go?" Devlin already had his hand on the doorknob, ready to exit.

Barak rose to his feet and offered Lacey his most formal bow. "Let me know when and where I should report for duty, Dr. Sebastian. My number is in the file that Devlin put together for you." Nodding curtly in the direction of Dr. Louis, he followed Devlin out the door.

When they were safely out of hearing, Devlin slowed his steps. "Look, Barak, I know this sucks for you, but it's for the best. We both know that."

"I agree."

Bane looked at Barak as if he had expected more of an argument, but Barak wasn't in the mood to fight. Working in the Geology Department certainly involved considerable risk on his part, but right now it seemed worth it. That might change as the days played out, but at least for now he'd be working alongside one of the few human women who apparently wasn't afraid to touch him, even if she did hate him.

For the first time in days he felt like smiling. Maybe a small celebration was in order.

"I don't know about you, Devlin, but I'm thirsty. What do you say about stopping somewhere, as you would say, for a cold one?"

Devlin didn't hesitate. "You're on."

Isolating herself in her office failed to soothe her. A hot cup of tea didn't help, either. Finally, Lacey pulled out the big guns and went straight for the chocolate. Half a dozen miniature candy bars later, the knots in her stomach and the pounding behind her eyes began to ease up. Leaning back in her desk chair, she closed her eyes and savored the last two bars in the bag.

She promised herself ten extra minutes on the treadmill later for her sins, but she couldn't bring herself to regret one single bite. She had far more important problems to worry about than a few extra calories. Like what she was going to do with an Other haunting her every working moment. She'd grown up hearing about Penn's encounters with the monsters from the world across the barrier, and she felt betrayed at a gut level where trust would never come as easy again.

No one had ever told her how very human the Others looked—or that one could be so handsome. She had no idea what exactly she'd been expecting when she'd stepped into the conference room, but Barak q'Young certainly wasn't it.

Those silver eyes had shown no signs of madness, only a quiet intelligence that saw far too much. If she hadn't been honor bound to hate the man and his entire race, she might even have thought him attractive despite his pale coloring.

It was hard to guess his age, with that dark hair shot through with silver highlights. Thirty? Forty? Maybe his kind aged slowly, like the Paladins did. But none of that mattered. She had no reason to be thinking so much about Barak, except to decide what duties he would be best suited for.

Taking out the trash? Mopping floors? Cleaning bathrooms?

She took some malicious pleasure in the idea, but she also knew that her boss would not allow her to get away with such nonsense. If the man really did have some knowledge of geology, then she would avail herself of his talent as much as possible. With the department's limited resources, she couldn't afford not to. It was hard enough to get Professor Louis to fund any of her research because he didn't believe she'd ever find a way to predict eruptions or earthquakes. The only reason he gave her any support was because her brother was a Paladin. That relationship carried considerable weight within the Regents' organization.

The outer lab door opened and slammed closed. She sat up straighter and wiped her mouth with a napkin to hide the evidence that she'd been indulging herself in a pity party of massive proportions. The soft squeak of athletic shoes on the concrete floor made it easy to track her guest's approach to her door, and Lacey smiled in anticipation. A knock wasn't long in coming.

"Hey, Ruthie, come on in."

Ruth Prizzi, departmental secretary and unofficial mother hen to all, popped into the room like the whirlwind that she was. No one knew Ruthie's exact age, but there wasn't a person in the lab who could keep up with her. She perched on the chair closest to Lacey's desk.

"So, did you get to meet him?"

There was no use in playing coy. There were hard-bitten police detectives who could learn a thing or two from Ruthie about interrogation techniques.

"Yes, we were introduced."

Ruthie frowned at her over the top of her half-glasses. "Details, my dear, I want to hear details."

How much could Lacey tell her friend without giving away the turmoil that still churned in her stomach? But better to chance revealing too much than to let Ruthie get the idea she was trying to hide something.

"His name is Barak q'Young. He bowed when he left, although he didn't act quite so respectful to Dr. Louis."

"Smart man. We both know where the real brains of the department are."

"Ruthie! Don't say things like that. Dr. Louis is a well-known authority in his field." That was true, but he only looked at what could be measured and quantified. Number crunching was an important part of any scientific endeavor, but she couldn't re-member the last time he'd worked out in the field. The Earth was a living entity, moving and changing all the time. To her way of thinking, if they ever hoped to find a way to predict earthquakes and vol-canic activity, they needed to get their hands dirty once in a while.

"I don't care how good he is. You and I both know that he isn't up to handling problems of this magnitude. If he were, he wouldn't be shuffling this . . . this Other off on to you."

"I *am* the junior member of the team."

Ruth wagged an arthritic finger at Lacey. "Well,

we will argue about that more later. Right now, I want to know what this Barak looks like so I'll recognize him when I see him. Wouldn't want to embarrass the department by treating our newest member to an unscheduled body search by the guards."

Lacey couldn't help but laugh. "You are so bad, Ruthie."

"I'm just trying to do my job, Dr. Sebastian." The twinkle in her bright blue eyes belied the outrage in her voice.

"We certainly wouldn't want to risk an incident," Lacey agreed.

Lacey's ruffled feathers soothed a bit, and Ruthie sat further back in her chair, all ready to listen. Lacey knew she'd put it off as long as she could. The longer she dodged Ruthie's questions, the more likely she was to arouse the older woman's suspicions.

"He's tall, maybe six-two, muscular without being bulky. You know, more like Cullen Finley than Devlin Bane. His eyes are a striking silver with a black ring around the iris. His hair is long, although he wore it tied back. The color is unusual—black mixed with shades of silver. It looked strange on a man I would guess to be in his midthirties."

"You're giving me facts, Lacey, but not context. Is he good looking or not?"

"I didn't notice."

She'd noticed all right, but she still hadn't figured out the strong reaction she'd felt when their hands had touched. The simple, businesslike handshake had haunted her for the hours since their brief meeting.

Luckily Ruthie's cell phone chose that moment to ring. The older woman stood as she snapped her phone shut.

"His Majesty is calling. He's probably mislaid a paper clip or something else equally important." She gave Lacey a piercing look. "Don't think this conversation is over."

"Yes, ma'am," Lacey said, executing a mock salute.

"Don't be pert with me, not if you ever want to see your grant money again."

After Ruthie disappeared, Lacey closed her eyes and listened to the fading sounds of squeaky shoes. When the doors were firmly closed again, she reached for the telephone. She was determined to operate from a position of power as much as she could. Waiting for Barak to give up and call her would be both weak and petty.

She punched in the phone number he'd left for her and crossed her fingers. With any luck she'd get his voice mail, meaning she could leave him a terse message and hang up. But after only two rings, he picked up.

"Barak q'Young speaking."

His voice brushed lightly over her nerve endings, sending a shiver right through the heart of her. The unsettling feeling left her mouth cotton dry, resulting in a prolonged silence while she fumbled for her water bottle.

"Dr. Sebastian, are you all right?"

She forced a swallow of water past the lump in her throat. "How did you know it was me?"

"No one else would be calling." The words were said with brutal honesty, but no self-pity.

"Ah, um, I see." She didn't *want* to feel any sympathy for him. "I would like to review your duties with you. When can you start?"

"I'm available now if that isn't too soon, Dr. Sebastian. Otherwise, whenever you find convenient."

"How about an hour from now? That would allow me enough time to finish up a few things." Like figuring out what she could trust him to do. After all, no one really knew what his agenda had been in crossing the barrier.

"That would be fine. And Dr. Sebastian?"

"Yes."

"Thank you for not refusing the offer of my assistance."

Better to start off with the truth. "I had no choice."

His sigh came across loud and clear. "I feared as much. I will speak with Devlin Bane immediately."

Was that a faint note of hurt in his voice? She surprised them both by saying, "No, don't. I really can use the help."

This time the silence came from his end of the line. "Are you certain? That you could use *my* help?"

"I don't think I could swear to that, Mr. q'Young, but there is certainly more to do around here than one person can keep up with."

"Then you may expect me in an hour. And please call me Barak. I have yet to grow used to my new surname."

"I'll meet you outside the alley entrance and escort you inside." She disconnected the call before she gave in to the temptation to take it all back.

Barak paced the perimeter of the gym, wishing like crazy that the hands on the clock would move. If he didn't know better, he would have sworn that they had been frozen in place for the past fifteen minutes. He could leave for the Center after another two laps. Maybe the hour would have passed more quickly if he'd reported back to Laurel's lab and offered to stock supplies for her, but he didn't want her to see him right now.

She was the only human who knew him well enough to sense his moods. If she suspected that his reasons for leaving her lab weren't purely for his own selfish reasons, there would be hell to pay, to quote one of the Paladins' more colorful expressions.

One more lap to go before he would start the brief walk down to the Center to meet Lacey Sebastian. As her image filled his mind, his feet sped up. He liked the way her hair carried the warmth of the sun in its color, and the way her bright blue eyes had widened in surprise when she'd first seen him. It was as if she'd reacted to him the way a woman reacted to a man she found attractive, not a man she saw only as the enemy. Maybe he was reading more into her reaction than he should, but he could hope. With effort, he resumed a slower pace. Finally, he turned the last corner and left the gym behind.

As usual, the guards pointedly ignored him as he walked out the front door of the building. He pulled on his sunglasses, still not adjusted to this sun-bright world. The warmth felt good on his skin, but he always took care to wear a sunblock since he had no idea what prolonged exposure to such intense light would do.

The walk would do him good, though. He spent so much time alone that it pleased him to lose himself in the throng of tourists and locals crowding the sidewalks.

How would they react if they discovered the truth of his existence? Panic? Hatred? It still amazed him to know that the Regents and their warriors, the Paladins, had managed to keep his world and its people secret from their fellow citizens. Devlin had told him that it had been easier in more primitive times and had grown harder as technology continued to shrink their world. Even so, Devlin insisted most people wouldn't believe what was right in front of them unless forced to do so.

That was fine with Barak. He had no desire to be used for experiments by some government agency.

He only wanted to be allowed to live out his solitary life in peace—even if it was lonely.

He slowed as he turned the last corner before the Center. On this morning's earlier visit with Devlin they had managed to avoid running into any Paladins, but this time it was unlikely that he'd be able to approach the Center unchallenged. Bracing himself for the worst, he entered the alley that sheltered the secret entrance of the underground labyrinth that housed the headquarters of his mortal enemies.

As he scanned the area for possible threats, he walked by one of the many homeless people who haunted the streets of Seattle. The unmistakable click of a handgun told him he'd just made a mistake, possibly a fatal one.

"Where do you think you're going, you alien bastard?" The man reeked of filth and fury. "One wrong move and you're dead—which you would have been weeks ago if Bane had been thinking with his brain instead of his prick." The hatred was emphasized by the painful jab of a gun barrel into Barak's back as a grimy hand grabbed his collar.

There had been a time when he would have welcomed death, even at the hands of a hated Paladin, but no longer. As Barak shifted into battle position, a familiar voice rang out.

"Penn! Let him go this minute."

"Stay out of this, Lacey. I caught him sneaking around the Center. Even Devlin Bane can't protect him now."

Lacey came closer, her feminine scent filling Barak's senses. If he attacked this Penn now, she might get hurt.

"Back off right now, Penn. And don't tell me that you've forgotten that Barak was coming to work in the lab with me."

"No one told me he was expected today." Penn released Barak's collar and shoved him forward.

Barak spun and shoved back. "I do not report to the likes of you, Paladin."

Despite the layers of dirt, there was no mistaking the Paladin for other than a warrior. He came charging right back, murder in his eyes. Barak moved into an attack stance, ready to meet the bullets with his bare fists if necessary.

Lacey Sebastian shoved her way between them. Did the woman have no sense at all? Barak snagged Lacey's arm to pull her behind him, only to realize his opponent was doing the same thing.

"Let go of her, Paladin. Or does your kind fight behind their women?" he sneered, his temper talking now.

"I don't need her help to teach you some manners, scum."

Penn managed to get past Lacey long enough to slam his fist into Barak's jaw, snapping his head back. Retaliating, Barak landed a solid kick to the Paladin's gut.

"Enough!" Lacey grabbed both of them by the front of their shirts and used their own momentum to fling both of them to the ground. She stood over them, glaring down at them.

"Darn it, Penn, do you want to end up getting hauled off to jail again? Devlin said that the next time it happened, he'd let you rot in there. And you!" she said, turning her anger in Barak's direction. "Is this going to happen often? If so, you can just find yourself another job. I don't need this crap."

"Aw, Lacey . . ."

"Don't start with me, Penn Sebastian. You know I can take care of myself—you're the one who taught me!"

The other man's name caught Barak's attention. "Penn *Sebastian*?"

"Yeah, he's my brother." She shot Penn a dirty look. "Although right now I'm not too proud of the fact."

"In that case, I offer you my sympathy, Dr. Sebastian." Barak pushed himself back up to his feet and brushed off his jeans.

"Go to hell, Other." Penn also stood up, ignoring the new layer of dirt on his clothing. "I don't want the likes of you near my sister."

Barak sneered. "You have no say in the matter. Why don't you go back to playing with trash, where you belong?"

Lacey snapped, "Shut up, Other, or I'll have you scrubbing the lab floor with a toothbrush for the next month."

She stared at him for several seconds in angry

silence before stepping back. "I hope you two are ready to quit acting like five-year-olds, because I don't have time for this. And you both should know better."

Barak took a step backward to show his willingness to end the confrontation. "My apologies, Dr. Sebastian. I spoke out of turn."

Penn shot Barak one more defiant look before doing the same. "Next time, warn me when he's supposed to be here, Lacey. If he shows up unexpectedly, he's fair game, the Regents be damned." He stalked away, shoving his gun back in his waistband.

"Penn—"

"Not now, Lacey. Take him with you and get the hell out of here."

Lacey stared after her brother, a look of raw pain on her face. Barak turned his eyes in the opposite direction, knowing it would embarrass her that he'd witnessed such a private moment between the two siblings.

"Come on, Barak. We're overdue in the lab."

He fell into step beside her, wishing there was something he could do to make up for this inauspicious start. He cursed Devlin Bane for not warning him that Dr. Sebastian had a brother among the Paladins. No wonder she wasn't thrilled to have him thrust upon her. They continued on in silence for another minute or two.

"I suppose I should apologize for that whole mess, Barak."

Her comment startled him. "You were not the one who was acting, as you said, like a five-year-old."

"No, but I did know that my brother was on duty today. He's . . . well, his temper does a Paladin proud. If I had been on time, none of that would have happened."

And if Lacey had been *his* sister and a Paladin had gotten near her, he would have reacted the same way Penn had—not that he liked having anything in common with the man. But why was a Paladin doing guard duty? All the other guards he'd encountered had been mortals.

He attempted to lighten the mood of their conversation. "So other than scrubbing the lab floor with my toothbrush, what duties have you assigned to me?"

Her smile was a bit forced, but it was still a smile. "I thought today I would show you the equipment we use to monitor the volcanoes in our region. You know, seismographs and the like." Then she frowned. "Or maybe you don't know. I keep forgetting how strange all of this must be for you. We know so little about your world."

And he would keep it that way. Any knowledge the Paladins gained would only be used as a weapon against his kind.

"Despite the differences, Dr. Sebastian, there are many similarities. I'm sure that I will be able to make the necessary adjustments." Just as he had made so many already in this bright and complex world.

She opened a door in a long hallway full of such doors. He made note that it was the third one down. At this point, he still had no idea if they would allow him entry to the Center on his own, or if he'd have to be met and escorted every day. That would grow tiresome, for both him and Dr. Sebastian.

"Welcome to my little bit of the world." Lacey stood back to let him enter.

The room was crammed with a great deal of machinery, the purpose of which he could only guess at. He closed his eyes and let the constant hum of so much electricity shimmer along his nerves. Hopefully, she would allow him ample time to understand what all of the dials and graphs and chattering computers were measuring.

Lacey stopped to study a series of instruments that had needles tracing out patterns in ink on paper. To him, the markings looked much like the heartbeats printed out by the machines that monitored Laurel's patients.

He risked a guess. "I would assume that these track land movements on the volcanoes? Mount St. Helens and Mount Rainier, perhaps."

Just as he spoke, one of the needles began swinging wildly, scratching out a jagged pattern on the paper. At first, he thought Lacey hadn't heard him. She stood staring at another monitor on the far wall as its readings turned blood red. His stomach roiled as if the floor had lurched and swayed beneath his feet. With effort, he ignored the powerful urge to grab on to something for support. The tremors were too far away to affect the Seattle area, yet he felt them deep in his gut and in his bones. Luckily, Lacey didn't question his startled reaction to the alarms sounding.

Lacey met his gaze with a grim smile. "You guessed right. That's Mount St. Helens saying hi." Then she pointed to the other screen. "And that's the barrier going down."

Which meant his people and hers were battling in the tunnels where the two worlds collided. The two of them could only watch the brightly lit dials and wonder how many would die.

Chapter 3

$\mathcal{B}$arak drew a shuddering breath, his empty sword hand clenched at his side. Perhaps if the Paladins were successful in restoring the barrier quickly enough, no one would have to bleed. His kind had lost so many already, and he couldn't wish death for those of his world who were driven to seek the light.

Even worse, now that the Paladins had names and faces that he knew, he found it impossible to wish them all dead in the never-ending battle between their two peoples. The confusion made his gut ache.

Lacey stood next to him, her eyes flickering between the machine marking the heartbeat of the restless volcano and the one tracking the barrier's ups and downs. The emotions crossing her expressive face were riveting: grief, fear, and sheer determination.

When the readings from the mountain settled

and held, she turned her full attention to the barrier readings. Finally, after what had been only two minutes by the clock, the readings regained stability, all solidly back in the green. Relief washed over her face.

"Now that that's over, we can get back to business." Her attempt to sound matter-of-fact and businesslike would have succeeded if not for the slight quiver in her voice.

He let her think he hadn't noticed. "I assume you monitor all the volcanoes and fault lines."

Lacey nodded. "That's why we're here."

She led the way into her cluttered office, gesturing for him to sit down. He lifted a pile of textbooks and set them in a neat stack on the floor to clear a space for himself. Lacey rooted through some files before finding the one she'd been looking for.

"I've made up a schedule for you for the next couple of weeks." She held out a piece of paper to him. "Until we figure out exactly what your duties will entail, I've matched your work shifts to mine. Once I know what you can do, we can work you into our normal rotation. I like to have someone on duty here around the clock."

In his experience, trust was a gift to be given only sparingly. She might think he was here to prove his worth to her department, but that road ran in both directions.

"Whatever you say, Dr. Sebastian."

Leaning back in her chair, she stared at him, her

troubled eyes studying him. "I think we should make it 'Lacey,' don't you think? After all, you've seen the Sebastians at their worst, squabbling out in the street. I apologize for Penn again. His attack on you was unprovoked."

Had the roles been reversed, his own people would not have tolerated a Paladin loose in their streets.

"There is no need to apologize for your brother, Lacey." The use of her first name was a gift he would savor. "And I appreciate your willingness to let me work here. It will feel good to be of use again."

She looked puzzled. "But what about Dr. Young? I thought you had been working in her lab."

"Yes, she was kind enough to keep me busy."

Understanding was quick in coming. "Ah, busy but not especially productive. Well, my budget is such that I need to squeeze as much as I can out of every minute, especially in times like these, when the mountain is so restless. I'm glad to have someone to help shoulder some of the load. I'm scheduled to do some field work this week; how do you feel about hiking tomorrow?"

"I would enjoy some time spent in the out-doors." Especially alone with this woman, out in the fresh air and warm sunshine, just the two of them far away from the prying eyes of the entire Regents organization. Maybe for a little while, Lacey would forget *what* he was and see him for *who* he was: a man enjoying the company of an attractive woman.

Knowing how her Paladin brother would feel about it only enhanced his pleasure in the idea.

"Give me your address and I'll pick you up in the morning. Say, around six?"

"I'll be ready."

But first he'd have to call Devlin and find out what one wore to go hiking.

Lacey knew Barak was hurting from the long day, but petty as it was, she deliberately kept up the grueling pace back to her truck until thirst forced her to stop. When she paused to take a swig of water out of her bottle, Barak immediately sank down on a boulder, another sign that he regretted coming along on this little expedition.

Well, too bad. She'd been hauling equipment up and down these trails by herself for years. While she'd been doing that, how many Paladins had Barak killed? It was about time the mountain exacted a little revenge.

She reluctantly admitted to herself that he'd done everything she'd asked of him without complaint. The few questions he'd asked had been intelligent and to the point as they'd checked the field equipment set to monitor earth movements around Mount Rainier. Lately Mount St. Helens had commanded most of the department's attention, but with Rainier looming over Seattle, it never paid to get complacent. If the big mountain ever decided to blow, thousands of people would be in the path of destruction.

She shifted her pack to keep it from digging into her shoulders. Her back itched due to the day's increasing warmth, but that was easier to take than the biting cold on the mountain in the winter.

She stashed her water bottle back in her pack and set off down the trail. Barak wasn't quite so quick to get started, but she heard the crunch of gravel as he fell in behind her.

"We're almost there."

"That is good news."

Barak sounded a bit breathless. Maybe if she grilled him on what he'd learned, it would distract him from his aching feet and sunburned nose.

The trail had widened, so she waited for him to step up beside her. "So tell me, what data are we hoping to gather?"

Barak kept his eyes firmly on the trail ahead. As he replied to her questions, his responses impressed her, though she didn't want them to. Her sudden surge of sympathy for him wasn't a welcome feeling either. But judging from the stubborn tilt to his jawline, he wouldn't appreciate any sympathy.

The trailhead was about a quarter of a mile ahead. As much as she looked forward to shedding the weight of her backpack, she wasn't relishing the thought of being shut up inside the cab of the truck with Barak for the long trip back to the city. Normally she stopped to eat along the way, but that would only prolong their time together.

When they made the last turn in the trail, she

glanced at her silent companion. His normal pallor was worse than usual and she slowed her footsteps, concerned that he might not make it as far as the truck. The last thing she wanted was to have to call for an emergency pickup just because she'd been taking cheap pleasure in her new assistant's misery.

"When's the last time you drank something?"

"I ran out of water shortly after we reached that last checkpoint." His pale eyes met hers.

That was over two hours before. She didn't know which one of them was the bigger fool: Barak for not complaining, or her for not keeping a better eye on him. He stumbled slightly, his feet dragging slightly as he struggled to keep his balance. She muttered a curse as she caught him in her arms. When he tried to resist she tightened her hold, but she realized her mistake as their bodies came together in an unexpected rush of heat. Her lungs forgot how to breathe as she stared up into his handsome face. His eyes met hers briefly before glancing down at her mouth. Was he about to kiss her?

"Barak?" His name came out in a whisper.

He started to lean closer, but then shook his head as if to clear it and stepped back. Afraid he might still stumble, she wrapped one of his arms across her shoulders, ignoring her body's response to his nearness. The sudden ache in her chest reminded her that it was the wrong time, the wrong place, and this was definitely the wrong man. Surely it wasn't disappointment she was feeling, but relief.

When he resisted her help, she said, "Don't fight me, Barak. We're almost to the truck. I have extra water there."

"I'll make it." His words were slurred, but at least he was still moving.

They managed the last distance in a series of short spurts, stopping frequently to allow him to catch his breath before trudging onward. Her small pickup had never looked better to her, dents and all.

She helped Barak drop his backpack to the ground and all but shoved him inside the cab. Handing him a bottle of water, she ordered, "Sip that slowly."

After stowing their gear, she started the engine, then turned on the air-conditioning to aid Barak's recovery.

He was leaning back in the seat, his eyes closed. Every so often, he'd lift the bottle and take another slow drink. Before putting the truck in gear, she poured some of her own water on a clean cloth she had in the back.

"Here. Hold this on your forehead."

Barak did as he was told. When the cool water touched his skin, he sighed with relief. "Thank you."

She didn't want his gratitude; not when she was partly at fault for his condition. "You should feel better as soon as it cools off in here and we get some fluids into you."

His color gradually improved as they drove down the mountain. Was his kind more sensitive to the altitude?

"Feeling better?"

At first she thought he wasn't going to answer, but then he looked at her out of the corner of his eye. "Yes."

"Good. I guess we overdid it for the first time out." Well, she hadn't, but she was used to the mountain and its ways.

"It does appear that I'll have to work harder to acclimate myself." He closed his eyes, thus ending the conversation.

There was a myriad of questions she would have asked him if he hadn't been the enemy. Why had he crossed the barrier in the first place? What was his homeworld like? What was so terrible that it was worth risking almost certain death to escape across the barrier?

But those questions would go unanswered for now as her unwanted companion fell into an exhausted slumber. She drove down the mountain and back to Seattle with only an oldies station for company.

If Barak could have lifted his head from the carpet without falling on his face again, he would have asked the gods to end his misery right then and there. He'd managed to salvage at least some dignity by walking unassisted from Lacey's truck into his apartment before collapsing. Even now, hours later, he couldn't focus enough to see the clock. Judging by the glow of the streetlight coming through the window, though, it was well into the evening.

He counted to ten, then pushed himself up into a kneeling position. When his head didn't start spinning in circles, he drew a steadying breath and pulled himself up to his feet with the support of the couch. Closing his eyes, he waited for the world to right itself before risking a step toward the kitchen.

One step, two, and then three and four. He was all the way across the living room and into his small kitchen. In bad need of both food and water, he yanked open the refrigerator door. Just as he suspected, he should have gone grocery shopping days ago. He mainly ate fruit and vegetables, but there was nothing inside the fridge that looked inviting.

He grabbed a sports drink and reached for the phone. He didn't know what it said about his new life that he had the local pizza parlor on speed dial. After placing an order for his usual vegetarian pizza, he sat down in his favorite chair and counted off the minutes until the pizza would be delivered.

Only five minutes had passed when there was a knock at the door, too soon to be his food. He reached for the stout stick he kept stashed next to the door. It wouldn't protect him against a gun or rifle, but it was all he had. After a quick glance through the peephole, he set the stick down and opened the door to greet his unexpected guest.

"What do you want?"

Devlin took one look at him and said, "You look like hell."

"Thanks. If all you came to do was insult me, this conversation is over." Barak started to slam the door in Devlin's face, but the Paladin shouldered his way into the room.

"Why are you here?" Barak growled.

Devlin helped himself to one of the three beers in the fridge. "I wanted to hear how your first full day went."

Barak gave up on getting rid of the Paladin anytime soon. He picked up his own drink and settled back into his chair. "Why do you care?"

Making himself comfortable on the couch, Devlin popped the top of the beer. "Because if this deal isn't going to work out, we need to start making other plans."

"I can make my own plans, Bane. You are not my keeper." A surge of temper washed through Barak, hot and bright red. "Now tell me the real reason you're here. We both know it isn't for the company."

"Laurel wanted me to check on you." Devlin's lip curled up in a sneer. "She's worried."

For the first time in hours, Barak felt like smiling. Despite Devlin's well-earned reputation as a cold-blooded killer, his mate had him spinning in circles. The way might never be smooth for the Paladin and his lover, but there was no doubt that it was a love match.

"Tell her that I am thriving."

Devlin looked at him for a long time. "Which is why you look like hell? What happened?"

Barak was not about to tell Devlin the truth, so he used the words Lacey had used to describe Barak's adverse reaction to the mountain. "Altitude sickness. Dr. Sebastian and I made a trip up to Mount Rainier today. Evidently I have not adjusted enough to this world yet to handle the extreme elevation. I should be fine after I eat."

As if his words had conjured the pizza delivery out of thin air, the doorbell rang again. He resigned himself to having a Paladin for a dinner companion. At least he'd ordered an extra-large pizza, figuring on eating the leftovers for a day or two.

Good manners in this world dictated that he ask, "Would you care to join me for dinner?"

Eyeing the large box, Devlin responded, "What kind did you order?"

"Vegetarian." Barak hid a smile, waiting for Devlin's reaction.

Just as he expected, Devlin looked thoroughly disgusted. "Laurel has definitely been a bad influence on you, but I can choke some down. I missed lunch today, and Laurel had to cancel our dinner plans."

Barak set the pizza box on the coffee table and brought two plates in from the kitchen. "Help yourself."

Neither of them felt the need to maintain polite conversation while they consumed all but one piece of the savory pizza. Devlin eyed the remaining wedge, then smiled at Barak.

"Since it's your pizza, I'll leave that one for you."

"How very generous of you. Now go home. I want to go to bed."

The smile disappeared. "Do you need help?"

"No, I can manage alone." Even if it killed him.

"Are you working tomorrow?" Bane asked as he picked up the pizza box and plates and carried them into the kitchen.

On another day, Barak might have protested, but it would take all the energy he had left just to make it to bed without crawling again. He pushed himself up out of the chair while Bane was out of sight.

"Yes, I am expected at ten o'clock. Dr. Sebastian is having me work the same hours she does until I learn my duties."

Bane's green eyes saw too much. He started to offer a steadying hand, but he caught himself at the last second. "Did Dr. Sebastian tell you that her brother is a Paladin?"

Barak struggled to keep his voice neutral. "We met yesterday."

The Paladin frowned. "I take it the experience wasn't exactly fun."

"No, I enjoy having a street person jam a gun in my back and punch my jaw. I look forward to chatting with him again tomorrow."

Devlin sighed. "That fool never makes it easy on himself. I'll have a talk with him."

"That will not be necessary. The man was attempting to protect his sister. I would have done the same if the situation had been reversed."

"You have a sister?"

Barak gritted his teeth for letting that slip out. "I didn't say that. I just meant that if I were to see an unknown Paladin approach a female that I cared about, I would have responded in a similar manner."

"If it continues to be a problem, let me know."

That wasn't going to happen. Either Penn Sebastian would learn to accept Barak or they would come to blows again. He couldn't have Bane or Laurel always standing between him and trouble. It would only make things worse for him.

Hiding the effort it took, Barak followed Devlin to the door. "I didn't think to ask. What caused Laurel to cancel your dinner plans?"

"One of the newer Paladins took a sword to the gut when the barrier went down yesterday. It's his first time with a major wound and he isn't handling it well. She was hesitant to leave him yet."

"Do we know him?" Not that he cared. Much.

"Yeah, it was that boy you cut on the face the other day. Roy, I think she said his name was. He'll be fine in another day, but the first time you go down like that is tough." Devlin opened the apartment door. "Keep me posted on your progress. And watch out for Penn. He might not be able to handle a sword, but he's a damn fine shot and throws a mean knife."

"Thanks. I feel so much better now."

Devlin's laugh was wicked. "You can handle him."

Barak watched out the front window until Devlin drove away. The big Paladin was no longer his enemy, but he wasn't exactly a friend, either. It was difficult enough to live in this strange world, but not having anyone to confide in was the worst part. He should be used to it, because he'd been very much alone in his own world. It was a place of darkness, and secrets were a way of life.

But here, it seemed as if most people lived surrounded by the noisy camaraderie of coworkers, family, and friends. With a few notable exceptions, conversations ended abruptly when he walked by, only to resume again when he was out of hearing—or so they thought. Leave it to these humans to assume that because he looked like them, his senses were like theirs.

While his eyesight was no more keen than the average human's, his sense of smell and hearing were far more acute. If he had lashed out every time he'd overheard a snide remark, he would have been fighting from dawn to dusk. Such slights were not worth the effort. Besides, his own kind hated all humans, as if each one had been the same as the next; he could hardly blame the humans for feeling the same way.

His bed was calling. The sooner he crawled in

between the sheets, the sooner this aching weariness would end.

For the first time, he had something to look forward to, working with Lacey Sebastian tomorrow. He owed her for her unexpected help coming down off the mountain. Without it he could have died up there on the steep slopes. She had obviously thought his illness had been due to the altitude. Perhaps that had been part of it, but geological phenomena of all kinds resonated deep inside him.

His body was not yet in tune with the pulse of the local mountains, and even a relatively quiet volcano such as Mount Rainier took some getting used to. Eventually he would be able to judge its mood without becoming ill. He could only hope that he could continue to hide his affinity for the moods of the mountains.

On that cheery note, he turned off the lights and sought out the refuge of his bed, hoping to dream about how it had felt to hold Lacey in his arms.

The shrill ring of the phone startled Ben, even though he'd been expecting the call. He let it ring a few more times before he answered.

"Hello."

"Another shipment is coming in the next time the barrier drops."

Ben swiveled his chair around to watch the door. It was unlikely that someone would enter his office uninvited, but he hadn't gotten this far by being careless. "Tell your friend that the quality of that last batch was crap. The damn stones fell apart a few hours after they arrived."

The voice on the phone sounded completely indifferent. "I'll tell him, but I don't know how much control he has over what they bring."

The older man shook his head. "I don't give a damn about his problems, and you can tell him so. I'm the one risking my neck here. If Devlin Bane or Blake Trahern manage to backtrack Ritter's trail, I'm a dead man. If you can't make it worth my while, I'm out of here."

The silence coming across the phone line was chilly. "I believe I have reminded you in the past about not mentioning names. I do not like having to repeat myself."

"Sorry, sir. I wasn't thinking."

"Yes, you were," the voice corrected. "But you were only thinking about yourself and not the big picture. We're all in this together. If you screw up, we all go down. I won't let that happen. Do I make myself clear?"

Hell, he should have retired two years ago. He should have said no when they'd first approached him. He should have stayed away from the track. There were a *lot* of things he should have done. Now all he could do was say, "Yes, sir. Very clear."

"Good. I'm glad we have that settled. Is there anything else I should know about? How about that stinking Other? What is going on with him?"

"They keep shifting him around, probably because no one wants that filth around for long."

"I hear he made a trip to the Missouri facility with Bane. No one seems to know why." Again the silence hung heavily between them.

"I hadn't heard that. I suppose I could make a few inquiries, but I'm afraid that would draw unwanted attention to us. I do know he's been reassigned to the Geology Department. Perhaps I'll learn more about his movements now."

"Good. He's a complication, and I hate complications."

"Yes, sir. I know."

As if to throw a favored pet a bone, the caller said, "The money has been transferred into your account. The amount was slightly higher than expected."

Ben took all the risks, yet he was supposed to act grateful for the few extra crumbs they threw him. "Thank you. I appreciate it."

"See that you do." Then the phone went dead.

Ben waited a few seconds, then dialed a number from memory. "I want to place a bet on Saturday's race."

Chapter 4

*E*arly the next morning Barak stood down the street from the Center, holding a cup of Starbucks coffee and trying to blend in as the river of commuters swirled around him. A few muttering under their breath about him being in the way, but he had more important things to worry about than causing someone to be late for work.

How was he going to enter the Center without another confrontation with Penn Sebastian? He didn't give a damn about the Paladin, but after yesterday's fiasco on the mountain Barak didn't want to give Lacey Sebastian another reason to reject his help.

Unfortunately, Penn Sebastian was firmly planted near the entrance. Bracing himself, Barak finished off his coffee and dropped the cup in the trash. If he had to fight, he wanted both hands free.

He matched his pace to that of several other people headed in the same direction, hoping the small knot of strangers would provide cover until he had to make that final turn down the alley leading to the entrance. So far, his ruse seemed to be working since Penn's attention was directed toward the opposite end of the street.

Barak's luck held long enough for him to cross the street unnoticed, but at that moment Penn slowly turned his head to stare right at him. Had the Paladin been aware of him the entire time? Judging from the smug look on his face, it was entirely possible. Barak shed all attempts at blending in with the crowd and met the Paladin's angry gaze head-on.

Penn rose to his feet, ignoring the way the rest of the early-morning commuters stepped sideways to avoid contact with him. More than one yanked out their cell phones, perhaps to dial 911 for assistance if Penn made a threatening gesture in their direction. The poor fools had no idea just how dangerous Penn really was, or that Barak was at least his equal.

"I see you came back." Penn's teeth flashed whitely against his grimy skin.

"I am expected." Although not wanted.

"So my sister told me," Penn sneered. "Seems you have a habit of letting women fight your battles for you, Other. First Dr. Young and now Lacey."

That did it. Barak dropped all pretense of civilized behavior and went right for Penn's throat. "Keep their names out of this, Paladin."

Penn grabbed Barak's wrists, trying to pull them away from his neck. His face was turning an interesting shade of red when another pair of hands appeared from behind Barak and yanked him back away from Penn.

Penn struggled to catch his breath. "I'll kill you for that. I meant what I said. Quit using my sister to hide behind."

Trahern shook his head in disgust. "Shut up, Penn. As usual, you don't know what you're talking about."

Barak stepped to the edge of the sidewalk to glare at Blake Trahern. Where had he come from? Judging from the look on Penn's face, he hadn't been aware of Trahern's approach, either.

"Go to hell, Trahern. This isn't any of your concern," Penn spit out.

Obviously Barak wasn't the only one who brought out the worst in Penn.

"Been there; done that. We all have." Trahern turned his ice-cold gaze in Barak's direction. "Bane sent me for you. He has something for you to look at."

"Tell him I'm busy right now." And if these two Paladins didn't get out of his way, he was going to be late. Barak started forward, turning his back on both Penn and Trahern.

Trahern's big hand clamped down on his shoulder and yanked him back a step, sending his temper soaring. If it took a street brawl to convince the Paladins to leave him alone, fine. He took a quick swing at Trahern, who managed to sidestep Barak at the last second, sending him barreling right into Penn. The two of them fought for their balance, barely managing to keep their feet.

Trahern separated them again, glowering at Barak. "Listen, Other, you want to go one-on-one with me fine, but not out here."

"He won't be much of a challenge, Trahern. Not after I get finished with him." Penn tried to shove Trahern out of his way, but the bigger man stood his ground.

Before they could outmaneuver him, a feminine voice entered the fray. "Damn it, Penn—I told you yesterday to leave Barak alone!"

Barak took advantage of Lacey's intervention to shove Penn, sending him stumbling into the street. A cab blared its horn as it swerved around him, while Barak tried to rein in his anger before he said something to Lacey he might regret.

Trahern intervened before Barak could string together anything coherent to say. "Dr. Sebastian, I was just looking for you. Devlin Bane would like to borrow Barak for a few minutes. One of us will make sure he gets back to your lab when we're done with him."

"Gee, thanks for asking, Trahern." Lacey glared at all three men equally. "Knowing Bane, he sent you here to kidnap Barak before he could report for duty. Fine. Take him if you have to, but tell Devlin that we've got work to do, so make it quick."

After shooting them another dirty look, she walked away.

"That went well. I'm sure she's going to be in a pleasant mood the rest of the day."

Trahern's dry comment eased the last of Barak's tension enough to allow him to regain control of his temper. He forced himself to stop admiring the feminine sway of Lacey's hips as she walked away from them. As much as he enjoyed the view, he was sure that Penn Sebastian wouldn't appreciate him staring after his sister.

"Shall we go find Devlin?" Barak put in. "I have a feeling the longer I'm gone, the worse her mood will be."

Penn was already settling back down on the ground in his nest of filthy blankets. "Lacey carries a mean grudge, too. With any luck, she'll be waiting to gut you both with one of my old swords." Then he closed his eyes and pretended to doze off.

Trahern jerked his head toward the other end of the alley. "Let's go."

Barak fell into step next to Trahern. "If I might ask, how is Miss Nichols adjusting to life here in Seattle?"

Trahern's eyes warmed up a few degrees at the mention of his woman's name. "I'd guess better than you are."

Considering the fact that Brenna had only traded one big city for another, that was no doubt true. Barak had stepped across a line to enter a new universe. He had to wonder about Brenna's taste in mates, but there was no doubting the strong feelings Trahern had for her. And from what Barak had heard, few had ever seen the tough Paladin smile until Brenna Nichols had brought him to heel. Although Barak had only met her briefly, he had no doubt that she was as strong a woman as Dr. Young.

Trahern keyed in the entrance code to the building, then stood back and allowed Barak to enter ahead of him. Inside, Barak waited for Trahern to lead him to Devlin Bane's office. He was surprised that he was being allowed to venture so far into the Paladins' stronghold without someone raising the alarm.

"What does Bane need me for?"

Trahern shrugged. "He told me to hunt you down. I did. That's all I know."

The finality in his words discouraged any further discussion, leaving Barak no choice but to follow along beside Trahern in silence. Instead of worrying about what Devlin had in mind, he concentrated on his surroundings. It only made sense to be aware of any potential escape routes from the Center. He was relatively sure that neither Bane nor Trahern posed any real threat to him, but he couldn't say that for the majority of the Regent organization.

"Devlin's office is just ahead on the left."

Trahern made an abrupt turn and walked back the way they'd come, leaving Barak to cross the last distance on his own. Cullen Finley looked up from his keyboard long enough to glare briefly in Barak's direction before turning his attention back to the screen full of numbers in front of him. D.J. was sitting next to Cullen, but he either hadn't noticed Barak's approach or else didn't care.

That was fine with Barak. He'd had enough of fighting Paladins for a lifetime. Besides, he wanted to get back to the geology lab and Lacey Sebastian. She might not like him any better than these guys did, but she was definitely easier on the eyes, to use one of Devlin's expressions.

He knocked on the office door. He could hear Bane talking, probably to someone on the phone, since he could discern only one heartbeat beyond the door. Although Barak couldn't make out what the person on the other end of the line was saying, Devlin wasn't liking it. Barak knocked again.

"Damn it, quit pounding on the door and come in!"

"Thank you as always for your courtesy," Barak murmured as he entered and sat down in one of the chairs facing the desk.

Devlin shot him a dirty look as he paced back and forth across the room with his cell phone in his hand. Then he gestured toward a bunch of small bags piled in a messy stack on his desk.

Barak hadn't needed him to point them out. He'd felt their cold pull as soon as he'd stepped through the door. Rather than immediately exam-

ine them, he sat perfectly still and closed his eyes,
ignoring the faint stirrings of power dancing over
his skin.

Except for some residue, the bags were empty,
but there was no denying they'd been used to trans-
port more blue stones from his world. The thievery
continued. He'd tried to warn the Guild elders, but
they had not been willing to listen. Rather than police the barrier, they had claimed that no one would
be so vile as to rob their already dark world of its
remaining light.

Another lie, one of so many.

Because he would not show fear in front of Devlin Bane, he leaned forward and picked through the
bags. Luckily, there was so little dust left in them
that the glow his touch generated was almost too
faint to be seen. When he heard the click of Devlin disconnecting his call, he dropped the bags and
sat back, willing the small flickers of light from the
dust to fade back into darkness before the Paladin
noticed them.

Although Devlin had already seen Barak cause
one stone to glow, he didn't know how rare that ability was among Barak's people. Or what other gifts
came along with it.

"Those are from your side of the barrier."

Barak wasn't sure if Devlin was making a statement of the truth as he knew it or asking a question.
He chose to answer anyway.

"Yes, they are."

"And the blue dust inside the bags comes from those stones like the one Jarvis showed us back in Missouri."

Another non-question.

"I would assume so."

"Don't try the enigmatic alien routine with me, Barak. Just remember: I'm the one who brought you into this world, and I can take you out again."

He grinned. "I've been dying to say that to you."

There was much about human humor that Barak didn't understand, so he remained silent and waited for Devlin to get to the point.

"Okay, seriously, I wanted to know if the bags themselves have any special significance in your world."

Barak shook his head. "Not particularly. They are often used to carry personal belongings. Perhaps there might be a way to determine if they were all made by the same hand, if we were to run chemical tests on them. But without some kind of norms to compare them to, that would seem pointless."

Devlin dropped down in his chair, making it squeak in protest. "I was afraid of that. We're grasping at straws here."

Yet another expression that made no sense by itself, but the frustration in Devlin's voice spoke for itself. "May I take a couple of the bags to see if I can do anything with them?" Barak asked.

The Paladin studied the pile in the center of his desk for a few heartbeats before lifting his gaze to meet Barak's. He picked a couple of the bags at random and tossed them across to Barak.

"Why not?" Then he glanced past Barak to the door behind him. "Don't mention that I've given them to you."

Barak understood Devlin's reasons for caution, but he didn't like it. Always being on the outside, first in his world and now in this one, grew tiresome. "Of course not. We wouldn't want anyone to think you might have asked me for a favor."

His barely suppressed venom startled Bane into sitting up straight. "Damn it, Barak, that's not what I meant. We're trying to keep a lid on this whole mess. Only a handful of the locals, and Jarvis back in Missouri, know what we suspect is going on. Until we know who can be trusted, we're not talking."

Barak didn't know what was more startling: that Devlin Bane had just apologized or that he might actually trust Barak.

"I'll see what I can tell about the bag and get back to you," Barak replied quickly. He slipped the two small bags into his jean pocket. "Now I need to get to the lab."

Before Devlin could respond, his desk phone rang. He looked at the caller ID screen, snatched it up, and snarled, "Whatever you want, it can wait." Then he nodded in the direction of the door. "See if Cullen or D.J. can show you the way. Otherwise, I'll take you when I get off the phone with Col. Kincade's idiot assistant."

Barak wasn't about to beg one of the other Paladins to show him to the lab. Besides, Cullen was no longer at his desk, and D.J. was staring at his computer screen with a big grin on his face. Barak waited until D.J. murmured something under his breath, his fingers flying across the keyboard, before slipping past him and around the corner.

Rather than backtrack the way Trahern had brought him, Barak followed his own instincts. Just as he'd thought, they'd taken several unnecessary turns before arriving at Devlin's office. Had that been Devlin's idea or Trahern's? It didn't matter. It took more than a few wrong turns to confuse him. Unlike the Paladins, who only spent time underground when they had to, it was the way of life in his world.

He kept going until he reached the entrance from the alley, where he paused to test the air. Closing his eyes, he breathed in slowly, sorting out the various scents. He noted the faint remnants of Trahern's aftershave. Penn Sebastian had left his particular stench in the hallway. It led in the direction of the men's room down the hall, so Barak ignored it. Another man had recently come in the door, but it was no one he recognized.

He angled his head to the left and breathed in again, tasting the sweet fragrance that was Lacey Sebastian. She smelled of flowers and sunshine and a scent that was all things feminine and desirable. Although his body stirred in response, he paid it no heed. Turning in the direction of the geology lab, he wondered how Lacey would feel if she were to learn that Barak could track her in total darkness with the way she flavored the air.

But as with most of the humans who knew him, she'd been taught to look at him only as the enemy. They called him an Other, never asking what he called himself. His own people were as bad, ignoring the fact that the humans were a close cousin to their own species, with only small differences between them. Frustration and anger burned deep in his gut, constant companions for far too long.

He bit back a curse at the gods as he fought to control the need to strike out at someone . . . anyone . . . but no handy target presented itself. Instead he found himself right outside the lab door without remembering just how he got there. Out of habit, he tested the air once again. Lacey's scent was stronger here, making his blood heat up and pound through his veins in anticipation. He smiled. Penn's mistrust of Barak around his sister was well founded.

He opened the door and walked into the lab.

Lacey picked up the phone, about to rip into Devlin Bane for delaying her assistant so long, when she heard the lab door open. It was about time Barak showed up. As far as she was concerned, the Paladins had given up all claims to Barak's time when they had foisted him off on her.

And she was going to make sure he knew it.

She pretended an interest in the current readings from Mount Rainier, letting Barak cool his heels behind her. After a bit, she glanced over her shoulder in his direction.

"Glad to see you finally showed up."

His pale eyes narrowed and his lips twitched as if wanting to smile. However, his face remained impassive as he said, "My apologies. I would've arrived earlier if I'd known that Devlin Bane wanted to see me."

Darn, she hated it when she was full of righteous indignation and the target for her temper was both polite and apologetic. "Yes, well, don't let it happen again. Undependable help is worse than no help at all."

Barak nodded. "I will endeavor not to be late again, Dr. Sebastian."

There he went again, being polite when she wanted to fight. What was it about him that had her feeling all edgy? It wasn't as if he was crowding her, but it felt that way. She wrote down some numbers she didn't need and moved further down the counter. He followed her, still maintaining his distance.

"How are you feeling today?" she asked.

Barak frowned. "Fine."

His tone said clearly that he didn't want to discuss the subject. Too bad.

"Does your kind always get sick in high places?"

There was no mistaking the temper in those pale eyes now. "My kind, as you put it, vary in their reactions to things, just as your kind does."

So she'd hit a nerve. "Sorry." Not that she meant it. "I should have asked if you always get sick in high places."

"I don't know. That was my first trip to the mountain. Are there any other rude questions you want to ask?" He stepped closer, as if trying to intimidate her with his height.

Thanks to Penn and his friends, she'd learned early on to ignore such behavior. She stepped closer, crowding his personal space with her hands on her hips. "I'm not asking to be rude, Barak. If you're going to be a liability, I need to know that."

Standing so close to him made her painfully aware of him, just as she had been yesterday on the mountain. She'd lived her life surrounded by Paladins, all of them the biggest, toughest guys in town, and size and muscle meant little to her.

Yet something about Barak made him sexy and virile. She backed up a step, appalled that she would even think such a thing about him. Even though he was dressed in human clothing, and had learned some of their ways, he was still an Other—one who had killed her people and invaded her world. He should have died or gone back to his own kind.

Something of her thoughts must have conveyed themselves to him. He crowded her again, pinning her against the counter without even touching her.

"I will not be a liability to you, Lacey." His rough voice and odd cadence made her name sound like a caress, sending a deep shiver of awareness through her.

She had to regain control of the situation. "Look, Barak. I'm sorry that Devlin's interference got us off on the wrong foot this morning. Why don't you continue reading through those manuals on the machines while I finish calibrating them? When you're done, we'll talk about any questions you might have."

She slid to the side, turning her back to him. She could still feel the heat of him standing behind her, but he didn't speak for several seconds. Finally, he walked away. She let out a breath and willed her hands to stop shaking.

For several minutes she concentrated on her research until she gradually became aware of Barak staring at her with a puzzled look on his face. When she glanced in his direction, he looked away.

"Is there something you wanted to ask me?"

He frowned. "I was wondering if someone else had been in the lab this morning."

"Not that I know of, but it wouldn't be unusual for one of the others in the department to stop in to check the readings. Even some of the Paladins come in for the same reason if the mountains are restless. Why are you asking?"

"Some of my notes are out of order."

Lacey set down her clipboard and walked around

the end of the counter to where Barak stood. "Maybe it happened the last time you shuffled through them. I do that all the time."

"Perhaps you are right," he said, although judging by his frown he clearly didn't think so.

"Let me know if you notice anything else out of place. I don't always lock up when I'm just running down the hall for something, but I can." Most of what they did wasn't secret; still, she didn't like the idea of anyone messing around with their stuff. "I'll have a key made for you, too. It wouldn't hurt to tighten up security a little bit."

She didn't have to remind Barak that there were those who might not appreciate his sudden addition to the geology staff. Barak's intrusion into their close-knit community was bound to ruffle a few feathers.

When she'd contacted the IT department to set up Barak's access to the department computer programs, they had flat out refused. She'd asked her boss to intervene, but he'd been almost as bad. Finally they'd set up a restricted e-mail account for Barak, but that had been all.

How was he supposed to work without using the computers? She planned on talking to Devlin Bane to see if Cullen Finley or D.J. would be willing to perform a little of their magic on Barak's behalf. If not, she'd have to think about letting him use her password, although that idea didn't sit well with her, either.

As she moved away, she could have sworn she'd heard Barak sniff. Maybe he was developing allergies to this world. If so, she hoped they made him miserable enough to want to return home. If that happened, they'd all be better off.

Except perhaps Barak himself. Which bothered her more than she cared to admit.

What were those damned Paladins thinking of? It was one thing to have that freak emptying bedpans for Dr. Young, but now they'd given the Other a real job in the geology department. Ben hadn't believed it was true until he'd checked, and sure enough, the spooky-looking bastard had been escorted in by Trahern himself.

Penn Sebastian seemed to be the only one truly troubled by the decision to allow the Other into the Center, but he didn't like anyone getting near his little sister. More than one guy had been warned off asking her out, and they'd been human. Having his mortal enemy working right beside her must have the wounded Paladin ready to chew nails.

A weakness Ben might just be able to exploit. Maybe he'd offer to bring Penn a sandwich for lunch. He'd have to be careful how he approached the man, but a few lunches or a cup of hot coffee now and then would be a cheap investment in what could be a useful relationship. At the very worst, Penn would growl, but even the most wary of beasts could be tamed with patience.

• • •

Penn shifted, trying to find a more comfortable position. The hours dragged by as he watched over the alley that led directly into the Center. He rarely had to do more than simply sit in his pile of squalor. Most of the fine citizens of Seattle sped up slightly as they passed him, trying to act as if he didn't exist.

A very few dropped money in the rusty peach can he kept on the edge of his blanket. He supposed he should feel guilty about taking their money, but he didn't. Hell, he probably made their day for them, sending them on their way feeling good about their efforts to help the less fortunate. Besides, considering all that he'd risked and lost fighting an invisible war, the least they could do was buy him an occasional cup of coffee.

He doubted Lacey would approve of his attitude, but he wasn't too happy with her lately, either. What was she thinking of, working with Barak? When he'd found out that she'd spent a whole day with the bastard out on the mountain with no one along to protect her, he'd seen red. Then when he'd tried to talk to her—well, yell at her—about the stupidity of what she'd done, she'd rolled her eyes at him and walked away, leaving him staring at her back in frustration.

That stubborn determination to take care of herself was what worried him most. He understood her need for independence, but she wasn't like him. She could be killed all too easily. His hand flexed painfully, reminding him that even he wasn't completely impervious to injury.

Footsteps had him sliding his hand under the blanket to grip the Glock he kept there. He'd never had call to use his weapons to defend the entrance to the Center, but there was always a first time. Especially now when Devlin was letting a damned Other wander the streets of Seattle as if he belonged there.

"Relax, Penn. It's just me, Ben Jackson."

Penn glared up at the intruder, the man's face shadowed with the afternoon sun at his back. He eased off the trigger but kept the gun in his hand. "What do you want?"

"I'm going to the deli on the corner to get a sandwich. Coming out this side of the Center is closer."

"Next time call ahead to warn me, or you might get your head blown off." Penn was only half kidding.

"Sure thing, Penn. I should've thought of that." The man took a few steps, then turned back. "Hey, since I'm coming right back by here, do you want me to bring you anything?"

Normally Penn might have accepted immediately, but the words seemed practiced, making him wonder if the man's whole purpose in coming down the alley was to make that offer. But to what end? He reluctantly nodded. "Sounds good."

"What would you like?"

Again, that subtle note of eagerness. "Whatever you're having will be fine."

"Sure thing."

Penn leaned back against the wall, keeping one eye on the technology specialist until he disappeared around the corner. Maybe the man was just being friendly. As Lacey had pointed out all too often, his mood lately had been pretty bad. It wouldn't hurt to loosen up a bit.

He reached for his wallet, grimacing in pain when he forgot and used his sword hand. He hadn't been doing the exercises the doctor had ordered as much as he should. They were damn painful, and he'd only had limited success in improving the mobility in his hand. But if he was ever to return to the tunnels, he needed to get past the pain and work those damaged tendons. Biting his lower lip, he slowly began a double set of reps.

He was just finishing up when his lunch arrived. He accepted the sandwich and cold drink after offering his thanks and a ten-dollar bill to cover the cost.

When Ben tried to give back part of the money, Penn shook his head. "Don't sweat it. This is a far better lunch than I would have had. I appreciate it."

"Okay, if you're sure." Ben checked his watch. "I'd better get going. I want to finish this morning's crossword puzzle before I have to go back to work."

Penn grinned at him. "Let me know if you figure

out what eight across is. I must have some wrong letters in there because I can't make any sense out of that part."

Ben disappeared down the alley as Penn took a bite out of his sandwich. After washing it down with a long drink from his pop, he studied the crossword puzzle again, hoping for inspiration to hit while he finished his lunch.

Chapter 5

A sense of unease had plagued Barak all morning and afternoon because of the faint scent that might or might not have been out of place. He hadn't been in this world long enough to develop a feel for how things should have been. Until he did, he could only rely on his senses to keep him safe.

And his nose was telling him that it was no coincidence that the man whose scent he'd caught near the alley entrance that morning had also been the one who had rifled through his notes, leaving them slightly out of order. Had he done so on purpose, as a warning? He could have just been waiting to talk to Lacey and picked up the papers out of curiosity.

Barak didn't think so. Or why would the intruder have gone to such lengths to avoid being seen by Lacey? No, someone was checking to see what Barak was doing in the geology lab—perhaps someone who thought he might be a threat.

There had been no trace of the blue stones in the

man's scent, but that didn't mean much. Unless the stones came into direct contact with someone with the talent for working them, they acted just as any other jewel might, reflecting available light and not much else.

The Regents weren't about to allow a manhunt through the underground offices, so he'd have to rely on luck to find his elusive quarry.

"Why don't you break for lunch, Barak?"

Lacey walked out of her office, bending from side to side to stretch out her back. The action emphasized her soft curves and narrow waist and his body flashed hot and hard with need. Ever since meeting her, his nights had been plagued with dreams of her in his bed, her bright blue eyes filled with smoky desire and those long legs riding high around his hips. He glanced back at his notes to keep her from seeing the heat in his gaze.

He about fell off his chair when she put her hand on his shoulder as she reached past him to flip his book closed. "Come on, Barak, you've been reading those manuals for almost four hours without a break. Not even I could stand to study them for that long without giving myself a headache."

"I have to admit my attention has wandered a bit the past few minutes."

"I can see why. I'm surprised you can keep your eyes open." Lacey stepped back, giving him room to stand up.

"I believe I will go out for a bite. Would you care

to join me?" The invitation slipped out before he could help himself.

For a long second, he thought she considered accepting, but then she frowned and shook her head. "No thanks, but I appreciate the offer. I brought something from home."

The idea of going out just lost its appeal, but he couldn't very well change his mind without making her suspicious. That he would also have to contend with Penn Sebastian going and coming increased his reluctance to leave the building.

He headed for the door, wishing that he could come up with a legitimate excuse to stay. At the doorway, he paused for one last look in Lacey's direction. To his surprise, she was watching him walk away. She blushed when he gave her a parting nod before stepping out into the corridor. For the first time in hours, he felt like smiling.

That lasted as long as it took him to reach the door that led to the alley. He'd rather not fight with Penn Sebastian, but the alley was the only way in and out of the Center that he'd been shown. It was unlikely that anyone would allow him free access through the rest of the complex to find another way out.

But that wasn't all that was bothering him. That elusive scent was back. He slowly turned in a circle, testing the air in each direction. The sickening sweet smell of cheap aftershave combined with male sweat came from the direction opposite the geology lab, reinforcing Barak's conviction that the man had been snooping around rather than having been here on legitimate business.

The real question was why.

To his surprise, the scent was strong in the alley as well. It would be a simple matter to ask Penn who had recently passed by him; the hard part would be to get the irascible Paladin to give him a straight answer. Even if Penn liked Barak, which he didn't, the Paladin would wonder why Barak wanted to know. No, until he had more concrete evidence that something was amiss, he would have to keep his concerns to himself.

Not even Dr. Young or Devlin Bane knew what Barak was capable of when it came to the five senses, or that he had one or two extras thrown in for good measure. He planned on keeping it that way.

He made sure to make enough noise walking down the alley to alert the quick-tempered Paladin that he was coming. However, he had almost reached the street end of the alley before Penn Sebastian even noticed, because he was too busy eating a sandwich.

Barak walked by him without saying a word, thinking it was the first time he'd have managed to get by Penn without a fight. Barak's luck ran out at the sound of a gun being cocked. He froze between one step and the next. Careful to make no sudden moves, he slowly turned back around.

"Thought that might get your attention." Penn's

teeth gleamed whitely. "No one said anything about you leaving the building alone."

"I'm on my lunch break."

"You're still leaving alone."

Barak grew weary of having his every action watched. "So?"

"So, I don't like the idea of you contaminating any of the local restaurants. You'll just have to go back to work hungry." Penn nodded back in the direction of the alley. "As much as I'd love to shoot you right where you stand, I'd rather not have to fill out all the paperwork to explain why you deserved to die."

That did it. He had to take orders from Devlin and even Trahern, but damned if he'd listen to the likes of Penn Sebastian. The man might have the right to be bitter over the injury to his hand, but he didn't have to wallow in his misery, let alone take it out on everyone around him.

For Lacey's sake, he wouldn't kill the obnoxious bastard, but he'd sure enjoy leaving him bruised and battered.

"Who's going to stop me from leaving?"

"We are." Penn aimed dead center at Barak's chest. "One shot from this little baby, and we'll be hosing your blood off this sidewalk." And liking it, too, if the smile on Penn's face was any indication.

"Do you use this same charm on everyone who passes by, or do you save it just for me?" Barak held his breath, hoping to get the answer he needed.

"Just you, freak. When one of the IT guys walked

by a while ago, I was the picture of charm. Now get back inside or bleed. Your choice."

No way that was going to happen. Barak took a couple of reluctant steps back toward the alley, all while sensing Penn following his every movement, his gun aimed straight at him.

At the last possible second, Barak charged Penn directly. Just as he thought, the Paladin was reluctant to use the gun in such a public place. Instead, he came boiling up from his blankets to meet Barak head-on, both ready to beat each other senseless.

Barak had no intentions of coming out the loser. He used every step of the ha'kai he could to keep Penn off balance while at the same time avoiding Penn's down and dirty street fighting tactics.

Barak slammed a fist into Penn's stomach at the same time Penn managed to land a thundering blow to Barak's jaw. The coppery taste of his own blood filled Barak's mouth. He spit as he wrapped his hands around Penn's throat and squeezed. Only the realization that Lacey would hate him forever kept him from shutting off Penn's breathing permanently, and he settled for rendering the man speechless long enough to make him listen.

"If you want to draw another breath, Paladin, you'd better listen. I'm the stuff your nightmares are made of. Keep messing with me, and I'll make that hand wound feel like a paper cut." He eased off the pressure.

The embarrassed fury in the man's eyes spoke

volumes. "Get . . . off . . . me . . . now!" His words
were as ragged as his breathing.

Barak eased back enough to let Penn regain
some of his dignity, but he stayed close enough to
keep Penn under control. When Penn didn't immediately start swinging punches, Barak backed away
completely. They glared at each other, neither one
wanting to be the first to blink. Penn lost. Barak's
smile showed lots of teeth and no humor.

"Paladin, you have every reason to hate me, but
I don't give a damn. I plan on building myself a
life here. Interfere with those plans and you'll die.
Again. Permanently." He bit out each word with as
much venom as he could.

Penn's nostrils flared, and his eyes narrowed in
cold fury. "Your kind has already tried and failed.
Come after me, and we'll see which one of us walks
away."

Barak stood up. "Right now, *I'm* walking away.
Then I'm going to be coming right back." He held
up Penn's gun. "And I'll have this. You even look at
me wrong, you dumb bastard, and I won't hesitate to
pull the trigger."

Penn wasn't about to cower. "I've got more where
that one came from."

"A bullet is a cheap way to kill. A blade shows the
true test of a warrior. Anytime you want to face me,
let me know.

Then he walked away, wondering each step of
the way if a bullet would tear through his back to

explode in his chest. Even so, he maintained a steady pace, refusing to show weakness in front of his sworn enemy. By the time he turned the corner down the street, it felt as if he'd been running for hours rather than strolling the length of a city block.

He slipped the gun in the back of his belt and tugged his jacket down to cover it. For the time being, his only problem was deciding where to have lunch. Then he caught a look at himself in a nearby window. He had dark red splotches of dried blood on both his face and shirt. If anyone saw him, they'd be more likely to call the police than take his order.

He scrubbed at his chin with his hand, hoping he'd gotten the worst of it off. Lacey would have a fit if he showed up looking like this. The last thing he wanted was for her to have to choose between him and her brother, especially when he knew whose side she'd take.

He headed for his apartment to change clothes. Luckily, most of his clothing was black, which meant it was unlikely that Lacey would notice if he'd changed shirts. If she did ask any questions, he would tell her part of the truth—he'd spilled something on his shirt.

Several blocks later, he pulled his keys from his pocket before heading up the stairway to his small apartment. He preferred not to linger in the hallway any longer than necessary. To date, none of his neighbors had objected to his living in the building.

The increasing immigrant population in the country had been making headlines lately, but he made a point to be polite and quiet, having no desire to draw attention to himself.

The dim interior of his apartment soothed his eyes. He was slowly adjusting to the brightness of this world, but too much of it gave him headaches. Because of his alien physiology, Dr. Young was leery of giving him any of the normal human painkillers until she had more time to figure out what effects they might have on him.

Although her intentions were good, he feared any information she accumulated might find its way into the Regents' database. That was the last thing he wanted. Worldwide, the Paladins would exploit any weaknesses she might uncover, using them as weapons against his people. As much as he respected Laurel, he didn't trust her with his secrets.

It made for a lonely way to live. After splashing blessedly cool water on his face, he dried off and grabbed another black shirt out of his closet. If he hurried, he might just be able to get something to go at the small grocery store down the street. A salad coupled with a power drink should hold him for the rest of the afternoon.

At the grocery, at the last minute, he grabbed a second bottle. He had serious doubts that Penn would accept the peace offering, but he felt an unexpected need to try.

• • •

Trahern stretched his long legs out in front of Devlin's desk. "So did your pet have anything interesting to say about the bags?"

Devlin glared at his friend. He was getting sick and tired of his buddies yanking his chain about Barak. But if they were teasing him now, it was nothing compared to what they'd do if he rose to the bait. "No," he said calmly. "Barak did admit they were made in his world and that they were used to carry small personal items."

"Think he knows more than he's telling us?"

"Since we don't know jack, I'd have to say yes to that." Frustration tied Devlin's stomach in knots. "I let him take a couple, just in case he could tell us more after studying them. I don't hold out much hope for that."

Trahern's eyes turned a shade colder. "Do you think he crossed over to get his share of the money out of the stones?"

Devlin shrugged. "I wish I knew. He couldn't have known that we wouldn't kill him, no matter what Laurel wanted. Even if we didn't gut him down in the tunnel, accidents happen all the time."

Trahern's smile was cold. "And if it becomes necessary, they still can. But as near as I can tell, so far he's walked the straight and narrow since we let him live. A couple of minor run-ins with a few of the young recruits, but that's to be expected. By all reports, he's a hard worker and keeps to himself most of the time."

Devlin pinched the bridge of his nose, wishing this never-ending headache would just go away. "Yeah, seems that way to me, too, but I wish we knew more about him and why he crossed over. Even if he's not part of the smuggling ring himself, I'm betting he knows more about the stones than he's letting on."

"We could always persuade him to talk to us." Trahern turned his attention to the collection of knives and swords that hung on Devlin's wall. "I'm sure it wouldn't take us long to convince him."

"Maybe not, but I suspect Brenna and Laurel would have our guts for garters."

They would, too. He'd never thought to see the day that he and Trahern would have women who knew what they were, and loved them anyway. Trahern had been that close to crossing the line into madness before Brenna had dragged him back from the edge.

"I'll give Jarvis another call to see if his crew has found any more of the blue stones. He won't risk sending me the one he has—not that I blame him. He did promise me a copy of any information he was able to find out about the damn thing. I expected to hear from him before now."

Trahern frowned. "Why don't you let me ask him for you? He might be more likely to respond to me."

Devlin managed a small smile. "I'd appreciate it. Col. Kincade has demanded another revised schedule, and of course he wants it yesterday. I don't know what was wrong with the last schedule I sent him, and the way the barrier's been acting, there's no use in trying to plan on anything anyway. Just as soon as I post a schedule, the mountain blows and everything goes to hell."

There wasn't much sympathy in Trahern's quick grin before he managed to hide it. Everyone in the organization hated Col. Kincade, but especially the Paladins. It was hard to tell if the man was incompetent or if he really didn't give a damn about those whose lives he controlled.

Trahern stood, stretched his arms over his head, and yawned. "I'd better get going before I fall over. Keep your fingers crossed that the mountain decides to behave herself for a couple of days."

"Go get some sleep. Calling Jarvis can wait until tomorrow."

"I'll let you know what he says."

Devlin watched his friend walk out the door. The barrier had acted like a yo-yo the night before, so it wasn't surprising that Trahern looked like hell. But it was good to see him acting more like his old self, a feat due to the reappearance of Brenna Nichols in Trahern's life. He was a lucky man. They both were.

There was a soft knock at the door just as Devlin started looking over the schedule for Kincade. Any distraction would be a welcome reprieve. "Come in."

A familiar face peeked into the room. "Am I interrupting anything important?" Laurel didn't wait for an answer. Slipping inside the room, she locked the door behind her.

Devlin's mood improved immediately, especially after spying the bag in her hand. "What's that?"

"Your dinner."

She set the bag on his desk, then sauntered around to his side of the desk, unbuttoning her lab coat. She wasn't wearing much under it, and the scraps of lace looked damn good on her. Laurel's smile had all of his blood pooling low in his body as she straddled his lap. "Do you want me to be the appetizer or dessert?"

"Both—I seem to have worked up a big appetite."

Laurel trailed her hands down his shoulders. "I missed you last night."

He held her close. "I missed you, too. It was a tough one." He tugged her closer for a deep kiss as she rocked against him.

Then he lifted her up onto the edge of his desk after sweeping the stacks of papers onto the floor. Kincade's schedule floated to the ground, where Devlin planned on leaving it until all of his appetites were satisfied.

"I would go with you." Barak kept his voice respectful but firm.

Lacey had just made the unexpected announcement that she needed to set up equipment in the labyrinth that wound along the fault lines and near the volcanoes in the region. Her intent was to compare readings at various distances from the most active of the local volcanoes, Mount St. Helens. The tunnels below Seattle were the logical place for her to place her seismographs.

They were also the last place a woman should be wandering in alone, and she should have known that. Paladins were the best-trained warriors in the world, and *they* routinely died in those same tunnels whenever the barrier went down. Lacey would be helpless against the onslaught of Barak's crazed kin when they crossed the barrier with swords in hand and murder in their eyes.

At the very least, she needed someone to guard her back. But since she hadn't asked permission to use the tunnels in the first place, she wasn't about to approach any of the Paladins, knowing they'd turn her down flat.

She set down her toolkit and glared at him. "I don't need a babysitter. I'll only be gone a couple of hours tops. You can stay here and monitor the readings. If they start going haywire, call me. I'll have my cell with me."

He moved to block her way. "Cell phones don't work near the barrier." He didn't know that for a fact, but he suspected it was true. Besides, he wanted time down in the tunnels, and this might be his only chance.

Her blue eyes met his gray ones head-on. "Devlin will have my head if I take you down there with me."

"And your brother will have mine if you get hurt—or worse—and I could have prevented it."

"Not even Penn could blame you if I screw up."

Barak arched an eyebrow and waited for her to admit the fallacy behind her logic. Penn blamed Barak for breathing the same air she did. If he let her go into a dangerous situation alone, the Paladin would take great pleasure in carving Barak into small pieces. And Trahern and Devlin would likely help him.

She picked up her kit again and moved to step around him. "I'm going. Get out of my way."

"No."

"Barak, step out of my way or find another job."

Barak had seen the stubborn tilt to her chin on her brother's face too many times to not know that she was going to fight rather than surrender, even if it meant risking her life.

Too bad. He stood in front of the door, ready to do battle if necessary. "Take me with you or I'll call Devlin. Or better yet, your brother."

Lacey didn't accept defeat easily. "I don't see you sporting any weapons. What are you going to do if we run into some of your friends? Glare them to death? At least I carry a gun."

"You can't use a gun near the barrier. Which entrance to the tunnels do you plan to use?"

"The one under the Regents' headquarters."

"Fine. We'll stop in the gym for me to pick up a sword." Practice swords weren't meant to be used in actual combat, but it was the best he was going to come up with.

He knew he'd won when she held out her toolkit. "Fine. You can carry this and I'll get the other stuff."

So far, so good. She and Barak had managed to bluff their way into headquarters, lift a sword, and reach the staircase down to the records room without being challenged. Barak had taken a lot of time to pick a weapon out of the rack, but when she'd complained, he'd pointed out that their lives might very well depend on his choice.

The barrier near where she planned to set up shop had a long history of stability. However, there was no guarantee it would continue that way, especially after a rogue guard had done his best to bring it down permanently. The Regents had tried without success to keep that little bit of information secret, especially with Barak as living proof that something had gone horribly wrong.

"Well, no time like the present." She started down the steps with Barak right behind her.

"I would think the Regents would have some form of security to keep their records safe."

"They normally do."

But she'd managed to find out when Brenna Nichols was scheduled to be working in the environmentally controlled record room several floors below. Lacey was counting on the woman being new and unfamiliar with all the protocols. If Lacey and Barak acted as if they routinely used the record room to access the tunnels, Brenna wasn't likely to question it. And even if she did, Lacey planned on being in the elevator going down to the tunnels before Brenna could summon help.

At the bottom of the long staircase, Lacey was relieved to see that the security pad on the wall was dark, meaning it was turned off. The door swung open easily. No one was in sight, but that didn't mean anything. Since the lights were triggered by movement, the pool of light on the far right side of the room marked Brenna's current location.

Lacey glanced over her shoulder at Barak, who stood behind her with his usual calm demeanor. But she wasn't fooled for one minute by his stoic expression or his silence. The man was capable of violent outbursts when provoked. Not for the first time, she wondered why that didn't bother her like it should. His kind was known as crazed killers: the few that escaped the tunnels went on killing sprees that spared no one, not children and especially not women. Yet, she trusted him as she did the Paladins she'd grown up around. Her gut instinct was that he wouldn't hurt her, at least not intentionally.

"Let's go." She led the way into the records room, carrying her equipment and a load of butterflies in her stomach. The building plans she'd unearthed in the Regents' computer system with some dedicated hacking showed the elevator to be in the far left corner.

Neither of them spoke as they walked through the room, the dim lights flickering on and off with their passage. The storage cabinets were too tall to allow Lacey to track Brenna's whereabouts, but so far all she could hear were her own heartbeat pounding in her ears and the soft whisper of their footsteps.

They almost made it when Trahern stepped out from behind the last row of cabinets. He had a smear of lipstick on his cheek, but that didn't soften the suspicious expression on his face. She might have charmed Devlin into letting her continue on her mission, but nothing would work on Trahern if he decided that she was up to no good.

"Hi, Blake," she tried. The use of his first name didn't soften his expression at all. He had definitely shifted into warrior mode.

"Dr. Sebastian, what the hell are you doing in here with him?" He glared past her to Barak.

"I'm doing my job." A less than subtle reminder that it was unlikely that he'd been assigned to guard the records.

"The only thing back here is the elevator down to the tunnels."

"Yes. I'm on my way to set up equipment to monitor the areas that were damaged by Sergeant Purefoy. It's important for us to know if he rendered the area more unstable."

"And why haven't we heard anything about this?"

"About what?" Brenna Nichols walked out from behind Trahern. When she touched his arm, he looked down at her, his gaze softening. "I thought I was the only one crazy enough to want to spend hours down here."

Lacey held out her hand. "I'm Lacey Sebastian, Penn Sebastian's sister. I'm a researcher in the geology lab. This is Barak q'Young."

Brenna smiled brightly. "Barak and I have already met. How are you doing in your new home?"

"I'm well, Miss Nichols. I'm sorry we interrupted your work."

Lacey fought the urge to giggle when Brenna blushed and linked her fingers with Trahern's. "That's all right. I needed a little break, but I should get back to the files."

When she tugged on Trahern's arm, he shook his head. "I'll be right there. I made note of right where you left off."

The smoldering look he gave Brenna was so full of hot promise that Lacey was surprised the smoke alarms didn't go off. She couldn't help being a bit jealous; no one had ever looked at her like that. Well, except for that taste of heat she'd shared with Barak on the mountain.

But then Trahern was back to being the fearsome Paladin. "Let me see your authorization to wander in the tunnels."

Barak spoke up before Lacey could think of a believable answer. "Regrettably, I left that folder back in the lab. We had no reason to think that our presence would be challenged."

Trahern's eyes narrowed. "Even if you do have permission to enter the tunnels," he replied, his tone clearly questioning the likelihood of that, "I know for a damn fact that you don't have permission to carry a sword anywhere but in the gym upstairs."

Barak positioned himself slightly in front of Lacey. "No one has given me a set of rules to live by, Trahern. I will carry this sword to protect Dr. Sebastian, and will return the weapon to the gym as soon as we are finished. You'll have to be satisfied with that."

Trahern stared at him long and hard before turning his attention back to Lacey. "Do you need me to tag along?"

Barak held his breath, waiting to see if Lacey would depend on him alone for protection or if she'd feel better having a Paladin as an escort. He wasn't sure why it was so important to him for her to turn down Trahern's offer of help.

"We'll be fine, Blake. I don't plan to be down there long, and the area has been stable even after Purefoy tampered with the barrier."

Some of the tension in Barak's shoulders eased, but not all. Trahern was just as likely to insist on coming with them or on calling Devlin Bane for approval. Barak was willing to report any information he found in the tunnels about the small bags or the blue garnets, but only up to a certain point.

Trahern finally made his decision. "How long are you planning on being gone?"

Lacey smiled, knowing she'd just won the battle. "An hour, certainly no more than two."

The Paladin nodded. "Fine. I'll call the elevator for you, but send it back up in case you need help. If you run into trouble, use the land lines down there because your cell won't work that close to the barrier."

"I know that." Lacey shifted her equipment box to her other hand and then back again. "But thanks, Blake."

Trahern turned his ice-colored eyes on Barak again. "Get her back in two hours in one piece or I'll come after you." He narrowed his gaze. "And I won't be carrying a practice sword."

Tired of being ordered around, Barak gripped his sword, poor weapon that it was. "Don't make idle threats, Trahern. If you think you can take me down, do so. Otherwise, we're late as it is."

Chapter 6

*W*ithout waiting for Trahern to respond, Barak walked away, leaving Lacey to follow as she would. Trahern caught up with them at the elevator door. He punched in a series of numbers, then stood back out of the way as they waited for it to arrive.

Lacey rocked from one foot to the other, the only clue that the tension between the two men was worrying her. Of course, she was more familiar than most with the explosive tempers of Paladins.

The doors slid open and Trahern stuck his hand out to hold them. "You first, Lacey, and stand at the back of the elevator."

"And why is that?" Evidently she didn't like taking orders any better than Barak did.

Trahern answered, "So if any of Barak's old friends are waiting at the bottom, he'll have a better chance without having to maneuver around you. He knows how to fight, so let him if it comes to that."

She seemed to be mollified by Blake's explanation, if a bit more worried about the risks they were about to undertake. "I'll stay out of his way."

"See you in two hours."

Then Trahern reached in and pushed the button that would close the doors and send them plummeting down into the deep tunnels below. Barak's last glimpse of Trahern revealed the Paladin hitting the speed dial on his cell phone. There was little doubt in his mind that Devlin was about to get an update on Barak's current whereabouts.

As much as he resented the constant monitoring, this time it wasn't a bad idea. If the barrier did prove to be unstable, he'd prefer that someone knew he and Lacey were down there.

His stomach lurched slightly, the unexpected speed of the elevator a surprise—yet another marvel built by these people. In his world, they depended on staircases because of the energy cost involved in running machinery.

He could feel the heat of Lacey's body directly behind him, even as her scent overpowered the stale-air smell in the small compartment. He found his awareness of her on so many levels soothing in some ways and arousing in others.

What would she say if she knew that he could hear the rapid trip of her heart and the way she breathed through her mouth when she was nervous? The need to reassure her was riding him hard, but he knew she'd only resent it if he thought her weak.

"What will you do if some of your . . . uh . . ." Her voice trailed off as she struggled to find a polite way of asking her question.

He saved her the trouble. "I will protect you, Lacey, even from my own people."

She blushed. "I meant no offense, Barak. It just occurred to me that I have never heard anyone call your kind anything besides 'Others.' I assume that's not what you call yourselves."

"You're the first person to bring that up."

She looked genuinely surprised. "Not even Dr. Young? I thought you two had become, um, close friends."

What had she been thinking? He spun around to face her. "Dr. Young and I had a working relationship, not unlike the one I have with you." That was a lie. He'd never wanted to push Laurel up against a wall and kiss her senseless. That idea crossed his mind every time he saw Lacey.

He forced himself to speak with a calm voice. "She was kind enough to teach me the ways of this world with the help of Devlin, her mate."

Lacey giggled. "He's her mate?"

"What else would you call him? The bond between the two of them is a powerful one, as is the one between Trahern and Brenna Nichols."

The sparkle in Lacey's eyes faded away. "Paladins are not known for fidelity, especially once they've got a few deaths behind them."

"I cannot imagine Devlin looking at another

woman in the same way he looks at Dr. Young. You can feel the pull of the link between them whenever they are together." As soon as he said the words, he knew he'd made a mistake. He was relatively sure that humans did not sense the emotional commitment between two lovers in the same way he did.

Lacey arched an eyebrow. "And you can tell they are mates by feeling this link?"

There was no use denying it now, but perhaps he could play it down. "It is part of their body language—the way they stand, and the way they look at each other."

"Yeah, I know." There was a note in her voice that he didn't recognize.

Before he could investigate any further, the elevator settled at the bottom of the long shaft. Immediately, he put aside all thoughts except the need to protect Lacey.

With his sword at the ready, he waited for the doors to open. Even before that happened, he closed his eyes and reached out with all his senses. The subtle clanking of machinery made it difficult to discern if there were any unexpected heartbeats in the area immediately outside the elevator, but he didn't think there were.

As the doors opened he drew a deep breath and tasted nothing but the damp, stone smell of the tunnel. So far, so good. He stepped out of the elevator and repeated the drill, ignoring how odd he must appear to Lacey. He felt her move up to stand just off his left shoulder, knowing not to block his sword arm.

For several seconds, the two of them stood in silence: he because he was still reaching out to make sure they really were alone in the tunnels and to test the health of the barrier; she because this was her first trip down into the tunnels. With Penn for a brother, she must have heard tales about the life-and-death battles that were fought here.

Probably the last thing she would have expected was to get her first peek at her brother's world in the company of his lifelong enemy. The gods always did love irony.

"Which way shall we go?" There didn't seem to be much difference in the tunnel in either direction.

Lacey immediately turned left. "This way. I studied the maps before coming down. I want to set up my equipment in a small offshoot from the main tunnel. Close enough to the barrier to get some readings, but far enough away so that its energy doesn't interfere with the machines."

Barak frowned as he sheathed his sword and picked up his share of the equipment. She'd gone ahead a few steps, so he lengthened his stride to catch up with her. "How do you know you'll be able to take accurate readings this close to the barrier?"

But she wasn't listening. They'd just come to the first turn in the tunnel and the barrier hummed and shimmered just ahead, its colors ever changing. He tried to see it through her eyes, with the innocence of that first view of the barrier's incredible beauty.

He hated it for the fickle bitch that it was.

Lacey let out a rapturous sigh. "No one told me it was beautiful."

"Probably because those of us who have spent our lives defending it or trying to cross it have had too many other thoughts on our minds to be poetic about it."

She frowned and opened her mouth as if to ask a question, but then thought better of it.

"Go ahead and ask what you will, Lacey. If I can answer, I will."

"Why do they come?"

He noticed she'd used "they" rather than lumping him in with the rest of his kind. Did that mean she had accepted him as a part of her world and trusted him on some level? She'd be a fool to think of him as harmless, but he wasn't about to point that out to her.

He realized he still hadn't answered her question. After casting around for some version of the truth that she would understand, he settled for, "Because they must."

Before she could demand a more thorough answer, they reached another split in the tunnel, which distracted her. "This is where I wanted to set up the first set of meters."

He'd been hoping they'd stumble across the area where he'd first encountered Laurel Young and the guard, Sgt. Purefoy, who had been intent on destroying the barrier in that area for all time. Luckily, Devlin Bane had killed the traitor before he'd been able to accomplish his goal.

During that encounter, Barak had lost his family's sword somewhere nearby. Someone had probably found it—either some of his own kind, or one of the Paladins. Though none of the Paladins besides Devlin had come this far down the tunnels, since they usually entered from the other end.

Perhaps there'd be time after he and Lacey got the equipment up and running to explore a short distance further along the passage. The sword had been the last thing he'd owned that had been his father's.

The old man hadn't approved of Barak's beliefs, but he'd never denied his son's right to carry the symbol of their family. His father would've hated knowing that Barak had dropped the sword without hesitation to protect a human female, giving him one more reason to have cursed his only son for a fool.

"Hand me that big screwdriver."

Lacey was bent over adjusting the balance on a spider-shaped piece of equipment. Her jeans traced the feminine curves of her backside with loving detail, making it difficult for Barak to make sense of her simple request. When she looked up to see what was taking him so long, she realized the kind of view she'd been offering him. She immediately shifted to the other side of the spider after getting the screwdriver for herself.

He stifled the urge to grin when she blushed. So the woman wasn't immune to a man's open admiration, even his. Rather than stand there staring at her, as much as he would have liked to, he picked up another of the miniaturized monitors and began unfolding its legs. The small machines were a tribute to her ingenuity.

"Where do you want this one?" he asked, but before she could answer, he held up his hand to silence her. She slowly straightened up, turning her head this way and that, trying to see what had caught his attention.

He pitched his voice for her ears only. "Someone is heading this way."

"But who? . . ."

There was no time for explanations, not if they were going to manage to hide their presence from the unexpected intruders. The tunnel lights were motion-activated. If they held still long enough, the lights would cycle off, hiding them in the shadows. He reached out and grabbed Lacey, clapping his hand over her mouth to silence her protests.

"Be still or we die. If they weren't up to no good, they wouldn't be muffling their footsteps and speaking in whispers."

Lacey's blue eyes filled with a touch of temper at being ordered around. She did as he'd told her, but with an unspoken promise that there'd be a reckoning later. As the intruders approached, he pressed her back against the nearest wall, sheltering her body with his. He drew his sword and turned to face the enemy. Keeping his eyes on the far end of the passage, he tried to ignore the delicious feel of Lacey's warmth trapped between him and the cold stone walls.

The enemy drew close; he could all but taste their greed. If he'd had a Paladin with him, he wouldn't have hesitated to confront the intruders, no matter whose side they belonged to. But he would not risk Lacey's safety for a chance to see who might be involved in the illegal trade of blue light. His fingers flexed on the grip of the sword, imagining the pleasure of making them bleed for their rape of his world. Lacey stirred behind him, a reminder that now was not the time. At least he could listen and perhaps learn enough to help Devlin trace their footsteps back to their leader.

He leaned back close enough to mouth a whisper to Lacey. "I will die before I will let harm come to you."

Lacey believed Barak's promise, although she still wasn't convinced that they were in any danger. The motion-sensitive lights nearest them finally blinked out, leaving the two of them tucked safely in the darkness beyond the glow of the barrier. She closed her eyes, struggling to hear whatever had convinced Barak that they were in danger.

There, she heard something, maybe just the rush of her heart as they waited in the deep silence.

It came again—the hushed noise of rubber-soled shoes on the tunnel floor. Two, maybe three men walking. Men who had no legitimate purpose in the tunnels.

Paladins swaggered; they didn't give a damn if the whole world heard them coming. That left either Barak's people or else someone who had no legitimate reason to be in the tunnels in the first place. The Regents would have posted notice if there had been some kind of maintenance going on. As far as she knew, there had been no such announcement.

As her eyes grew more accustomed to the dim light from the barrier, she could see that Barak had his head tilted toward the far end of the tunnel. She wanted to ask him what he was listening to so intently, but she suspected he wouldn't appreciate her interfering with his concentration.

Finally, three men passed by the front of the small tunnel where she and Barak stood huddled in the shadows. Although she couldn't make out their features very clearly, she was certain that they were all strangers. What really caught her attention were the high-tech guns they wore slung over their shoulders with careless ease.

Even she knew how much damage a bullet could do to the barrier. Either these men didn't know the risks, or they flat out didn't give a damn. One stopped to light a cigarette before continuing on. For the space of a heartbeat, that small flare of light from the match seemed to light up the whole area, leaving her feeling exposed instead of cocooned by the shadows.

She held her breath, realizing how much danger they were in. As if sensing her sudden surge of fear, Barak reached back to take her hand in his, silently offering her the reassurance of his touch. She knew that her brother and his friends would be horrified to see her readily accepting comfort from their worst enemy, but Barak was not *her* enemy.

At that moment, she had more to fear from the human men who had just passed by. A few seconds later, she could no longer stand the silence. She leaned forward slightly to whisper, "Are they gone?"

She felt Barak shake his head. He squeezed her hand, again reassuring her. Finally, though, most of the tension drained away from his stance, and he sheathed his sword. Slowly he turned to face her, his movement triggering the closest of the lights. The sudden brightness had her instinctively burying her face against his shoulder. Immediately his arms wrapped around her, cradling her against his chest.

As she waited for her heart to quit racing, she realized that she wanted far more than comfort from the man who embraced her so gently. Slowly, she forced herself to look up. His pale eyes held her gaze as his hand came up to cup the side of her face. Her knees weakened with the sure knowledge that Barak was going to kiss her.

And that she'd waited her entire life for a man to

look at her just the way that he was looking at her—as if by looking into her eyes, he'd found the answer to every question he'd ever asked. She offered him a small smile, and traced the masculine line of his jaw with trembling fingers.

As he closed the last little distance between them, her eyes fluttered closed, waiting for the touch of his lips to hers, knowing without question that her life was about to change forever.

Her breath mingled with his as Barak lightly brushed his lips across her mouth, making feminine desire coil deep within her. She slid her hands up to his broad shoulders, needing his strength and craving his heat.

She sighed, parting her lips in invitation to deepen the kiss. His tongue swept across hers as he gathered her closer, letting her learn the fit of his powerful body against hers. Her skin ached to be shed of the layers of clothing that held them apart even that small distance. She nibbled at his full low lip as she wrapped her leg around his; he growled in response and started to kiss her again.

Then a shout startled them both. They jumped apart, leaving her feeling guilty and disappointed. Trahern and Devlin were coming to find them, and she wasn't sure if they'd just saved her, or cost her something precious that she might not find again.

Chapter 7

*B*arak gave her a gentle shove toward the small pile of cases. "Work on the equipment. I'll distract them."

Normally she would have resented his taking charge, but at that moment she was only grateful.

She watched him intercept Bane and Trahern before she turned her attention to the work at hand. He stopped them a short distance away while she tried to make the final adjustments. Inside the box were the various pieces of equipment she used to monitor and record earth movements in the surrounding area. Out on the mountains, she used a larger version to accommodate the bigger batteries required to power the instruments.

She'd modified the original design to make this smaller, more portable, version for more protected areas like these tunnels. If this one worked as well as she hoped, she wanted to install them throughout the tunnel system that the Paladins had to guard.

Her hope was to learn how to predict the earthquakes and volcanic eruptions that caused the barrier to come down. Even a few minutes of lead time could help save Paladin lives. She'd watched them sacrifice so much—their very sanity—for a battle they could never completely win.

She had to wonder what Barak thought about the research she was doing. If she was successful, the lives she helped save would be at the cost of his kind.

"Get out of my way," Penn snarled as he tried to get past Barak, who had put himself squarely in Penn's path. Just great, another testosterone-laden pissing contest.

Devlin glared at Penn. "Back off, Penn."

"Like hell I will, Bane. This is your fault."

"What's my fault? That you're acting like a major asshole?" Devlin joined Barak in blocking Penn's access to the tunnel. "No one gave you permission to be down here, you damn fool. If this gets reported, you'll be on laundry duty for the next six months."

Oh, yeah, name-calling and threats were going to calm her brother right down. She latched the lid on the case and reached for the second one. Barak had already done most of the work, so it took only a couple of seconds to have it up and running as well.

She dusted off her hands and packed up her tools. "If you all are done acting like idiots, I could use some help here."

Barak immediately left Devlin and Trahern to deal with Penn. As Barak leaned down to pick up the tool case, he met her gaze. In a soft voice, he whispered, "I'm sorry about all of this."

The words hit her like a splash of cold water. What was he sorry about? That her brother was being a jerk—again—or that her decision to monitor the tunnels had stirred up a hornet's nest? Or that they'd kissed? Even now, she could remember how it felt to be in his arms and to taste his kiss.

And that scared her right down to her bones. He represented everything she'd been brought up to hate, yet Barak was a far cry from the monster her brother and the other Paladins had made his kind out to be.

She said calmly, "If you'll pick up that one, Barak, we'll take it a short distance farther down the main tunnel and finish setting it up."

Devlin stood in front of her, his hands on his hips, looking scarier than she'd ever seen him. "Lacey, what the hell are you doing down here? And who authorized it?"

She wasn't impressed. "I'm doing my job. Now, if the whole bunch of you would get out of our way, we could finish up and get out of here."

"Damn it, Lacey, there are reasons we don't let just anyone go wandering around down here. What would have happened if the barrier had gone down?"

"I would have protected her." Barak had set the box back down and stood with his hand on his sword.

She was tired of their arguing over her like a pair of dogs fighting over an old bone. "In fact, he did keep me safe, Devlin. Three men carrying rifles went strolling by here no more than ten minutes ago. If Barak hadn't heard them coming, they would have seen me for certain."

Bane's green eyes snapped from her to Barak. "When were you going to tell me about this?"

Barak glared right back at the Paladin. "I wasn't sure how much you wanted Penn or Trahern to hear. I would have told you as soon as I had you alone."

Some of the anger drained out of Devlin's expression. "Fine. I'm listening."

"I heard their voices carrying down the tunnel. I pushed Lacey deeper into the small tunnel and told her to hold still so that the lights would go out. I drew my sword and waited for them to appear."

"Were they members of the Guard?"

"They wore no uniforms, but that doesn't mean much. They seemed relaxed even though they carried weapons, as if they expected to have the place to themselves. They didn't sense our presence, although it was a close thing."

"Son of a bitch." Devlin ran his fingers through his hair. "Were they carrying anything they shouldn't have?"

Lacey had been following the discussion right up to that point. "Like what? They had some kind of machine guns. Isn't that bad enough?"

Barak and Devlin exchanged looks, but neither one seemed inclined to offer up any explanations.

Trahern spoke up. "Where do you need that equipment put, Dr. Sebastian? I can carry the stuff for you while these two hash things out."

He was trying to distract her, and there wasn't much she could do about it. Paladins played their cards close to their chests, and right now she was too mixed up inside to argue.

"This one stays," she said, pointing at the closest case. "I want to take the second one farther down the tunnel enough distance that I can compare the readings."

For once she got no argument, which spoke to how worried Devlin and Barak were about keeping their conversation to themselves. She picked up her tool kit and followed Trahern down the passage. Barak watched her leave, but maybe she was only imagining it.

"So what did you do with Penn?" She should have thought to ask where he'd disappeared to before now.

Trahern shrugged. "Devlin ordered him back to the elevator. I thought I might have to knock him out cold and drag him there." The tall Paladin looked down at her. "He wasn't too happy to hear that you'd come down here alone with Barak."

"Then why did you and Bane tell him? You had to know how he'd react."

Trahern stopped short. "We didn't tell him. I called Devlin myself, but neither of us spoke to Penn at all. I figured he must have seen you and Barak leave the lab."

"I knew better than to let him find out. Otherwise, we'd never have gotten past him in the first place. We left by the other door and went straight through the building without stopping to talk to anyone."

Her companion muttered something that sounded suspiciously like an obscenity. "I'll have to tell Devlin and let him talk to Penn. It will be interesting to see who was watching you or maybe Barak."

She sighed. It was bad enough that her brother still treated her like a child half the time without him enlisting others to help him spy on her.

"If he's having his friends watch me, I'll kill him. I've been threatening to for ages. Maybe it's time I show him that I'm serious."

Trahern laughed, although it sounded rusty. "I'd love to watch. If it's any comfort, my money would be on you."

She gave him a suspicious look. "Because of his hand?" Because that would really make her angry.

He looked shocked that she'd think such a thing. "No way. I've just learned to have a healthy respect for what a strong woman can accomplish."

He looked back to where Devlin was still talking to Barak. "Whoever thought Bane could be hog-tied by a woman?"

Lacey had to laugh. "Some might have wondered the same thing about you."

His harsh features softened a bit. "We're not talking about me."

But he didn't deny it, either. Brenna Nichols had worked a miracle with Blake Trahern, and Lacey was genuinely happy for both of them.

They'd reached another branch in the tunnel. "Let's set this one up in there."

"Not that one!"

Trahern reached out to stop her, but she'd already gone far enough to trigger the lights. There wasn't anything to distinguish the short space from the previous one—until she spotted a dark brown stain on the floor. It looked like . . . Then she recalled the stories she'd heard about the day that Barak had crossed over from his world and Devlin had killed a traitor from among the Guard. Oh, Lord help her. It was blood—old and dried out—but blood, all the same. The stain was puddle shaped and ran right up to the small area of the barrier that ran through the tunnel. It ended abruptly at the edge of the barrier.

"Blake, is this where? . . ."

"Yeah," he admitted reluctantly. "This is where Sgt. Purefoy chained Laurel to Barak and waited for the barrier to come back up. It would have killed them both." Devlin had killed him instead, with Barak's help.

It seemed appropriate to set up her equipment right where Barak had earned the right to live in her world. She swallowed hard and set down her tool kit. "Let's get set up."

The chill of the tunnels had made her fingers stiff, making it hard to fine-tune the last settings. Finally, though, she had the small machine running properly.

"Would you mind if I looked around a bit more? It won't take more than a minute or two for me to see if I can find other places to set up more equipment on my next trip."

He frowned at that. "You can look. That's no guarantee that you'll be allowed back down here anytime soon."

She rolled her eyes. She'd managed to get down there once; she'd do so again. Rather than argue the point, she did a hurried inspection of the next hundred feet of tunnel. There was only one more offshoot of any size. After waving her hands to set off the lights, she blinked her eyes against the sudden brightness.

Except for a rusty bed with a broken headboard, the tunnel was empty and would do for another station. If Devlin refused to let her come back, maybe she could get Trahern to accompany Barak down to set up the equipment. As she was about to ask him, she spotted something glittery out of the corner of her eye and turned to see what had caught her attention.

It was a sword, but one like none she'd ever seen before. She approached it with caution, knowing it had to have come from the wrong side of the barrier.

"Blake, come look at this."

He joined her, kneeling down to look at the sword. The two of them studied it for a few seconds before he reached out a cautious hand to move it out from the wall to get a better look.

"It had to have belonged to an Other."

"But according to the files, there hasn't been any fighting along this stretch for years." The words were out of her mouth before she could stop them. The only way she'd know that was if she'd been accessing secret Paladin files.

"I mean, uh—"

Trahern shot her a knowing look. "Don't sweat it, Lacey. Devlin's already figured out that you've been reading the files. He sicced D.J. on your trail."

She'd be lucky if her boss didn't have her up for disciplinary action. "I needed the information."

"Next time just ask for it. We all have a vested interest in your work."

"Thanks, I will," she replied, surprised by his answer.

"I won't promise that Devlin will allow you free access to everything. But if you can convince him that your need to know is legitimate, he'll listen."

Trahern pulled out a handkerchief and used it

to pick up the sword by the hilt. "I've never seen inlays like that before. I would guess that this little beauty belongs to your friend back there."

"Is Barak allowed to carry a weapon?"

Trahern arched an eyebrow. "He's carrying a sword right now, isn't he? Your doing, I assume."

She felt a blush rising up her face. "No, actually, it was his idea to come with me in case I ran into trouble. He said that the practice swords in the gym were the only weapons he had access to."

"Well, let's go see what he has to say about this one." Trahern stood aside to let her lead the way.

Devlin stood glowering, his hands on his hips. "Damn it, Barak. I can't have you wandering all over creation. The Regents would have my head for it."

Barak frowned. He was still learning to differentiate the meaning behind some of the expressions used by the Paladins and other humans he came into contact with. There was nothing in his experience that made him believe that the Regents would kill one of their fiercest champions because of Barak.

No, logically speaking, they'd be more likely to order his death instead of Bane's. Devlin was exaggerating again.

"Was I supposed to allow Dr. Sebastian to come into the tunnels alone?" Barak kept his tone reasonable, but he was growing weary of having to defend his actions.

"Hell, no, but you could have called me instead of letting her go traipsing all over the place." Devlin gestured widely with his hand. "The barrier could have gone down."

"As you've already said."

"Well, it doesn't appear to have sunk in yet, has it? You're standing here arguing with me, and she's still acting like she has the right to be using these tunnels as her own private geology lab."

It occurred to Barak that Devlin was ranting on and on because he'd been worried about the two of them. "I'm sorry we worried you. Next time we'll call."

"Next time? Haven't you been listening? Hell, if you hadn't happened to hear those bastards coming right at you, it could have been a bloodbath!"

"*No!* I would have protected her!" Barak drew himself up to his full height and met Devlin glare for glare. He was willing to take a certain amount of bad temper from Devlin, but he had pride in his own abilities. Lacey would have been safe, or he would have gladly exchanged his life for hers.

"With what? That practice sword?" Devlin wasn't going to back down anytime soon.

"It's the only weapon you allow me. If you want to make sure I can keep her safe, then allow me the tools to do my job!" He rarely yelled, but dealing with an irrational Paladin sure called for a show of strength. "Give me a sword, and I will use it. You may be a Paladin, Bane, but I was considered a formidable warrior in my own world. I can be in this one as well."

Before Devlin could respond, the ice-eyed Trahern stepped back into view. Barak knew without looking that Lacey was right behind him. He'd caught her scent on the air, and something else. Something that resonated inside his head and his heart. Before he could speak, Trahern did.

"If you're going to give him a sword, Bane"— Trahern shot Devlin a look daring him to contradict his words—"you might want to give him one that he knows how to use."

Lacey stepped out from behind Trahern and held up a sword. Not just any sword: Barak's father's sword. He fought the urge to shout out his relief. He held out his hands, and Lacey's smile brightened as she gently placed it there.

"I've never seen a blade that wide or one curved like that. It's beautiful, Barak. Almost a work of art."

He supposed it was, but its real value was as a weapon that had been handed down from father to son for generations upon generations. He would be the last of his line to own it.

"Where did you find it?" His voice sounded rough.

Trahern leaned closer to study the weapon. "Near where you crossed over, I would guess. Lacey spotted it looking for more places to put her toys."

He got the predictable rise out of her. "Those 'toys' might just save your life one of these days, Blake Trahern."

Devlin had evidently gotten over his mad. "Yeah, they just might, squirt." He ruffled Lacey's hair before crowding in to admire the sword, too. "The workmanship on that inlay is unlike anything I've ever seen."

"Quit that!" Lacey batted Devlin's hand away from her head. "That blue scrollwork is beautiful against the dark metal."

It was. Only someone with the gift for the blue stone could have worked the metal and stone in such a way. If Barak concentrated hard enough, he could make it glow, a trick he was not anxious to share with anyone.

"Thank you for finding it, Lacey. It is a piece of my home that I've missed." He offered her a small smile. If Devlin demanded that he surrender it to his safekeeping, he would, but at the cost of much pain.

"We'd better get out of here before those men come strolling back this way." Devlin held out his hand. "Give me back the practice sword, so I don't have to report it stolen."

For the first time since his arrival, Barak felt balanced, with the familiar weight of the sword in his hand. If he and Lacey continued their work in the field and in the tunnels, he would carry a warrior's weapon that would keep them both safe.

He nodded in the direction of the elevators. "I would suggest we leave. We were lucky enough to avoid those gunmen once."

As the four of them walked in companionable

silence, Devlin glanced down at Lacey. "Next time you're ready to go down into the tunnels, schedule it with me. I'll send D.J. or Cullen with you to set up some cameras in the same area. I'd like to catch up with whoever you two saw today."

"Barak and I can set up the cameras, Devlin. We don't need your guys for babysitters."

"Damn, Lacey, did you have to inherit your brother's stubborness, too? I'm sending them because they can interface the cameras with our computers. You'll do your thing and they'll do theirs, but I'd like to make sure that there's more than one sword on hand if you cross paths with the gun-toting fools."

Barak had told Devlin everything he could about the strangers that he and Lacey had encountered. Both he and the Paladin were certain that they were involved in the theft of the blue stones. The trouble would be in catching them in the act, because there was no telling how often they passed through the area.

A familiar sound caught his attention. He tilted his head slightly forward and closed his eyes. "Devlin, they're coming back this way."

Neither of the Paladins questioned his word. Warriors all learned to trust gut instincts, or they didn't survive long. Devlin brought the practice weapon up into fighting position as Barak drew his father's sword.

"How far away are they?"

"I can't really tell, with the way that sound echoes in these tunnels." He centered himself inside and reached out to listen with all his energy. "I'd guess not far, but we might make it to the elevators if we run."

The three men automatically shielded Lacey as they took off, letting her shorter legs set the pace. As they neared the elevator controls, Trahern outdistanced them to enter the necessary codes to operate the elevator.

"Damn it, Penn left it topside!"

Keeping Lacey behind them, they counted off the seconds as the elevator made the long journey back down. Devlin stood beside Barak as they faced the darkened tunnel.

"I can't believe I was stupid enough to come down here unarmed." Trahern looked thoroughly disgusted with himself.

Lacey set down her tool kit and lifted out the top tray, pulled out her handgun, and held it out to Trahern. "Are you any good with one of these?"

He didn't dignify her taunt with an answer. Instead, he checked out the gun with an efficiency that spoke of lots of practice. "Thanks."

They could all hear the footsteps now. If the elevator didn't arrive in the next few seconds, the four of them would be trapped in the open.

"Let me distract them." Barak separated himself from the others.

"I'll come with you." Devlin started to follow.

Barak waved him off. "They'll think I'm a strag-gler from the last fight. If they see you, they're more likely to panic and start shooting."

It was the only sensible plan, and they all knew it.

"Keep Lacey safe," Barak murmured.

"Barak, no!"

Lacey tried to push past Trahern, but she might as well have been trying to move a mountain. "Stop him, Blake. He could be killed!"

The pain in her voice warmed Barak like nothing else had in a very long time, for he knew it meant she did care about him. It soothed the bitterness in his soul to know that if he was about to die, he would not move into the spirit world unmourned in this one.

He'd gone no more than about twenty feet when he heard the elevator doors open. A quick glance back verified that Trahern had dragged a struggling Lacey inside with Devlin offering what cover he could as they'd backed up. He waved to Barak, motioning him to retreat to the safety of the elevator.

But before Barak could slide back more than a step or two, the same three men he'd seen earlier charged into sight. If their guns had looked deadly when they'd worn them slung carelessly across their backs, it was nothing compared to how they looked aimed straight at him.

He screamed out a battle challenge and lunged

forward, surprising them with his direct attack. The closest one fell back a step, stumbling into his nearest comrade. Evidently they had been cautioned against firing their weapons near the barrier, since they didn't immediately open fire.

He circled around to keep the barrier at his back, trying to take advantage of their reluctance. A single shot rang out, and the man farthest from him stumbled backwards as a circle of red blossomed on his chest, spreading fast.

One down, two to go, thanks to Trahern. The noise distracted Barak's last two opponents long enough for him to attack again, this time allowing him the exquisite pleasure of feeling his blade slice through human flesh. The man's scream was drowned out by Barak's own triumphant bellow. His sword, already dripping with bright red blood, thirsted for more of the same. He twirled around to his left, the blade singing through the air on its way to yet another target.

The last of the three men would have screamed if his throat hadn't just been cut. Instead, the only sound was a noisy gurgle as he tried to hold back his blood and breath with only his fingers. His bewildered eyes met Barak's only seconds before the life drained out of them, just as his blood had drained from the slit in his throat.

Barak stood still, waiting for his heart to slow back down to a rate somewhere near normal. It had been some time since he'd claimed a human life as his prize for a fight well done. The victory tasted sweet right up until he realized that he'd let the battle fever claim control over him again.

He let his sword drop down to his side as the familiar pain of regret filled his heart. Granted, these men had given him no choice, and had he not fought them, they could have caused great harm to him and his companions. Killing in self-defense held no sin, he knew.

But taking pleasure in it did.

A whimper cut through his thoughts, as sharply as his sword had cut through his enemies. Slowly, he turned to face the elevator, all too aware of the blood pooled on the floor of the tunnel, the scent of it metallic and pungent. All of the horror he should have been feeling—and wasn't—was there to be seen in Lacey's bright blue eyes brimming full of tears.

In a choke of sobs, she turned away from him, burying her face against Trahern's hard chest.

"Get her out of here." Barak's voice came out little better than a growl. What had Trahern been thinking by letting the door open again? Finally the elevator door slid closed, hiding him from her pain.

"She'll get over it. She's tough."

Barak jumped. He'd almost forgotten about Devlin. "How much did she see?"

"Enough." Devlin knelt beside the man Trahern had shot and checked his pulse. "This one's still alive. Come put some pressure on this wound while I put in a call for the cavalry."

Barak had to assume he meant he was sending for help. "I regret not taking at least one more prisoner."

Devlin looked at him, his green eyes jade hard. "I don't. They got cocky. We'll get more out of this one, now that he knows we don't like to take prisoners." Then his smile turned nasty. "Or keep them for long."

Barak knelt down and held Devlin's handkerchief over the gunshot wound. He felt nothing at all for the injured man, not caring that his eyes were full of pain and fear. The bastard had threatened Lacey's safety; if he died, this world would not be any worse off.

He drew some pride from the fact that Devlin had included Barak in the "we" when he'd spoken. But that would do little to restore the innocence lost when Lacey had looked at him and seen him for the killer that he was.

Chapter 8

*S*on of a bitch! Penn kicked a can as far as he could. The small act of violence did little to ease his need to hurt someone, anyone, but especially that fucking Other. Penn had seen red the second he'd found out that the animal had followed his sister down into the tunnels.

What would have happened if Trahern hadn't intercepted them? Sure, everyone else thought of Barak as Laurel Young's tame little pet, but he knew better. He'd seen the same hatred in Barak's freakin' eyes that he'd seen in all the Others he'd crossed swords with over the years. The bastard might have fooled Bane and Trahern, but not him.

What if Barak's plan was to drag a human woman back into that nightmarish world he'd come from? He'd failed with Laurel Young, but now he had another candidate in Lacey. Well, that wasn't going to happen, not if Penn could help it.

The soft whir of a camera panning the alley

reminded him that he wasn't really alone. No, Big Brother was always on duty. If he continued to act agitated, they were bound to send someone out to check on him. Rather than risk being relieved of duty, he slowed his pace as he walked back to his pile of blankets.

After rearranging them, he plopped down. For now he would man his post, counting off the minutes until his shift was up. Then he'd go home and take a hot shower, eat a big, bloody steak for dinner, then pay a courtesy call on his little sister to deliver a simple message.

Either she jettisoned her lab-rat Other, or he'd take pleasure in doing that little chore for her.

Two cups of tea and a handful of chocolates had done little to calm Lacey's badly shaken nerves. Finally, she'd added something a lot stronger than a teaspoon of sugar to the third cup of tea to see if that would work. So far, it had only further upset her already churning stomach.

She would have lain down, but every time she closed her eyes all she saw was blood, pools of it surrounding those dead bodies. She shuddered and took another sip of her doctored tea.

The doorbell was not a welcome interruption. It could only be one of two people, neither of whom she wanted to see, so she ignored it. But between chimes, she heard a woman's voice calling her name.

She pushed herself up off the sofa, letting her afghan drop to the floor. Her oldest sweats weren't exactly what she normally wore to entertain company, but right then she didn't care.

A quick look through the peephole had her fumbling to release the chain and throw back the dead bolt. What was Dr. Young doing on her front porch? Lacey ran her fingers through her still damp hair, trying to tame the curls a bit before opening the door.

Cold fear for her brother washed over her. "Dr. Young? Is Penn all right?"

Laurel looked puzzled at first, then horrified. "Oh, Lord, it didn't even occur to me that you'd think that. He's fine, Dr. Sebastian. I'm here because Devlin asked me to stop by." She crossed the threshold to put her hands on Lacey's shoulders. "I'm sorry if I scared you."

As a Paladin's sister, Lacey had lived most of her life knowing her brother could be killed for the final time with no warning. Laurel Young's dark eyes were filled with sympathy, reminding her that because of Devlin, she also lived on that razor's edge. Worse yet, she was the one who might just have to kill the man she loved.

It was a hard life, but one neither of them would give up even for a minute.

"Call me Lacey."

"And it's Laurel, please. I get 'Doctored' enough at work."

Lacey mustered a bit of a smile. "Come on in. I

just made a fresh pot of tea. Would you like some?"

"If it's not too much trouble, I'd love a cup. Today's been a real bear."

Lacey gestured for Laurel to have a seat at the kitchen table. She poured her a cup of tea and set out a plate of homemade cookies. "Trouble in the lab?"

"Yeah, to put it mildly." Laurel took a sip of the tea and sighed with pleasure. "Darjeeling! My favorite. But I'm not here to complain about my day. Devlin mentioned what happened down in the tunnel with you and Barak today. We both were worried about how it might have affected you. Are you okay?"

How could she answer that? She was alive and unharmed, at least physically. She'd known there'd be a certain risk in going down in the tunnels, but she'd never expected a scientific expedition to erupt into violence and death. Or a moment of passion. Would she have actually done more than kiss Barak if they hadn't been interrupted? She feared the answer was a resounding yes.

"I'm all right, or at least I will be." She couldn't hide the shudder that ran through her, or prevent her confession, "Those men died because of me."

"No! That's not what happened at all!" Laurel's expression grew fierce. "Those men had no business being there in the first place. Devlin told me everything, and nothing he said cast any blame on you. He was a tad upset," she said, softening her words with a slight smile, "that you went down there without permission. But even if you had asked, that doesn't change the fact that those men could have killed all of you."

"Instead, Barak and Trahern killed them. It wouldn't have happened if I hadn't dragged Barak down there."

By the time the elevator doors had reopened, two men had already been down, but she'd seen him kill the third. He hadn't even noticed the spray of blood that had stained his clothes, and she could've sworn he'd been smiling. How could anyone be happy about killing someone, even if they deserved to die? There had been a fierce joy in his expression before he'd looked up and seen her.

"He saved lives down there, Lacey. That's the part you need to remember."

Lacey wished she knew Laurel better because she badly needed someone to confide in. "I don't understand Barak."

Laurel sighed and took another long sip of her tea. "I don't think anybody does, Lacey. I certainly don't. Ever since I came to work for the Regents, all I've ever been told about the Others was that they were monsters. But I've never seen that side of him."

Neither had she, not until today. "I've known Paladins my whole life. Each and every one of them is a fighter. Lord knows my brother Penn has a well-deserved reputation for being volatile. I guess

I've just never seen any of them in their real role before."

Laurel nodded. "That first glimpse is a tough one. I've patched them all up, mending wounds that would have put a normal man in his grave a dozen times over. But until Sgt. Purefoy kidnaped me, I'd never seen Devlin with his game face on. We were already lovers by that time, so it was a tad upsetting, to say the least. But despite it all, I knew he would never hurt me.

"Devlin did what he did because he loves me." Then she reached out her hand to touch Lacey's arm again. "But Barak almost died down there in the tunnels with me. He laid down his sword and took a gunshot meant for me when he didn't know me at all. Keep in mind that his people hate us as much as we've been taught to hate them. And yet he's offered up his life not just once, but twice, to prevent harm to you and me."

Yeah, but Lacey bet he hadn't kissed Laurel.

"I appreciate the reminder. I guess I didn't expect my expedition to end that way." Lacey shuddered again, still unable to forget the pools of blood on the floor. She had a feeling that they'd be haunting her dreams for some nights to come.

Laurel refilled her cup. "Devlin also asked me to tell you that it might be awhile before it would be safe for you to go back down into the tunnels, even with an escort. Until they know what those men are doing down there, nobody is safe."

"I figured as much, but it makes me mad. I've finally got a shot at making some real progress in my research, and this had to happen." Lacey poured herself another half a cup of tea and left the rest for Laurel.

"I know just how you feel. I believe Devlin said you're looking for a way to predict earthquakes and eruptions more accurately?"

"So far without much luck, but I'm trying to develop a more sensitive monitoring system. That's the first logical step in the process. My boss doesn't seem to think it's possible, so he keeps me operating on a shoestring budget, which is why I was willing to take on Barak as an assistant. The extra money he brought into the department was a godsend."

Laurel set down her cup so hard that it rattled the saucer. "What money was that?"

Oops! Was she not supposed to mention the financial bribe that Devlin had offered the Geology Department? If so, why hadn't Devlin warned her? "I, uh, meant that having them budget his time to work with me has helped me keep up with my research."

Laurel's eyes narrowed, as if to indicate she didn't quite believe Lacey's explanation but wasn't quite willing to call her on it. As far as Lacey was concerned, if Laurel had questions about the money, she could bring them up with Devlin. And she wouldn't want to be in his shoes if he didn't have a good answer.

The idea of the big Paladin being brought down a notch or two by his girlfriend lifted Lacey's spirits.

"I really appreciate your coming over here tonight. It's really helped to have another woman to talk to."

Laurel's smile was warm. "You're welcome. And we should do this again soon. We both live surrounded by these big, tough men—not that I'm complaining, mind you. At least not much. They need women like us and Brenna Nichols to help keep them grounded. I'm convinced that it makes a difference."

"It must, because Trahern was almost chatty today. He even asked me about my work." Lacey hadn't really thought about it before, but he *had* seemed different. Another memory surfaced. "When he caught Barak and me heading for the elevator in the records room today, he had a lipstick smear on his cheek!"

That set both of them off in a fit of giggles. Laurel snickered. "What is the world coming to? If it wouldn't embarrass Brenna, I'd give Blake a hard time the next time I see him. He has no idea how lucky he is that I'm not going to go straight home and tell Devlin."

Then she looked at her watch. "Well, I'd better go. I left Devlin a note, but you know how these Paladins are. If we're five minutes late, they're ready to call out the troops."

Having grown up with one for a brother, Lacey

knew exactly what Laurel meant. If she hadn't learned early on to push right back, Penn would have kept her under his thumb forever.

After walking Laurel out to her car, Lacey was about to turn out the porch light when she spotted Penn heading straight for her. She was tempted to lock the door and pretend to be in bed or gone, or anything to keep from having to fight with him. But he had a key to her house, so there was no way to keep him out short of nailing the doors closed from the inside.

She didn't want him to feel too welcome, so she left the door open slightly and went back inside. After filling the kitchen sink with hot water, she was busy washing dishes when he came stomping through the door.

"Lacey!"

Before he could launch into whatever he had to say, she held up a sudsy hand to forestall him.

"I'm in no mood for any of your lectures, Penn. If you haven't eaten, I'll heat up some leftovers for you. Or there's a fresh batch of sugar cookies in the jar if you want something sweet."

Then she turned her back on him and went back to scrubbing her skillet clean. Penn muttered under his breath before reaching for the cookie jar. He flopped down in the chair that Laurel had just vacated and prepared to wait her out. Well, he could wait for a long time.

After wiping down the counter, she decided to

dry the dishes rather than let them sit in the drainer until morning. Then of course the sugar bowl needed filling, as did her salt and pepper shakers. She was about to alphabetize her spice bottles when Penn gave up and spoke first.

"All right, Lacey, this is the bottom line: I don't want you running around alone with that—"

She shot him a look over her shoulder to warn him to watch his mouth.

He tried again. "I don't want you running around alone with Barak."

Penn still managed to say Barak's name as if it had been an obscenity. She rolled her eyes and braced herself for the fight she knew was coming. Reasonableness wasn't likely to work with her brother, but she'd give it a shot.

She turned to face him but didn't accept the chair that he pushed toward her with his boot. Like all of the Paladins, he towered over her. By standing while he sat, she at least had a small advantage.

"Penn, I understand why you worry, but I don't tell you how to do your job. I don't want you to tell me how to do mine. Though today didn't turn out exactly as I had planned, that was hardly Barak's fault. In fact, if I hadn't given him back his sword, I don't know what would have happened."

Judging by her brother's thunderstruck expression, he hadn't heard about what had happened after he'd been banished back up the elevator. He sat up straight in the chair, his hands clenched in fists.

"Back up and tell me exactly what the hell you're talking about."

She might as well sit down now. There wasn't going to be any chance of glossing over the details when he could just go ask Devlin or Trahern and get the truth.

"After you left, Trahern and I finished setting up the equipment while Devlin talked to Barak. You see, right as Barak and I had gotten started working on the first piece of equipment, some armed men came down the main tunnel. We hid in the darkness until they were out of sight."

"You were trapped in a dark tunnel with an Other." He bit out each word separately, as if speaking to someone who had a difficult time with English.

He hadn't exactly asked a question, but she nodded anyway. "Before we got back to the elevator, Devlin and Trahern showed up. You know, you were right behind them. After you left, Trahern helped me set up my gear," she repeated, hoping Penn would be happier that she'd been with the Paladin rather than Barak. "But when the four of us were leaving, the men came back. Trahern shot one of them with my gun, while Barak killed the other two with his sword."

"And you saw all of this?" Again his tone was unnaturally calm.

"No. I was in the elevator when the second man was killed, but I heard the shot and saw Barak cut down the last guy. Trahern took me up the elevator while Barak and Devlin waited for help to arrive. I don't know if the third man died or not. I hope not." Even if his reason for being in the tunnel was shady, he didn't deserve to die. It was bad enough that the other two had been killed, even if it had been self-defense.

Penn remained absolutely quiet for a handful of seconds before he exploded in rage. After an impressive string of obscenities, he began ticking off her transgressions on his fingers.

"You went down in the tunnels with an Other. You hid in the darkness with an Other while armed killers strolled by. You managed to see two men get killed. And unless I'm mistaken, you don't see that you've done anything wrong."

Technically, she only saw one man die, but she didn't think now was the time to point that out. "I admit I should have checked in with Devlin before going down in the tunnels."

Penn slammed his fist on the table hard enough to rattle the windows. "Damn it, Lacey, you haven't got the sense God gave a goat! You could have been killed down there—if not by those men, then by that damn Other. What if he'd decided he was tired of this world and dragged you back across the barrier with him? Did that thought even occur to you?"

She was in no mood for this. "No, it didn't, because he wouldn't do that."

"And you know this how?"

Because she trusted Barak, but Penn wouldn't want to hear that. She was so tired of arguing with her brother, especially when it got her exactly nowhere.

"You need to leave, Penn. I love you because you're my brother, but you are not my keeper. I'm a grown woman and capable of making my own decisions. Until you understand that, I suggest you not come back here."

She stood up and walked to the door, opening it to emphasize her point. "I've already told Devlin that I won't go down in the tunnels without letting him know ahead of time. He's asked me not to go at all until he knows more about the men we ran into. That's a reasonable request, so I've agreed to wait until he says it's safe for me to do my job. Now go."

Penn looked as if he wanted to fight some more, but then he took a closer look at her. "You look like hell, so I'll go. But this isn't over."

She sighed. "Yes, it is, Penn. I don't mind having discussions with you, but we're done with the ultimatums. Now good night."

She slammed the door closed a little harder than necessary.

The night sky was cloudy, but a few stars still managed to peek through. Barak stood on his small balcony and stared up into the darkness. He'd have to buy a book on the stars of this world so that he could learn their names. He drew comfort from their presence, because light of any kind warmed his soul.

The day had been a disaster. His first real chance to prove his worth to Lacey Sebastian, and what had he done? He'd cornered her in a darkened tunnel and kissed her. Despite hours of personal debate, he still had no idea if he was relieved or regretful that they'd been interrupted before they'd gone too far.

More times than he could count, he'd reached for his phone to call her to make sure she was all right. She'd been through a lot down there in the tunnels, but she seemed to have handled it well. At least she hadn't . . . how had Devlin described it? Ah, yes, she hadn't fallen apart, an appropriate image.

But the look in her eyes when she'd seen him kill that last fool would be hard for either of them to forget. He half expected to get to the lab in the morning only to be sent away, perhaps for good.

And then where would he go?

He'd managed to save a small amount of money, but not enough to pay for food and shelter for more than a month. He'd gotten rather good about starting over, but he had set down roots in this city of Seattle. He was learning his way around and even had a few friends. Laurel for certain, Devlin didn't seem to hate him anymore, and even Trahern was usually civil. He'd hoped to add Lacey Sebastian to that list, but only time would tell.

And only the passage of hours until morning

would tell whether he still had a job. Weariness settled heavily on his shoulders, telling him that it was time to retire for the night. Sleep would not come easily.

Combat always left him restless and horny, another funny expression he'd learned from listening to D.J. talk with Cullen. It hadn't been difficult to guess the meaning of the word, and he'd found it a fitting description of his condition. He'd chosen a life of celibacy for the past few years for a variety of reasons. Horny—that was him.

He thought back to those precious few seconds when he'd held Lacey in his arms, touching the smooth skin of her face as he'd stared down into her blue eyes. The rest of the world had disappeared into the distance, leaving the two of them alone, with only the hunger for the touch and taste of a kiss surrounding them.

Barak cursed Devlin and Trahern's bad timing. If they hadn't come along, he would have savored the sweet flavor of Lacey's kiss as well as how she'd felt in his arms. Even now, hours later, he could close his eyes and remember exactly how her body had fit against his.

How much more exquisite would it feel to have her beneath him, cradling him in the warmth of her arms and in the heat of her body? He very much wanted to know the answer to that question. It had been so long since anyone had touched him, even just out of friendship. The females of his world had long ago turned their backs on him, not understanding the road he'd chosen to follow.

But Lacey had reached out with her sensitive fingertips and touched him with such gentleness. Her golden hair had slipped through his fingers like silk, her breasts had felt so right pressed against his chest.

Had it been only a moment of weakness on her part, or was she feeling the same fascination for him? He'd had little experience with seduction in his world, and none at all in this one. Perhaps a trip to the library would provide some credible information. Maybe tomorrow after work . . .

The shrill ring of the phone drew him back inside his small apartment. The phone rarely rang unless it was a wrong number. Most of the time he just ignored it, but the need to hear another voice, even a stranger's, anything to distract his thoughts from Lacey Sebastian, had him reaching for the receiver.

"Yes?"

"Barak? It's Lacey. Lacey Sebastian."

As if he wouldn't know that. "Is something wrong?"

Her laugh sounded nervous. "No, nothing's wrong. I just wanted to make sure that you were all right."

"I'm fine." Other than his body hurting with the need to bed her. Even the sound of her breathing was stirring his body into full readiness to mate.

"I was worried. That whole experience down in

the tunnels was so awful." There was remembered fear in her voice.

He hurt for her. "I regret you had to see what happened when those men returned."

"Yes, well, better them than you or Devlin or Trahern." She paused. "Or me. I just wanted to let you know that I'm grateful that you insisted on coming down with me into the tunnels. I'm sorry that it had to end on such a horrible note."

"I was honored to serve as your bodyguard." He pulled a chair closer to the phone so he could sit down. The darkness in the room lent a certain intimacy to their conversation. "And I'm grateful that you found my sword. I'm relieved to have it back."

"I'm happy we found it."

Silence settled between them, and for the moment the only connection between them was the distant hum of the power in the phone. Words never came easily to him, but he didn't want her to think he was reluctant to talk to her. And there was something in her voice that made him think there was more wrong than she was telling him.

"Have there been repercussions from the incident?" The need to protect this woman boiled up in his blood.

There was a definite hesitation before she answered. "No, not really. It's no surprise that Devlin said we can't go into the tunnels while he investigates why those men were there. And Laurel Young stopped by to make sure I was all right. That was kind of her."

"She is a kind woman. Did it help to talk to her?"

"Yeah, until my brother stopped by to yell at me. I sent him packing." Pain and anger colored her words.

"I would have liked to have seen that. You do know he just wants to keep his sister safe." He considered his next words. "And I would think he hated you experiencing some of the violence that is so much a part of his life."

"I'm not a child."

"No, you're not, and Penn knows that. If he didn't, he wouldn't hate me being around you so much. Big brothers often have a problem with men desiring their beautiful sisters, no matter what their age. That he considers me his enemy makes it even worse for him."

There was a sharp intake of breath on the other end of the line. He knew the question she wasn't asking. And the answer.

"Lacey, I've wanted to kiss you from the first moment you walked into that meeting room, ready to do battle. Instead, you took my hand." Even now he could remember the burst of pleasure at the surprise he'd felt at her touch.

"It was just a handshake."

So she'd felt it, too, or else she wouldn't be trying to convince herself otherwise.

"But down in the tunnel today, it was so much

more than a simple handshake." He was playing with fire. Either she'd admit to the powerful attraction they both felt, or she'd banish him from her lab for his presumptions.

"Yes, but it shouldn't have gotten that far."

He heard regret in her voice, but was it because she was sorry they'd been interrupted or because it had happened at all? Before he could think of a response, she yawned loudly, then sighed.

"Sorry, Barak, that was rude. It's been a long day for both of us. I'd better be going."

To bed. He ruthlessly ignored the interesting picture that brought to mind. "Thank you for calling, Lacey."

"It was the least I could do. After all, you risked your life to keep the rest of us safe."

"No. To keep *you* safe," he corrected.

She ignored the distinction. "I'll see you in the morning. Good night, Barak."

"Good night, Lacey."

He waited until she disconnected before hanging up his phone, not wanting to lose touch with her a second sooner than he had to. Then he made his way through his darkened apartment to his lonely bed.

Perhaps now he could sleep.

Chapter 9

The pounding at the door matched the pounding in Penn's head. He squinted at the clock beside his bed and cursed as he threw back the covers. His robe lay on the floor at his feet, but damned if he'd risk bending over to pick it up, not the way his stomach was churning.

Wincing at the bright sunlight flooding into his kitchen, he cussed again when he saw Devlin staring at him through the back-door window. What in hell did he want? Even if the clock was pushing noon, Penn wasn't due for guard duty until two. Plenty of time for him to settle his stomach and clear his head.

After unlocking the dead bolt, Penn stepped back. "Before you start yelling about whatever you came by to yell at me for, I need coffee."

Devlin gave him a disgusted look. "Sit down before you fall down. I'll make it."

Penn would have argued, but he figured he'd only embarrass himself further. "I'll be back."

If Devlin wanted to talk to him badly enough to come to the house, then he'd wait around long enough for Penn to shower and dress. Besides, if he was going to get his ass chewed, he wanted to be wearing more than yesterday's boxers.

Ten minutes later he walked back into the kitchen feeling a helluva lot better. "Sorry to keep you waiting."

Devlin had already poured them each a cup of coffee. He'd even managed to scrounge up a couple of aspirin and had them sitting by Penn's cup. Penn nodded his thanks and swallowed them dry, then took a careful sip of the coffee. It was strong enough to melt nails, burning away the last of the cobwebs in his head.

After emptying the cup, he set it down. "So go ahead and yell. I'm ready."

Devlin's smile was not pleasant. "Penn, you've been screwing up so much lately, I ought to rip your fucking head off. God knows I've warned you enough about fighting. And it would help if you followed orders once in a while. Then there's yesterday's fiasco down in the tunnels."

Damn it, he wasn't the one who screwed up yesterday! "It wasn't *your* sister down in the tunnel where that son of a bitch could have dragged her across the barrier."

"I've already dealt with your sister over her lack of judgment, so you stay out of it. However, you were the one who didn't bother to send the elevator back down to us. If you had, we could have made it up without those bastards even knowing we were there. But because you had to be an asshole, Lacey saw Trahern shoot a man while Barak sliced up the others like ripe watermelons."

Penn blanched. "I didn't think about that."

"And damn it all, that's exactly what your problem is, Penn!" Bane leaned forward in his chair. "You don't *think*."

There wasn't much Penn could say to that.

Devlin stared at him a few seconds longer, then sat back and took a long drink of his coffee.

"But I didn't really come here today to yell—too much. I have a question for you and I didn't want to ask it back at headquarters."

Penn's stomach clenched with dread. "What is it?"

"How's the hand doing?"

This wasn't the time to lie. Penn held out his hand and clenched it, making a fist, but he couldn't hide the amount of effort it took. "It's better, but not great."

"How good are you at fighting left-handed?"

Where exactly was this conversation headed? "I've never tried it seriously. I'm a fair shot with both hands, though."

"That's good." The scowl on Devlin's face lightened up. "That's damn good. As of today, you're no longer on guard duty. Instead, I want you working more closely with the physical therapist on strengthening your right hand. And I want you in the gym every day with either me or Barak working on fighting left-handed."

Penn's good mood disappeared instantly. "*Barak?* Why the hell would I want to work with him?"

"Because I don't have time to work with you every day, and Barak's fighting style is closer to yours than Trahern's or Cullen's." Devlin finished his coffee. "This is your best chance at getting back into the fight, Penn. After this long, it's hard to know if your right hand will ever be normal. We've cut you a lot of slack, knowing how hard it must be to be so close to the barrier and not able to fight."

"You don't know. Nobody does." If he sounded like he was whining, too damn bad.

"Maybe that's true." Devlin met his gaze head-on with his best no-prisoners-taken glare. "Don't blow this opportunity, Penn, or we'll have to move your sorry ass somewhere far enough away from the barrier to keep you from driving everybody, including yourself, crazy."

Devlin stood up and held out his hand. "I need you back, Penn. All the way back."

A few minutes later, Penn watched Devlin drive away. Damn, he'd known the day would come that the decision would be made about whether he would rejoin the fight or else be shuffled off into some no-account job. Oh, they'd try to protect his dignity, but they all knew that a Paladin who couldn't fight would wither away. Already some of the Paladins avoided him because he reminded them how precarious their own lives were.

At least Devlin had offered him a chance. Turning away from the door, Penn flexed his hands and considered the irony of it all. An Other had taken away his ability to fight, and now he had to depend on one to give it back.

A sense of calm poured through his veins as he picked up his keys and prepared to drive to the Center to be fitted for a new sword. A new weapon, a new life, and an old enemy to face.

"Hey, Penn, you're looking pretty clean cut for sitting out on the sidewalk."

Penn clenched his teeth. Ben Jackson was at least the seventh person who'd made the same or similar crack since he'd come into the Center.

"I'm no longer on guard duty." And if Penn kept moving fast enough, Ben wouldn't have time to ask if that meant he was returning to the tunnels. The Paladins didn't bother to ask. If he'd been recalled to normal duty, the news would have flown through the ranks like wildfire.

"Hey, well, congratulations, Penn. That's terrific news. I bet you're thrilled to be back in the trenches." Ben slapped him on the back a little too enthusiastically. "What say I buy you a beer in celebration?"

It took some effort, but Penn managed to smile at the IT specialist. "I'll hold you to that offer, but I'm not back on the roster yet. Devlin has something else in mind for me than sitting on my ass out in the alley, though. I guess that's good news."

Ben's excitement didn't dim by even a flicker, making Penn more suspicious than ever. Why had he singled out Penn for so much attention? He'd taken to stopping and talking every time Penn was out on the sidewalk, almost as if he'd been watching for him. Maybe Penn shouldn't be so distrustful, but he hadn't been known for having a charming personality even before his injury. Now he could hardly be civil to anyone, including his own sister.

Ben's behavior was making Penn's hackles rise, enough so that he didn't want to blow the guy off. There'd been rumors about some pretty weird stuff going down lately, what with the renegade guard and all, and maybe Ben was part of it. But Penn wouldn't say anything to Devlin until he had something more solid than just his gut feeling to go on.

"Tell you what. If I get a chance, I'll stop in the bar up the street after I get done. If you're there, I'll let you buy me that beer."

He managed to dodge Ben's effort to slap him on the shoulder. "Great! I'll see you then."

Penn walked on toward Devlin's office, pausing to look back at the man. Yeah, something was up; he only wished he knew what it was.

• • •

Lacey shook her head to make sure she'd heard correctly. "Are you sure he said Penn? As in my brother, the one who hates your guts?"

Barak looked up from the data he'd been entering into the computer for her and nodded. "Yes, I am to meet your brother in the gym this afternoon after I finish here."

"But why on earth would Devlin pick you to spar with Penn?"

What kind of game was Devlin playing? Did he want her brother to kill Barak for him since he couldn't do it himself? No, that didn't make sense. Devlin Bane wasn't known for his subtlety.

Barak shrugged. "I would guess it has something to do with your brother's hand."

Oh, no! Lately, she'd suspected Penn hadn't been very diligent about doing the exercises the therapist had given him, but surely his hand had been improving. Maybe not, if Penn's increasing anger was any indicator.

"You're not a doctor or a therapist," she said, suddenly realizing how little she really knew about her new assistant. Except he had a way of making her hormones stand up and take notice whenever he walked into the room. Or when he looked in her direction with those spooky silver eyes. Or . . .

"No, I'm not." He turned to face her. "From what little Devlin said, your brother needs to change sword hands if he can. Like Devlin, I am able to fight with either hand. Perhaps that is what he thinks I can teach your brother."

"Penn's not going to like this."

Barak tried unsuccessfully to hide a nasty little smile. "No, he won't."

She crossed her arms over her chest and gave him a disapproving look. "I know he's been a total jerk around you, but he's had a hard time with this injury."

"What your brother needs is a swift kick in the ass, to borrow one of Cullen's colorful phrases. Penn isn't the only Paladin to suffer this kind of injury, and feeling sorry for himself won't help him get back his sword. Working out against me might."

She couldn't argue with his logic, but that didn't mean she had to like it. "Can I watch?"

"No."

"And why not?"

"Devlin promised your brother that we would give him privacy, especially at the beginning. At first Penn will be clumsy fighting left-handed. Spectators will only make it more difficult for him."

She grudgingly accepted defeat. "Fine. Just make sure that this extra duty doesn't interfere with your work here. And remember, we're scheduled for another trip to the mountains tomorrow."

"I'm looking forward to it. I've heard and read a great deal about Mount St. Helens. It will be nice to meet her in person." He picked up his clipboard and began writing down more numbers.

He wasn't the only one excited about the trip. It was a pretty drive, right up until the moment you reached the highest tourist center and looked right out at that brooding mammoth of a mountain. Mount Rainier and Mount Baker were volcanoes, too, but they hid their anger better.

It would be interesting to see Barak's reaction to the lady, as he called the volcano. She watched him work for a few more seconds before returning to her office. Ever since their trip down to the tunnels a few days ago, she'd found herself staring at him far too often.

Neither of them had mentioned their brief kiss or the phone call they'd shared that night. And Barak's thoughts were impossible to read. He was the perfect coworker: courteous, punctual, diligent.

She had nothing to complain about, but she found herself wanting to pick a fight. Yet whenever she criticized his work, he nodded and made the corrections without complaint. His eyes followed her whenever he thought she wouldn't notice, but she hadn't confronted him about it.

He was her brother's enemy, but not hers. From the first moment she'd met him, Barak hadn't fit the image of an Other that she'd grown up with. But just as she'd started thinking of him as a friend, the memory of him smiling over the corpses in the tunnels jolted her into remembering he'd probably killed his share of Paladins and Guards.

"How many of my people have you killed?" The

question had been hanging unasked between them from the beginning. She didn't regret its slipping out; she only hoped that she didn't regret his answer.

Barak stared at her with those odd eyes and slowly stood. He walked toward her, forcing her to either stand her ground or retreat to her office.

She took a step in Barak's direction and widened her stance. He stopped close enough that she could feel his body heat, and a deep breath filled her senses with his scent.

"Why do you want to know?" He cocked his head to one side and studied her face.

"We spend a great deal of time with just the two of us. I think I have a right to know what kind of man you are."

"I've been here for some time, Lacey. Why all of a sudden are you worried about your safety? Have I in any way threatened you?" His eyebrows snapped together, the first sign of real temper he'd ever directed at her.

"No, but—"

"Is this about that day in the tunnel? If I hadn't killed those men, Trahern or Bane would have. Would that have been easier for you to accept, one human killing another?" He inched closer, his anger coming at her in waves.

"No, it's not about that." But it was, and about so much more.

"Are you afraid I'll hurt your precious brother?

If you'll recall, he's always been the one to start the fight, not me."

He started to reach toward her, the sudden motion causing her to flinch. She knew he wouldn't hurt her, but he'd been pushed as far as he was going to be pushed.

His hands clamped onto her upper arms, but not hard enough to leave bruises. "I have given you no reason to fear me, Lacey. You want answers to your question. Fine." He pulled her closer, staring down at her with his pale eyes. "I have killed until the thought of it makes me sick, and I have seen my people die on your Paladins' swords for no reason other than the color of their eyes."

She wanted to protest the horror of the picture he painted with his words. "I didn't think—"

"That's right, you *didn't* think. Nobody does. All our two peoples know is endless death and butchery." He let go of her as suddenly as he'd grabbed her.

The grief in his voice melted into her heart. As he started for the door, she said, "Barak, stop."

She thought he'd ignore her, but he paused to look back at her. Something in the heat of his expression gave her the courage to say, "Come back."

"Why? So you can burden me with more of your questions? Why don't you seek out your brother instead and ask him how many of my kind he has spitted on the end of his sword, or why he's so anxious to kill more?" He took a shuddering breath. "At least I walked away from the madness."

He resumed his march to the door, but she caught up with him before he could open it. He stared at her hand on his arm. "Touch me at your own risk, Lacey. I have given you time to adjust to what happened between us in the tunnel, but I grow weary of waiting. Either step back or accept the consequences."

God help her, she couldn't retreat. This was the wrong man, the wrong time, the wrong everything, but she wasn't going to let him walk away.

She slid her hand up his arm to his shoulder, feeling the strength in his muscles and liking it. Sliding between him and the door, she smiled, even if it was a bit shaky. Some of the tension in his stance faded as he wrapped her in his arms, his mouth crushing down on hers, a warrior claiming his prize.

His kiss gentled, content to let the heat build at its own pace. Lacey teased his tongue with her own, smiling when he groaned with deep pleasure. She reached up and tugged the strip of leather off his ponytail. He murmured his approval as she fisted her fingers in his shoulder-length hair. It felt like rough silk to the touch.

His hands were doing a little exploring of their own, trailing down her ribs to her waist and on to trace the curve of her hips. When he cupped her bottom with both hands and squeezed, she thought she was going to come right then. Breathing was becoming difficult. He broke off the kiss long enough to pick her up and set her down on the nearest counter.

Without asking permission, he parted her knees and stepped between them. The counter was the right height to bring the center of her body in direct contact with his. When he flexed his hips, letting her feel the powerful strength of his need, she moaned and pulled him closer for a long, hot kiss.

His hand slipped between them to test the weight of her breasts. She was no innocent, but nothing she'd ever experienced had prepared her for such intensity from a lover. She wanted him to take her right then, right there on the lab counter. It was crazy and risky and she didn't care. But when she reached for the buttons on his shirt, he stilled her hands.

His breathing was ragged. "Lacey, we can't, not here."

He was right, but that didn't make it easy to hear. He rested his forehead against hers as he lifted her hands up to sprinkle a few light kisses across her knuckles. At least he was only banking the fire, not trying to extinguish it altogether.

"I want you, Lacey. I spend far too many hours thinking about how it would be to hold you naked in my arms as I pleasure you every way I can think of. The thought of taking you makes me *ache*." His silver eyes held hers prisoner.

The image had her demanding his kiss again. When she tugged him closer, he came willingly.

But then he said, "But before we go any farther, you have to make sure this is what you really want. I won't take a lover who is embarrassed to be seen with me in public, or who only takes me to her bed when she's sure that no one will know."

His words cut through to her heart, even though his intention was to protect them both. He was right. Kissing him in a fit of temper or even to offer comfort was one thing. Letting everyone in the organization—not to mention her brother—know that she'd invited their enemy into her bed would be a disaster.

He must have read her answer in her eyes, because he stepped away, giving her one more measuring look as he left the lab, letting the door swing shut behind him. She'd done the right thing; she knew that for a fact.

So why did it hurt so much?

The gym door opened. Barak picked up the sword he'd chosen from the rack and turned to face his opponent. He wasn't sure if he was relieved or angry that Penn Sebastian wasn't alone. Evidently Devlin felt that one of them needed a babysitter for this first practice session.

"Barak," Devlin said by way of greeting.

Penn glared at Barak and remained silent. Fine. Barak's encounter with Lacey back in the lab had left him irritable as hell. There was no better target for his temper than her jerk of a brother.

Devlin stripped off his shirt and tossed it down in the corner. Penn did the same, so Barak followed suit. The gym was hot and would only grow more uncomfortable as the afternoon wore on.

As usual, Devlin took charge. "I started Penn on a weight routine yesterday to help build up the strength in his arms. But he'll also need help learning to respond with his off hand."

Barak nodded in agreement before starting a series of stretches to warm up his muscles. After a few seconds Devlin and Penn stopped their own warm-ups to watch. Barak continued, letting the death dance absorb some of his anger. A fighter who let his emotions overrule his concentration stood a good chance of being hurt or killed, even in a practice match. After a bit, the other two resumed their own workouts, leaving him to finish undisturbed.

Barak ignored Penn and spoke to Devlin. "Do you want him working mostly with his right hand, or should he concentrate on his left?"

"He needs both."

"*He* is right here, Bane. If the Other has questions about me, I'll answer them."

"His name is Barak, Penn. Use his name or shut up. Barak has moves that I can't hope to duplicate. Maybe if you'd spend less time being an asshole and more time watching him, you might pick up a few tips."

"I know how to kill his kind, Bane. That's the

only tip I need." Penn picked up his sword in his right hand with a belligerent look on his face.

Barak didn't know what kind of game Bane was playing by pitting Penn against him, but he didn't like it. "I do not need this. I'm leaving."

Devlin promptly planted himself in Barak's path. "I don't give a damn what you need or don't need. The deal is that you will earn your keep around here, and the Regents have left it up to me to decide exactly what that means. I've decided that it means you'll teach Penn to fight left-handed. Tomorrow I might decide differently, but you're not walking out of here until I say you can."

Penn sneered, "And if I refuse to work with him? Will you send his ass back across the barrier where he belongs, or kill him like you should have in the first place?"

"Enough!" Devlin let loose a roundhouse punch that sent Penn stumbling backwards into the nearest wall. "Pick up your sword and do what Barak says."

He stomped out of the gym, leaving Barak and Penn to fend for themselves. Did he trust them that much, or had they pushed him so far that he didn't really care if they killed each other?

The idea was tempting. But as angry as he was with Lacey at the moment, Barak still could not bring himself to kill her brother. For her sake, and not Devlin's, he would teach Penn what he could.

Barak switched his sword to his left hand and held it up in a mock salute. "So, shall we kill each other and simplify Bane's life, or continue to aggravate him by surviving this little farce of his?"

Penn stared at his right hand as he opened and closed it a couple of times, each time forcing it closer into the correct grip. It obviously hurt him, but he seemed determined to make it work. Then he switched hands and held up his sword, trying to mimic the same grace that he had with his right.

"Bring it on, Other. I'm ready."

Chapter 10

The drinks were cold, which was all Barak could find to like about the dingy neighborhood bar. Glancing at Penn, he wondered which of them was more surprised at ending up sharing a booth and a beer.

Back in the gym, they'd worn each other out with blunted weapons. It had been some time since he'd served as an instructor, but the old habits were still there. He'd challenged Penn when he'd shown progress, and he'd used the flat side of the blade to correct him when he'd gotten careless or clumsy.

Afterward, when they'd been leaving the building, Penn had mentioned he was meeting someone at the bar right up the street. The comment hadn't exactly been an invitation, but when they'd reached the bar, Penn had offered to buy Barak a cold one.

Barak wasn't sure what the Paladin was up to, but one afternoon of swordplay did not mean they were friends, especially if Penn ever found out what Barak had been doing with his sister. Barak leaned back in the booth and took another long drink of his beer. The cold liquid slid down his throat, easing his thirst but doing nothing to erase the taste of Lacey's kiss or the memory of how the fullness of her breast had fit his hand.

His body stirred in memory of her sweet, hot response to his touch. Maybe he'd been a fool not to take what she'd offered, but she deserved better than a quick tussle on a lab counter. They both did. But if he'd blown his one chance to couple with her, he'd never forgive himself.

Penn was too busy watching the door to pay much attention to Barak. Who was coming that had the volatile Paladin on edge? Penn's fingers drummed a relentless beat on the tabletop as he sat up a little taller each time the door opened to afford him a view of the latest arrival. After he slumped back down in the corner of the booth for the third time, Barak drained his beer and set it down.

"So who are we waiting for?"

Maybe Penn would answer; more likely, he'd tell Barak it was none of his damn business. Before Penn decided which he'd do, the door opened again.

"He's here."

A balding, middle-aged man paused inside the doorway, probably waiting for his eyes to adjust to the dim interior of the bar. After a few seconds, he spotted Penn waving at him from the back. He started forward, his steps faltering when he realized that Penn wasn't alone. He pasted an insincere smile on his face as he approached the booth.

Sliding in next to Penn, he nodded in Barak's direction. "Sorry I'm late, but our departmental meeting ran overtime." Rather reluctantly, he held his hand out. "I'm Ben from IT. You must be that Barak fellow everybody's been talking about."

"I must be." Barak shook the man's hand. Was it fear or something else that had the man's palms sweating?

Something about the man teased at Barak's senses. He hadn't seen the man before, but there was something about him that was familiar. He closed his eyes briefly and drew in a slow, deep breath, tasting the air surrounding the booth. He'd smelled the same aftershave in the lab when he'd found that his notes had been shuffled through and left out of order. He met Ben's nervous gaze and smiled slightly.

It wouldn't hurt to prod a little. "You seem familiar, Ben. Have we met before? Perhaps in the geology lab?"

"No!" Ben immediately realized he'd overreacted to a simple question. "Sorry, I didn't mean that to come out the way it sounded. It's been a long day, and I guess I'm more stressed than I realized. I should have said that I haven't been into the research wing in months." He pulled a handkerchief out of his hip pocket and dabbed at the sweat on his forehead. "How about I buy the next round?"

Penn had been watching the interchange with interest. "That would be great. After that, though, Barak and I need to hit the road."

Why would Penn make it sound as if he and Barak had plans together? Barak didn't know anything about Penn's personal life, but it seemed unlikely that he and this Ben fellow were good friends. As a rule, Paladins hung out with other Paladins, especially when they were on the wrong side of too many deaths. Barak had to wonder if Penn suspected Ben was up to something.

Like stealing the blue garnets from Barak's world? Barak accepted the second beer and studied Ben as he and Penn got into a long-winded discussion about the Mariners' chances of taking their division. Barak had yet to develop an interest for the sports the humans seemed to be addicted to.

Lacey wore the occasional T-shirt with a team logo emblazoned across her chest and he always admired the snug fit of the shirt, though he knew little about the team it stood for. Perhaps it would be wise to study the various sports in greater detail in order to fit into society a little better. Maybe he could coax her into taking him to a game or two.

But right now, Penn had almost finished his second beer. It was time for him to do the same. As Barak lifted the bottle to his lips, Penn slid out of the booth with no warning.

"It's time." The Paladin nodded in Ben's direction. "Thanks for the beer, Ben."

Then he walked away, leaving Barak to follow or not. Since Barak had no desire to be left behind, he took one last swig of his beer and set the bottle down on the table. "I thank you as well."

If Ben was surprised to be abandoned, he hid it well. "You're welcome. Any time."

Somehow Barak doubted that, but it didn't matter. At least now he was reasonably sure that Ben was the one who had been sneaking around the geology lab. The problem was what to do with that information.

Outside, he spotted Penn standing a short distance down the street. What was going on? Penn was up to something, and there was only one way to find out what.

Barak deliberately crowded Penn and demanded, "When I first started working with your sister, why did you send Ben to search the lab?"

Penn had been leaning against the brick front of the tavern, but he immediately straightened, his fists clenched at his sides. "What the hell are you talking about, Other? I never sent him anywhere. I hardly know the man."

The temper rang true. So Ben had been exploring on his own. Again, why?

"Right after I started working in the lab, someone went through my papers. Until just now, I didn't know who it was," Barak replied, allowing a small smile to soften his words. "I even thought it might have been you."

Penn's blue eyes narrowed. "Well, it wasn't. How the hell do you know it was Ben?"

"I recognized his scent: sickly sweet cologne mixed with too much sweat." He doubted the Paladin would believe him, but that was his problem.

To his surprise, Penn nodded. "We need to move on before he decides to leave."

Barak fell into step beside Penn as they headed up the block.

"He's been hanging around me lately for no good reason." Penn kicked a small rock, sending it flying out into the street. "He wants something."

"It would seem that he's interested in both of us." And it had to do with the blue stones, but he couldn't tell Penn that yet. He only had Penn's word that he wasn't involved in whatever Ben was doing. He'd have to check with Devlin, since the Paladin leader was determined to limit the number of people who knew about the ongoing theft from Barak's world.

Penn continued on in silence. Finally, he stopped and turned on Barak. "If you're doing anything that would endanger or hurt my sister, you're a dead man."

Then he walked away, leaving Barak staring after him.

"We're almost there."

Lacey couldn't keep the excitement—tinged with relief—out of her voice, because sharing the ride with Barak had made the interior of the truck seem crowded and small. She loved studying all of the volcanoes in Washington, but Mount St. Helens was special. She glanced at her silent companion, wondering what he was thinking as they drove the switchback road that would take them to the visitors' center closest to the mountain.

She frowned, noting the tension in his expression. "Are you all right, Barak? I hope you're not getting altitude sickness again."

He shook his head slightly, all the time keeping his eyes firmly on the road and the periodic glimpses of the mountain. "I'll be fine." He glanced down the steep drop to the valley below. "After seeing the places that have been replanted, I'm surprised that so much of the area immediately around the mountain is still so barren. It hurts my soul to see it."

She tried to see how it all must look to him, and she nodded. "They show a film of the 1980 explosion in the visitors' center, if you'd like to see it. It doesn't last long, but it's pretty amazing."

"I'll think about it."

He craned his head to look behind them, once again letting the silence settle between them. Although he wasn't given to long conversations, he'd been unusually quiet since leaving the lab. It bothered her more than she cared to admit, because she suspected that it was due to what had happened between them.

Had he also had trouble sleeping, thinking too much about how wonderful that intense burst of passion had felt? Even when she had finally dozed off, her sleep had been filled with images of Barak's silver eyes and serious smile. Not quite the stuff for soothing dreams. Though she rarely bothered with makeup, today she'd needed some to hide the dark circles under her eyes.

The mountain directly ahead reminded her of Barak in some ways. For the moment, the volcano had only a few plumes of steam rising off the peak, a quiet reminder of the power and heat hiding behind that deceptive façade. But no one who lived in the Northwest would forget that the mountain was capable of violence. And Barak, for such a reserved man, was capable of some pretty intense moments.

The last one had left her shaken for hours afterward. As a result, she'd spent a good part of last night debating the wisdom of bringing him along today. But she wasn't a coward, and if they couldn't be lovers, then somehow they'd have to learn how to be friends.

She made the last turn that led into the parking lot at the end of the road. "Let's get the equipment unloaded, and then we can decide if we have time to watch the movie."

Barak looked like a statue, frozen in position as he stared out at the mountain. Finally, he closed his eyes and took a handful of slow, deep breaths.

"Are you all right?" She'd already asked him that once, but he was starting to worry her.

Without opening his eyes, he snapped, "Quit

hovering. I have already said I'm fine, Lacey. I'm just adjusting to the mountain."

Adjusting? What did he mean by that? She could be snarly, too. "Okay, fine. You just sit there and do whatever it is you need to do. Meanwhile I'll unpack the gear I promised to leave for the university students to disperse on their next hike."

But when she reached the back of the truck, Barak was already there to help her lift the equipment down to the ground. When they both reached for the same box, his hands covered hers. Once again a jolt of awareness shot up her nerves, making her jerk away. On the surface he seemed to either be unaware of the reaction his touch caused, or else he didn't care. Then she met his gaze and knew she was wrong. He'd felt it, all right, and was fighting the same rush of heat that she was.

"I'm sorry, Barak." Not for the accidental touch, but that neither of them could afford to give into temptation.

He went on unloading the boxes as if she hadn't said a word. That was fine with her. Really. "I'm going to go borrow a dolly from the rangers. I'll be right back."

When she walked away, she could have sworn that she could feel his gaze following her each step. When she reached the door of the Center, she risked one quick glance back to check. His back was toward her as he lifted another box from the truck bed. His dedication to his duties was to be admired; at least one of them seemed able to cope with the attraction between them.

Barak wondered at the number of people who were willing to venture so close to the mountain. Humans might not have his affinity for stone, but no one could look at the surrounding area and not recognize the volcano's taste for destruction. He stood near the seismographs, their needles etching the ground movements in ink. Only a few minutes before, the needles had swung wildly from side to side, indicating a slight quake. He'd held his hand out, tracing the energy back to its source. Murmuring under his breath, he siphoned off some of the tension and spread it out over a greater area. After a heartbeat, maybe two, the needles slowed their wild dance and resumed a more sedate pace.

Barak leaned against a handy counter, pretending an interest in the items displayed there as he caught his breath. It had been a long time since he'd last worked stone, and then it had been in his world. As he still struggled to learn this new world, even the simplest of techniques—like soothing the momentary spasm in the stone—took a lot out of him.

Even so, it felt good to stretch muscles he hadn't used in a while. Once he caught his breath, he looked around for Lacey. He spotted her standing across the room, talking to a group of children about a "spider," a clever piece of machinery vulcanologists used to monitor the mountain. This particular piece of machinery had been damaged when Mount St. Helens had been in one of her moods.

Lacey knelt down on the floor to speak to the children at their level. Right then she was listening intently to a little girl. Lacey frowned slightly, her eyes alight with intelligence as she answered the question in terms such a young one could understand.

He could have watched her all day, inspiring the small child with her love for her chosen field. Did she have any idea how beautiful she was? Somehow he doubted it. But even across the crowded room, he could feel her warmth, selfishly wishing he could keep it all to himself.

He'd overheard one of the Paladins bragging about a recent conquest, describing a night spent burning up the sheets. That's exactly what would happen when he convinced Lacey to share his bed.

As if she'd felt his scrutiny, Lacey glanced in his direction. Her smile faltered slightly as she gave him a puzzled look. He carefully banked the fires and turned away after a quick nod in her direction. He was trying to give her time to adjust to his presence in her life, but it was growing increasingly difficult. Her friendship was a double-edged sword. There was so much he had to hide from her while at the same time he badly needed her to trust him enough to let him get close.

He had secrets to protect. But, damn it, it hurt to be this alone.

• • •

The small theater was cool and comfortable—for her. Barak, on the other hand, was clenching the armrest between them in a white-knuckled grip. Telling herself she would have offered comfort to anyone, she gently pried his hand free and threaded her fingers through his, noting how chilly his skin felt.

She could understand his reaction to the movie of the 1980 explosion of Mount St. Helens; it was nature unleashed and destructive beyond description. But it had happened close to thirty years ago. Why was it bothering Barak so much?

The screen went blank and disappeared back up into the ceiling. The drapes covering the windows drew back, revealing the mountain in all of its deadly beauty. Her heart skipped a beat, just as it always did at the sight of all that barely controlled rage. She'd always wondered just how strong that glass was, in case the mountain decided to blow again.

Barak's hand squeezed hers almost to the point of pain, although she doubted he was aware of it. He slowly rose to his feet, his eyes never leaving the mountain. She let herself be tugged along in his wake as he slowly approached the windows.

When he stepped into the bright sunlight streaming in through the glass, she was surprised to see that his lips were tugged up in a slight smile. He drew a deep breath, letting it out slowly as the tension in his stance disappeared. It was only then that he noticed how hard he was gripping her hand.

"I'm sorry." He brought her hand up to his lips.

The warmth of his breath both tickled and soothed her hand, but it had a different effect on the rest of her body. Without thinking, she turned to face him, the desire to be held in his arms suddenly overwhelming her.

"Have you thought about what I said?" he whispered.

The reminder of the choice she had yet to make acted as a splash of cold water, causing her to back away from him. No, she hadn't thought, which showed how comfortable she'd become with him regardless of his alien nature. When she backed away, he let her go without protest. She cast around for something to say, something that would ease the renewed strain between them.

"We'd better be going. It's a long drive back home from here."

Barak's mood remained cold and angry all the way to where Lacey dropped him off in his apartment parking lot. He had spent the ride down the mountain silently cursing himself, cursing Lacey's understandable reluctance to accept the passion he could offer her, and cursing the mountain even more. He'd promised himself earlier that morning that he would make an effort to be casual and relaxed with Lacey.

He'd known beforehand that being shut up in the small cab of the truck with her would make it difficult to control his growing attraction to her. She warmed him in ways he'd thought gone from his life for good. If she'd been of his world, he would have known better how to court her, how to lure her to his bed.

He'd worried that he'd driven her away for good with his blunt statement that it had to be all or nothing for them. It was the simple truth, but he could have softened his words so they wouldn't have hurt her so much. It spoke of Lacey's innate kindness that as they'd approached the mountain she'd seemed more concerned about him than she was about herself.

He closed his eyes and thought about the mountain. He'd known Mount St. Helens was restless, but he hadn't known how powerfully she would call to him. He'd been able to sense the murmurs deep under the slopes as powerfully as if he'd reached out and touched them with his hands.

Even the movie had held him captive, reveling in the power of the rock and stone that made up the mountain's heart. And these foolish humans had watched as if it had been just another special-effects extravaganza. Lacey and the rangers who worked near the mountain were the only ones who understood the danger they were all flirting with by being so close to the restless volcano.

He walked up the stairs to his apartment, wishing he could find some release for the energy building up within him. Another good fight with Penn would help, but Barak couldn't very well call up the Paladin to say that he either needed to spar with Penn or bed his sister. Imagining the volatile Paladin's response made him smile for the first time in hours.

Devlin and Trahern would understand the strong feelings a man felt for a woman he wanted to claim as his own. But they weren't likely to accept Barak's pursuing a human female, especially a fellow Paladin's sister.

When Barak reached his door, he could hear the phone ringing inside. He charged through to the kitchen and snatched up the receiver.

"Barak here."

"Hi, Barak." Laurel Young's calm voice washed over him, soothing away some of the day's stress. "You sound breathless. Did I catch you at a bad time?"

"It is never a bad time to speak to you, Laurel." He pulled a stool closer to the phone and sat down, content to stay on the line with his friend as long as possible.

"I was wondering if you'd like to come to dinner tomorrow night. Devlin, Trahern, and Brenna will be there."

He could tell she was holding her breath, waiting for his answer. "I would enjoy an evening out, if you're sure the others won't mind."

"I wouldn't be asking if I didn't want you there."

And if the two Paladins had strongly objected to her inviting him, she wouldn't have been calling. If she'd bothered to mention the idea to them at all.

She played her trump card. "If it makes any difference, I've also invited Lacey Sebastian."

Clever woman: she had him trapped. If he refused the invitation now, Laurel would know something was up. "I'm sure Lacey will enjoy an evening in your company, Laurel. She reminds me of you in some ways."

"So she's both brilliant and stubborn?" Her words were laced with laughter.

He chuckled. "I was going to say that you are both charming, but I won't contradict your assessment."

He could hear the smile in her voice. "I'll be glad to see you, Barak. Tomorrow at seven."

As he hung up the phone, he pondered the significance of Lacey's acceptance of Laurel's invitation. She was a bright woman and adept at math. There would be six people, three men, three women, three couples. Should be interesting.

Ben Jackson mopped his forehead for the third time in ten minutes. Failure mixed with fear made a man sweat even in cool weather. The minutes on the clock were ticking away until he had to make the call. His coconspirator paid well, but he expected results for his money.

Ben didn't have any to offer him, and that was bad. Maybe real bad. His sole assignment had been to find out what the Paladins knew about the blue stones operation. He'd thought Penn Sebastian was the best one to approach, but so far the disgruntled Paladin had proved elusive.

When he'd convinced Penn to meet him after work at the local bar, he'd thought that he had finally made some headway. But the man had thrown Ben a curve by showing up with that spooky Other in tow. What was up with that?

It seemed unlikely that the two were in cahoots with each other, but stranger things had happened. Besides, if word about the blue stones had leaked out, what better partner than one of those pale-eyed bastards from across the barrier? After all, what did Penn have to lose? He'd spent the last few months sitting on his ass in a filthy alley. If that was the best the Regents could do for one of their own, Penn should be vulnerable to bribes, at least.

But, just when he'd thought things had been working out, Penn's status had changed with no warning. If he really was on the verge of returning to full duty, then Ben was back where he'd started: hunting for a chink in the Paladins' armor.

He mopped his forehead again, wishing he could think of an excuse not to dial that phone. Hating the way his hand shook, he punched in the number he had on speed dial and prayed for voice mail to pick up. Luck was with him; unfortunately it was all bad.

"You're late."

Groveling wouldn't help; neither would lying. "At least I called."

The heavy silence told him that his small show of

bravado did little to improve the man's mood. "But late; we've already covered that. What have you got for me?"

"I had a beer with Penn Sebastian. It's the first time he's been willing to do that." Of course, Penn hadn't said more than a handful of words the whole time.

"Did you get anything out of him about what the Paladins know or suspect about our operation?"

"No, but he had the Other with him. That Barak fellow." Ben shuddered; that freak had really given him the creeps. "There was no chance to talk with him sitting there."

"What was he like? The Other, I mean." There was renewed excitement in his boss's voice.

Ben thought back. Mostly he and Penn had dissected the last couple of baseball games. "He was quiet, but with the same edgy feel as a young Paladin—you know, before they learn to hide what they are. If he didn't have that strange coloring, he could have passed for just another guy stopping off for a cold one on the way home from work."

Ben frowned. "He and Penn were sitting together when I came into the bar, but I didn't get the idea that they were chummy. Last talk I heard, Penn was angry about Barak working with his sister. Can't see how that would have changed any."

"Then that's a weakness for you to prey on. That and his bad hand. I hear that it's not healing."

How had he heard that? He didn't work in the

same area as the Paladins. Even if he did, they didn't spread gossip, especially when it was bad news.

"I'll keep trying. But if I push too hard, he's more likely to get suspicious rather than friendly."

"We need to know what they know. It's up to you to find out. Try harder, or I'll find someone else who will."

Ben was sweating again. No one was allowed to just walk away from their little enterprise. You were either in or dead. Nothing in between.

The silence from the other end of the line was ominous. Ben closed his eyes as he desperately tried to offer up something that would placate the man. There was Penn, the Other, and Penn's sister.

Penn's sister—there was a thought. Lacey Sebastian was well thought of throughout the organization. The local Paladins treated her like a mascot, so threatening her would be like running on a razor's edge. They'd go after anyone who threatened her with their swords drawn, but they wouldn't risk her getting hurt.

Maybe, if he was really careful, he could trade information for Lacey. Then he'd have to run like hell, but that day was coming anyway. Hurting a woman wasn't his style, but he needed to buy himself some time.

He braced himself for the worst. "Listen, sir, how about this?"

Chapter 11

$\mathscr{H}$ello, Barak, come on in." Laurel smiled as she stood back and welcomed him into her home.

He handed her the bottle of wine he'd chosen. "I hope you like it. The guy at the wine shop assured me it was a decent vintage."

Laurel grinned up at him. "Listen to you! You're sounding more like a native-born Washingtonian all the time. I'm impressed."

Devlin loomed up behind her. "Damn it, Barak, I've warned you about flirting with my woman." He slipped his arm around Laurel's shoulder and pulled her against his side to nuzzle her neck.

Laurel did her best to frown up at her lover, but it was obvious that she couldn't stay mad at him long. "He wasn't flirting. I was just commenting on how well he was adjusting to our world."

Barak thought she was being optimistic, but that was Laurel's way. No one else would have taken on the daunting task of convincing Devlin and the other Paladins to suffer their lifelong enemy to walk among them safely.

"I'll take the wine into the kitchen. I need to check on dinner."

Devlin waited until she was out of the room before giving Barak a conspiratorial look.

"We may need all the wine we can drink. Laurel doesn't cook very often." Then he dropped his voice and shuddered. "Thank goodness. Vegetable dishes are pretty safe, but the meat is usually iffy."

Barak stifled a smile. "I will choose what I eat with care."

"What are you two talking about out there?" Laurel poked her head out of the kitchen.

Before Devlin had to come up with a believable answer, the doorbell rang again. "That's probably Trahern and Brenna."

The entryway was about to get crowded. Barak walked into the living room, hoping for a few seconds of solitude. But he hadn't been the first one to arrive, after all. Lacey looked up from the magazine she was browsing and gave him a tentative smile.

"Hi, Barak. I hope you don't mind me being here. Laurel was pretty insistent that I come."

"No, of course not. I've said before that I thought you and Laurel would make good friends. Brenna Nichols, too."

He was rather proud of himself for sounding coherent. He was used to seeing Lacey dressed in jeans and a T-shirt for work. Nothing had prepared him for seeing her in a dress, one that showed off her feminine curves to perfection. Her tan legs were long and graceful, and the heels she wore accented her trim ankles and pretty feet. She looked wonderful all dressed up, and he wanted nothing more than to strip every stitch of clothing off her.

He'd vowed to treat her no differently than he would either Laurel or Brenna—courtesy coupled with a cool distance. But there was nothing cool about the way he was feeling right now—especially when Lacey leaned over to put the magazine back on the coffee table, affording him a brief glimpse of her cleavage. Maybe he should leave while he could still walk out the door.

Trahern strolled into the room. "Hey, Lacey, what are you doing here?"

Lacey's eyes met Barak's briefly before facing Trahern. "They do let me out of the lab once in a while, you big oaf. I'm more interested in knowing who's holding your leash tonight. Has poor Brenna realized that you're barely even housebroken?"

A smiling Brenna Nichols stepped out from behind Trahern. "We're working on that. It's good to see you again, Lacey. You, too, Barak."

He doubted that, but he was willing to pretend if they were. "Are you still enjoying the archives, Brenna?"

"Yeah, although I promised Blake I wouldn't bore everyone to tears with it," she said, giving Trahern a mock frown. "I can't help it if he and his buddies like to be all mysterious and spooky."

Lacey giggled. "It's hard to consider them mysterious when you had to share a bathroom with one of them growing up."

Trahern rolled his eyes and yelled, "Hey, Bane, I need backup in here. Brenna and Lacey are ganging up on me."

Barak enjoyed the banter, wishing he knew how to join in. He had grown up thinking the Paladins were murderous monsters, but it was getting harder to remember that when he saw them with their women, relaxed and happy. Who could have ever imagined someone as hard as Blake Trahern being teased by a trio of beautiful women and enjoying it?

"And how about you, Barak? How is it working with Lacey in the geology lab?" Brenna stood next to Trahern, with his arm draped casually around her shoulder. "Laurel tells me that you've a special interest in the subject."

That was the excuse that he and Devlin had told Laurel, but it was truer than the Paladin leader knew. "I'm enjoying the challenge of mastering your technology. And Dr. Sebastian introduced me to Mount St. Helens yesterday."

He knew he sounded stiff and formal using Lacey's title, but he needed that small distance it gave him. He didn't want anyone to think of them as a couple, though if he'd been human, he would have encouraged everyone to think that way. Especially her.

Laurel joined in the discussion. "I've never been down there, but I understand it's an amazing sight. I keep planning on making the trip, but I never seem to find the time. Besides, the one time I mentioned it to Devlin, he looked at me as if I were crazy."

Devlin nodded. "And for good reason. I spend way too much of my time fighting because that bitch of a mountain can't settle down. Every time she acts up, I end up ankle deep in—" Laurel elbowed him in the ribs, bringing the Paladin's comment to an abrupt halt.

Ankle deep in Other blood. They all knew that the mountain's rumblings resulted in the Paladins having to face Barak's kin in one bloody battle after another.

Laurel broke the silence in a too-bright voice. "Devlin, I'd like to see you in the kitchen." Then realizing how that sounded, she amended her request. "I could use your help."

Devlin looked like he'd swallowed something foul, but he followed Laurel anyway. Trahern waited until his friend disappeared into the next room before laughing. "Does my heart such good to see someone call Bane on the carpet once in a while."

"I heard that, Trahern," Devlin yelled from the kitchen. "Keep that up and I'll run your ass ragged tomorrow in practice."

Trahern only laughed harder. From what Barak

had seen, the two men were pretty much equal when it came to fighting, either with or without weapons. Devlin had more style when it came to using a sword, but Barak would not have wanted to face Trahern in battle. He didn't underestimate his own skills, but Trahern fought with deadly determination.

Still smiling, Trahern looked at Barak. "I hear Devlin has pitted you against Penn. How's that going?"

Lacey moved closer to him, waiting for his answer, no doubt worried about her surly brother. Barak hesitated before answering, mainly because Devlin had wanted to keep the workouts private. Obviously, though, Bane didn't care if Trahern knew, and Lacey was Penn's sister.

"We've only had one workout so far. We started off at each other's throats, but that's no surprise. His right hand is still weak, but showing promise. He's never fought with his left hand, but he's learning."

Lacey offered him a tentative smile. "That's good news, Barak. He may not say so, but I'm sure Penn appreciates your working with him."

Barak laughed. "I wouldn't say that. Devlin was so disgusted with the two of us, he stormed out, leaving us to kill each other. We decided that would only make his life simpler, and we'd rather stick around to aggravate him some more."

"I heard that, too," Devlin said as he walked in from the kitchen. "Laurel says we can all come to the table. Dinner is served."

He met Barak's gaze long enough to remind him of what he'd said earlier about Laurel's cooking. Barak quietly sniffed the air and decided that Devlin was right. Judging by the slight burnt-meat smell in the air, it might indeed be safer to stick to the vegetables.

Besides, the food didn't really matter. For this one evening, he was being included as part of the close-knit group of friends enjoying themselves over dinner. He just wished he and Lacey Sebastian would be leaving together afterward.

The evening drew to a close. Lacey had to work in the morning, but she'd been in no hurry to leave. Laurel and Brenna were kindred spirits, who gave her hope that Penn might eventually find someone who brought happiness to his life.

But more importantly, she liked the way they both accepted Barak. Laurel had been the first to champion his cause, but Brenna didn't seem at all uncomfortable in his presence. Why that should matter to her she didn't know, but it did.

Maybe because she sensed a deep loneliness in Barak. Even in a crowd of people, he seemed to be set apart. Perhaps it was his own doing, but it had to be difficult to be the only one of his kind wherever he went. For her part, most of the time she forgot that he was different.

Except for the way he affected her. She had to wonder if Laurel had sensed that Lacey's feelings for Barak ran deeper than mere affection for a fellow coworker, especially when Lacey considered the fact that she and Barak had been the only unattached guests at the dinner. Although Laurel hadn't assigned seats at the table, the two couples had naturally chosen seats next to each other, leaving Lacey and Barak no choice but to do the same.

"Thank you again for inviting me, Laurel. I had a wonderful time," Barak said.

"I'm glad you could come."

Trahern's car had been blocking Lacey's truck, so he and Brenna had left first so she could get out. The temperature outside was still mild, but it had started raining while they'd been eating.

When Laurel saw how hard it was coming down, she stopped Barak from leaving. "Give me a minute to grab my purse, and I'll give you a ride home."

Devlin wasn't having any of that. "If anyone takes him, it will be me."

Lacey intervened. "No, let me. There's no point in you two going out in this weather when I'm going right by there."

"I don't want to be trouble for anyone. It will not hurt me to walk." Barak stepped past Lacey, heading out into the steady drizzle.

She caught his arm. "I wouldn't have offered if I didn't mean it. It's no trouble."

He studied her face briefly before slowly nodding. "All right then, thank you." Turning back to

Laurel and Devlin, he gave them one of his rare smiles. "And I thank you again for inviting me."

Devlin said, "We're both glad you came, Barak. I'll see you at the gym tomorrow afternoon."

"Bring your sword. It will be easier to show Penn what he should be doing if I have a victim to practice on."

Devlin laughed. "Don't you mean a volunteer?"

Barak arched an eyebrow. "That depends on which one of us wins. We'll find out tomorrow."

With that, Lacey led the way out to her truck. Once again the cab seemed small with Barak in it, but she didn't regret making the offer. It wasn't often she got to see Barak this relaxed and enjoying himself. She almost wished he lived farther away to stretch out their remaining time together. Tomorrow morning they'd be back to their usual roles of coworkers.

At a stoplight, she turned to face her silent companion. "I had such a good time. I'll have to think of something nice to do for Laurel for inviting me. I know she appreciated your bringing her wine."

"She is a kind person."

Lacey hesitated before bringing up her brother's name. "I want to thank you again for working with Penn."

"It's nothing." He turned to look out his window, clearly trying to avoid the subject.

"No, it's not nothing. I know it must be hard for you to help him regain his ability, considering how he'll put those skills to use." She reached out to touch his hand, offering what little comfort she could.

He immediately wrapped his hand around hers and gave it a gentle squeeze. "Laurel isn't the only kind one."

There wasn't much she could say to that, so they drove the remaining few blocks to his apartment in silence. She pulled into a parking spot even though that wasn't necessary to drop him off.

Barak didn't hurry to open the door. When he turned those pale eyes in her direction, it was as if he'd reached out to caress her face. The summer rainstorm shut out the rest of the world, leaving the two of them alone—and too far apart. She was playing with fire, waiting for whatever was going to happen next.

She only hoped it happened soon before she lost all courage and bolted for home.

"Lacey . . ." He made her name sound like a prayer, and maybe it was.

"Barak . . . ," she whispered and then giggled, partly from nerves and partly because they sounded like the beginning of a love scene in an old soap opera.

"I like your laugh." Barak reached across to tuck her hair behind her ear. "I want to kiss you."

Was that a challenge? Or simply a man warning his woman what was coming? His hand slid behind her head to draw her closer to him. She went willingly, sliding across the bench seat until her thigh brushed against his, sending a frisson of heat through her chest and spreading out from there, leaving her aching.

"Things haven't changed, Lacey. I won't be a guilty secret for you." He brushed his lips across hers, stopping short of actually kissing her.

Was this what she wanted? *Yes.* Was tasting the passion she saw flickering in Barak's eyes worth the risks? She didn't know and didn't care. Right now, right there, she wanted him.

But she had her pride, too. She wouldn't lie to him. "Barak, I don't know how to handle this; I'm not sure I can. But if you'll settle for what I can give tonight, invite me inside."

She crawled up on his lap without waiting for an answer. Using little flicks of her tongue, she coaxed and teased until he abruptly claimed her mouth, plundering it with his tongue and teeth. He lifted her up to straddle his lap and slid down in the seat enough so that his erection was riding and rubbing directly at her core.

His taste was headier than the wine they'd shared at Laurel's, making her head spin with the intoxicating heat they were generating. When he wrenched his mouth from hers, she whimpered, wanting more of the same.

"If I'm to have you but this once, Lacey I want to do it right. Come inside with me."

Somewhere in the past few minutes, she'd pulled

the tie off his ponytail. Running her fingers through his hair, she rested her forehead against his. "Take me to your bed, Barak. Please."

He caught her hands in his. "Get your purse, and we'll go inside."

His practical nature made her smile as she clambered off his lap and reached for her keys and purse. He was already around the truck to open her door for her. Luckily, his apartment was only a few steps away, giving them little time to think about what they were about to do.

Inside he took her purse and dropped it on a handy chair. "Would you prefer to have a cup of coffee or tea first?"

How sweet! But no, she wanted more of what they'd merely tasted out in the truck. She walked into his arms and raised up on her toes, leaning into his strength. A deep chuckle vibrated through his chest.

"I will take that as a no."

She gave him a woman's smile, the kind that said she was hungry for her man, and ran her hand down his chest, hesitating only briefly before continuing down the front of his pants to caress him. "You can take this as a yes."

His smile was purely male and pleased. "My bedroom is that way."

She took hold of his hand and led him in that direction, feeling daring and desirable. Once they crossed the threshold, he kissed her again, no holds barred, his tongue thrusting deeply into her mouth. His hands slid down her sides to catch the hem of her dress, tugging it upward. He cupped her bottom with only the thin lace of her panties between his callused hands and her skin. Her knees melted.

She wrapped her arms around his neck to keep from collapsing on the floor. His hand slid under the lace, tugging her panties down her hips. Oh, Lord, she was burning up.

"I want to lay you down and kiss you all over." He traced her ear with his tongue.

Sweeping her up in his arms, he surprised her with his strength. She wasn't a small woman, but she felt so very feminine in his embrace. He set her down on the edge of the bed and knelt at her feet. He slipped off her sandals, gently rubbing each foot.

Holding her gaze with his own, he slid his hands up her calves to her thighs to grasp her panties again, this time taking them off completely. She pulled her dress over her head and tossed it on the floor. Barak took charge of her bra, fumbling a bit with the front clasp. When it finally gave way, her breasts spilled into his waiting hands.

How did he know exactly how to tease her nipples exactly the way she liked it?

"You're still dressed," she complained.

"That can be fixed." He quickly stripped off his

shirt while she murmured her approval, but when he reached for the fly on his pants, she stopped him. "Let me."

She put her warm hands on his chest and slid them down toward his belt, taking her time, as if to memorize the shape and the feel of him. She undid his buckle and then, keeping her eyes on Barak's face, she slowly, oh, so slowly eased his zipper down. He closed his eyes briefly, praying for patience, sighing with relief when she finally finished. He stripped his pants and boxers off, glad to be rid of the burden of clothing.

This moment, when they would first lay skin to skin, was to be savored. He leaned over her, pressed a kiss against her forehead, then claimed her mouth; this time there was nothing innocent about it as their tongues tangled in a rhythmic pattern of thrusts and parries.

The scent of Lacey's growing desire perfumed the air. She scrambled back farther onto the bed, taking him with her. For far too many nights he'd lain in this same bed dreaming of having Lacey here beside him, but his imagination had failed him completely.

Her skin was living silk, sun-kissed to a golden color, smooth and supple and so warm to the touch. And her breasts—he could spend hours learning their weight and taste. He leaned toward her, burying his nose in the gold of her hair, and drew a deep breath before kissing his way down her jaw to nuzzle the pulse point at the base of her neck.

"Tell me what you want, Lacey."

"You," she whispered as she turned toward him, lifting her breasts up to him.

He kissed each one, liking the way her nipples beaded up and hardened. Swirling his tongue around the closest one, he finally gave in to Lacey's mute request and suckled her breast, tugging at it with his lips and teeth. Her legs stirred restlessly as his hand followed the slight curve of her belly down to the nest of curls below.

Lacey lifted her hips, asking without words for him to continue on. He kissed her belly and caressed her before easing a finger deep inside her slick passage. He smiled; her body was ready for their joining.

"That feels so good—but I want more." Lacey's eyes were half closed, her gaze heated. She pulled him back up to where they could kiss, this time with her sprawled over his chest.

He liked that she wasn't a passive lover as she moved from side to side, rubbing the pretty tips of her breasts against his chest. Placing his hands on her shoulders, he lifted her up high enough to be able to lave her breasts with quick flicks of his tongue and then suckled them harder.

In a quick move she straddled him, centering her wet heat right over his erection. His breathing came in quick shudders as the need to take her, to join with her, tried to wrest away the last bit of his control.

He rolled to the side, taking Lacey with him.

She pouted and tried to push him back, but he caught her hands and anchored them over her head. "We're getting too close. I need protection."

There was nothing he wanted more than to thrust into Lacey's welcoming body with only slick heat between them. But neither of them could risk creating a child. He reached for the bedside drawer and the box of condoms he'd bought the day he'd met Lacey.

She held out her hand. "Let me."

But instead of immediately opening the foil back, she laid the packet on his stomach and turned her attention to his penis. Lacey held him a willing prisoner: her feather-soft touch had him fisting the sheets and waiting to see what she'd do next.

Lacey smiled up at her lover, liking the power he'd given her as she leaned down to run her tongue down the length of him, feeling the way he strained to remain still. His body was all sculpted muscle and hard planes with the scars to prove his life hadn't been an easy one. He looked the part of a barbarian warrior with his dark hair spread out on the pillow.

And right now she wanted the power all those muscles promised. She tore the foil package open and gently rolled the condom down the impressive length of his penis, then skimmed her hand up and down it. Once. Twice.

Barak flipped her onto her back and knelt between her legs, bracing himself with his arms extended. "Look at me, Lacey. I want to see your eyes when we join."

She spread her legs wide in invitation. "Now, Barak. Take me now."

In two quick thrusts, he buried himself deep within her. She felt stretched by the length and width of him as he bit his lip trying to give her time to adjust. Rocking slowly, he pulled out a little and then pushed back in. She moaned with the wonder of it all, but she wanted more, faster, harder.

"Don't hold back, Barak."

He rocked again. "I don't want to hurt you."

"You won't."

He took her at her word, and she liked that about him. Barak lifted her legs high over his shoulders and began thrusting hard and fast as Lacey clutched the pillows and held on for the ride.

"Barak . . ." His name became her chant. He filled her as no other man ever had, his power and heat pounding deeper and deeper inside her, filling places she had never known were empty.

Suddenly he slowed his pace, almost withdrawing completely before pushing back deep inside of her.

"Barak! Don't tease."

He smiled down at her. "You don't like it this way?" He repeated the motion.

Oh, she liked it just fine, but the tension was building until she thought—no, she *needed*—to explode. She held up her arms, needed him to be closer. He eased her legs down to his waist and leaned down to kiss her. She reveled in the feel of his weight against her sensitive breasts.

Running her hands down his back, she grabbed his backside as once again he pounded into her. Ah, yes, this was what she'd needed all along. Heat and lightning coiled deep inside her, waiting for just the right touch to explode. Sweat-slicked skin slid over skin, as the pressure continued to build.

Then he raised up to look down between them. "Look, Lacey, to where we are joined."

When she did as he demanded, the sight of him sliding in and out of her made her smile. He rocked against her in a circular motion, the friction making her pant in anticipation. Then he did it again. In a burst of light and bright colors, she came, screaming Barak's name.

"Yes, Lacey, yes!" Barak drove forward hard, shuddering as his own release poured out deep inside her.

It took a minute, maybe two, for the world to right itself. Finally, Barak lifted his head and kissed her again, gently this time. His smile was a bit weary around the edges, but it warmed her heart. "Are you all right?"

How like him to ask. She answered him honestly. "I can't remember ever feeling this good."

He withdrew from her body and rolled onto his back, tucking her close to his side. He kissed the top of her head. "Good. Because as good as that was, it's only the beginning."

Several hours later, Lacey stirred and blinked sleepily at the clock on his bedside table. He knew that something was wrong, because she stiffened, then tried to ease away from his side without disturbing him. He fought the urge to yank her right back to where she belonged—in his bed, in his arms.

But too much was left unsettled and unsaid between them. She had offered him this one night, and it would only ruin what they'd shared if he made demands now.

Faint light streamed in his bedroom window and he could see Lacey's body, now as familiar as his own, as she furtively pulled her dress over her head and picked up her shoes. He watched as she paused at the foot of the bed, looking back at him. What was she thinking?

He'd expected her to have regrets; they both had good reasons to avoid a serious relationship. But he hadn't expected her retreat to hurt so damn much.

He waited until the front door opened and closed, then threw back the sheets and padded naked to the window. He pulled the blinds apart enough to watch his beautiful lover climb into her truck, and watched until her taillights disappeared around the corner.

A movement on the far side of the parking lot caught his attention. Had someone darted back into the deep shadows beyond the cars? He studied each vehicle, looking for a sign that someone was huddled in between them, but nothing moved, human or otherwise. Whatever it had been was gone now. Probably just a stray cat or dog, or one of the homeless men who shuffled through the Seattle streets at night.

Next time, though, if Lacey needed to leave in the middle of the night—if there ever was a next time—he would walk her out to her truck. Just in case.

He returned to his bed and buried his face in the sheets, which still carried Lacey's scent. Sleep would be a long time coming.

Chapter 12

*B*arak was late. Lacey chewed her lower lip and tried to concentrate on the last batch of readings from the monitors she and Barak had placed in the tunnels. Had it really been only a week ago? So much had happened since then that it didn't seem possible.

Why was Barak late? Was he even coming back?

Back to the reports. The numbers seemed stable, varying only a little from hour to hour and day to day. Once she had adequate readings from the remote tunnels, she'd need to retrieve the equipment and try placing it farther south, either closer to the tectonic plates or even near Mount St. Helens.

She'd need to bribe Devlin with something good to get permission to gain access to the more unstable areas near the barriers. Chocolate? Scotch? She started to turn the page when she thought she heard someone outside the lab door.

Oh, Lord, he had come back. She didn't know

if that was good or bad. How could she face Barak after enjoying hours of the best sex she'd ever experienced, only to sneak out in the wee hours of the morning without even saying good-bye?

Her face felt hot and flushed, much the same way it had during the night when Barak had made love to her, not once, not twice, but three times. This time, however, it was embarrassment instead of bone-melting passion that had her feeling that way. She'd already made two trips to the ladies' room down the hall to splash cold water on her cheeks.

Luck had been with her so far, because she'd been able to avoid seeing both her brother and Ruthie, the departmental secretary. Lacey might be able to fool everyone else, but those two would take one look at her and know something was up. And Ruthie would do her best to wheedle all the salacious details out of Lacey.

Penn, on the other hand, would do his big brother routine, demanding to know if the man involved was worthy of his little sister. Normally Lacey laughed at him, accepting his heavy-handed ways, but today that would be a total disaster, because she'd made the mistake of telling him about last night's dinner plans. Well, not the part about hot sex with Barak.

If Penn figured out that part, she and Barak were both in hot water. If everyone found out, she'd probably have to resign her job working for the Regents, but Penn would go after Barak with intent to kill. It would be her worst nightmare—her brother against her lover. No matter which of them came out on top, his life would be ruined. The Regents would be unlikely to allow the victor to survive.

What had she been thinking? She leaned back in her chair and studied the ceiling with visions of last night playing in her head. Here she was, hours later, and the memory of Barak's muscular, sleek body moving over and inside her had the power to have her stirring restlessly in her seat. No other lover had ever taken her to such heights.

Oh, God! What had she done? Temptation had been bad enough. Giving into it was possibly the biggest mistake she'd ever made.

The outside lab door opened. Leaning forward, she listened for any clues about who had just come in. The silence was deafening until she heard a telltale squeak. Ruthie, champion secretary and departmental snoop, coming this way.

There had to be some excuse Lacey could concoct to account for her frazzled appearance and flushed face. The thermostat? By the time Ruthie reached her office door, Lacey was standing at the thermostat and glaring at it as if it had been her worst enemy.

"Lacey?"

Lacey smacked the thermostat to achieve the right effect and pasted a surprised smile on her face before facing the older woman.

"Come on in, Ruthie—although I can't promise

how comfortable you'll be. The thermostat seems to be on the fritz. One minute it's too cold and then it's too hot." Lacey dropped back in her desk chair and took a long swig of water. "What brings you here?"

Ruthie wasn't buying it, not at all. "It feels just fine in here, Lacey. Are you sure you're not running a fever or something? The flu causes you to run hot and cold. Of course, so does menopause, but that's my problem, not yours."

"No, I'm fine. Really."

The lab door opened and closed again. This time it almost had to be Barak. She did her best to ignore his almost silent approach, concentrating instead on Ruthie. "So, what brought you down to my little part of the world?"

Ruthie frowned more, warning Lacey that she'd sounded a bit too chipper. Lacey tried again. "Seriously, what can I do for you?"

Ruth tossed a file on top of Lacey's already cluttered desk. "His Majesty wants an accounting of Barak's time here in the lab. Evidently His Majesty caught wind of Devlin Bane borrowing him to do something for the Paladins. Our lord and master doesn't want those hours to be paid out of our budget."

Lacey always wondered if Dr. Louis, their boss, had any idea how much Ruthie disparaged him. She didn't know how he could not know, but why did he put up with it? After all, he was in charge. She reached for the file; what a big waste of time. "As far as I know, he's only been over there twice: once before work and once after hours."

Neither of them noticed Barak in the doorway until he spoke, directing his comments to Ruthie. "That's right, ma'am. Devlin set it up that way. However, I'll be glad to keep track of any hours that I spend away from my duties here in the lab with Dr. Sebastian."

So far he'd done little more than glance in Lacey's direction. She was relieved—and mad at the same time. "Dr. Sebastian"? Whom was he trying to impress? They'd been on a first-name basis since day one.

He towered over Ruthie, but he was using that sort of Old World dignity of his to charm the older woman. That was a good thing, even if Lacey wished that he'd send some of that charm in her direction instead of ignoring her.

She butted into the conversation. "So, Ruthie, do you need me to submit a formal report or just a note at the end of a pay period?"

Ruth jumped, as if she'd forgotten that Lacey was even there. She'd been busy staring up at Barak. Maybe it was the first time she'd been this close to him. What did she see when she looked at him? Those beautiful silver eyes? The way his black and silver hair framed his chiseled face?

Or one of the legendary enemies of the Paladins and the rest of mankind?

"Mr. q'Young, why don't you go record the newest data and then enter it into the database for me?" Lacey put in. Two could play the formality game.

He finally looked directly at her, his eyes glittering with some powerful emotion, his nostrils flaring as he gave her an abrupt nod. "Yes, Dr. Sebastian. If you'll excuse me, Ms. Prizzi."

Lacey couldn't draw a full breath until he disappeared behind a bank of machinery. With that one look, her traitorous body was wanting his. She folded her hands on top of the desk, trying without success to slow her pulse.

"Ruthie, how did Dr. Louis find out about Barak doing some work for Devlin Bane?"

Ruthie stared out into the lab for another second or two before jerking her attention back to Lacey. The expression on Ruthie's face worried Lacey, as if Ruthie had a few questions of her own, ones neither Lacey nor Barak would have good answers for.

Lacey prompted Ruthie again, hoping to derail the inquisition. "Dr. Louis? How did he find out?"

"Someone from IT stopped by to load some updates on our computers. His name was Ben something. Although, come to think of it, why would he know anything about what Devlin was up to, and why would he bring it up to Dr. Louis?"

A good question. One that Lacey intended to investigate. Maybe Devlin would know something. Normally she would have asked Barak, but not this time, at least not now. He'd moved back in sight.

She watched him work with his usual quiet efficiency for several seconds. Eventually she'd have to talk to him again, but she still felt too raw after last night.

She also didn't want to arouse Ruthie's suspicions about Barak. "Maybe this Ben guy was only making small talk and didn't realize that it would cause trouble for anybody."

Ruthie wasn't buying it. "I think it's more likely that he was up to some kind of mischief, but we'll probably never know the why of it." She rose to her feet. "I'd better get back to my office. His Majesty gets testy if he actually has to answer his own phones, you know."

Lacey gave her friend a conspiratorial smile. "Should I call to tell him that you're on your way back, and that we've worked things out about sharing Barak's hours?"

Ruthie laughed. "No use in baiting the bear, my dear, but I appreciate the offer." She stopped in the doorway to watch Barak for a few seconds. "What's he like, Lacey? Barak, I mean?"

Lacey chose her words carefully, trying to sound like a coworker rather than a lover. Especially a one-night lover. With some effort she was able to shove that idea down deep, where it wouldn't hurt so much.

"He's punctual, methodical, and efficient. He still has a lot to learn about how we do things, but once you show him how to do something, he catches on quickly."

Barak snapped his pencil in half and gritted his teeth. "Methodical"? "Punctual"? She made him sound like some soulless machine. At least she'd given him credit for being a quick learner. Was she thinking back to last night, when he'd paid such close attention to the way she'd moaned when he'd touched her in just the right way?

He turned to watch the older woman go, counting the seconds until he and Lacey were alone. He thought about confronting her in her office, but he didn't want her to feel cornered. No, he'd wait out here in the lab.

It was another ten minutes before she ventured out of her office. Lacey wasn't the type to cower. She headed straight for him with an odd look on her face, one he couldn't quite decipher. The expressions on human faces were usually easy to read, even when the person in question was trying very hard to disguise what they were feeling.

Small clues in body language or the look in their eyes usually gave it away, but right now Lacey was a puzzle. He kept recording numbers until he finished before acknowledging her presence.

"Do you know someone named Ben? Works in IT?" She cocked a hip against the counter, her eyebrows drawn together in a frown.

"I've met him. I wouldn't say that I know him. He bought a beer for me and your brother the other night." That got her attention; her eyebrows lifted in surprise.

"You and Penn. Had. A. Beer?" She spoke the words as if each had been a sentence unto itself. "When was this and why didn't you tell me?"

"It was the day we sparred after work. He had already made plans with Ben and wanted me to come with him for some reason. I didn't mention it because it lasted all of half an hour and didn't seem important."

She pursed her lips and narrowed her eyes. "Well, it might not have seemed that way, but this Ben guy is the one that let it slip to Dr. Louis that you were spending time with Penn and Devlin Bane."

"I'm almost sure that we didn't mention anything about our workout. In fact, we were already at the bar when Ben came in, so he had no way of knowing for sure that we'd come in together." He stood up. "I need to share this information with Penn, but first I'll go talk to Devlin."

She caught his arm. When she realized what she'd done, she jerked her hand back, as if touching him had burned her. "No way you're leaving until you tell me why it's so important that you have to rush off to talk to Devlin Bane. He's the one who got us into this mess by yanking your leash back into his department."

"I'm not on anyone's leash." He took a step closer to her, trapping her against the counter. A brief flash of fear in her eyes only inflamed his temper. "Damn it, Lacey, don't do that! After last night, how could you think even for a second that I would hurt you?"

When she didn't answer, he walked out.

He managed enough control to avoid slamming the lab door; it might draw unwanted attention from anyone else in the area. But he burned to slam something. Paladins were always looking for a fight; maybe he could find one and prod him into trading blows.

For once, the area around Devlin's office was deserted. They couldn't be down in the tunnels, because Barak would have felt it if the barrier had gone down. Cocking his head, Barak listened to see if he could pick up any voices. Luck was with him. Some of the Paladins were headed this way. He recognized the voices: D.J., Cullen, and, yes, Trahern. If Bane was with them, he wasn't talking.

Cullen rounded the corner first, but D.J. was right behind him. Just as Barak expected, D.J. came charging up as soon as he caught sight of Barak sitting at his desk, playing with the odd collection of toys D.J. kept there. It took Cullen and Trahern to hold him back.

Barak was disappointed. He smiled at D.J., knowing that would only set him off again.

"Get the hell away from my desk, you son of a bitch!"

"You weren't using it." It felt good to taunt his enemy, even if D.J. really wasn't Barak's enemy anymore.

Trahern's eyes went ice cold. "I don't know what game you're playing here, Barak, but go back to the lab, where you belong."

Barak slowly rose to his feet. He stood a good chance of besting D.J.; maybe even D.J. and Cullen together. Trahern was a different matter, but right now he didn't care. He had to find some outlet for his pent-up anger. If it meant taking a beating, he'd give it his best.

"I'm not going anywhere." His smile was not friendly.

Trahern spared a glance for Cullen. "Get D.J. under lock and key; then track down Bane and tell him to come pick up the pieces of Laurel's pet Other."

When Cullen tried to tug D.J. away, the man screamed, "At least let me watch. There's nothing I like better than to watch one of them bleed!"

Barak watched Cullen drag his smaller friend down the hallway. The racket didn't draw a crowd: maybe these men were used to occasional Paladin explosions. When they were safely out of sight, Barak turned his attention to Trahern.

"Shall we?" Barak sneered at the cold-eyed Paladin.

Trahern stared back at him, a faint smile on his lips. "Something's got your tail in a wringer, Other. You've got a temper, but Devlin normally trusts you to keep it under control." An unholy glee lit up his face. "And I would guess that something is a woman. Lacey Sebastian, maybe?"

That did it. Barak charged Trahern, happy to finally have a target for his frustrations. He managed to get in one good kick, between a couple of Trahern's solid punches, before someone caught him by the collar and yanked backward. He twisted and took his new attacker to the ground with him.

Devlin Bane surged back up to his feet, having rolled clear of Barak. "What in the hell is going on here?"

With a nasty smile, Trahern wiped a drop of blood off the corner of his mouth with the back of his hand. "We found Barak sitting here as if he owned the place. When I asked him what was wrong, he attacked."

He sidestepped Devlin and offered Barak a hand up off the floor. "Feeling better?"

Barak gave the matter some thought. "As a matter of fact, I am." Despite the ache in his jaw and the sharp pain in his side.

"Good. Now if you'll excuse me, I've got to go help Cullen calm D.J. down." Before Trahern left the room, he turned back to give Barak a hard look. "This stays between us, Other. Is that clear?"

Barak nodded, staring after Trahern as he walked away. "Does that man ever make sense?"

"About as much as you picking a fight with him right out here where anybody in the organization can see you." Bane marched into his office, leaving Barak to follow at his own speed. "Now sit down and tell me what's going on."

If Trahern wasn't going to talk, neither would Barak, not about Lacey. "I came to tell you that someone is showing unusual interest in my business."

Whatever Devlin had been about to say about the fight was forgotten. "Give me a name."

"Ben. He didn't give me a last name the one time I met him, but he weighs more than he should and is losing his hair. Evidently he found a reason to work on Dr. Louis's computer. While he was there, he mentioned that you were having me spar with Penn Sebastian."

"Son of a bitch, how would he even know about that?"

This was the part that Barak didn't want to talk about, but he couldn't risk hiding important information. He debated if it was wise to tell the Paladin leader that it was Penn who had introduced him to Ben. But even if he did, that was no guarantee Penn had mentioned that they would be working together.

No, he'd wait and talk to Penn first. He would accuse no man of wrongdoing until he had proof. It was enough that Devlin had been warned.

"I'm not sure, but I do know that right after I started working with Lacey, he sneaked into the geology lab and shuffled through my papers."

"You saw him?" Devlin's temper was starting to flare.

"No, I smelled his cologne in the air." *Tasted* it was a better description, but Devlin was human and might not understand what he meant. "At the time I didn't know who the scent belonged to, but I recognized it when I met him."

Devlin rocked back in his desk chair and stared at the ceiling. "I'll have one of my men do some checking on the IT section; it shouldn't take long to figure out who he is and what his game is. If he contacts you, play along, but let me know."

"Fine. Now I need to return to work."

"And Barak?"

Now what? "Yes?"

"Laurel was really pleased that you accepted our invitation." Then he looked a bit puzzled. "The whole evening was fun."

If the man only knew. "It was. Thank you for allowing me to come."

"Tell Laurel. It was her idea."

"Yes, but if you had really not wanted me there, she would have invited me to meet her for lunch somewhere. She didn't have to invite me into her home."

"Yeah, well, get on out of here before D.J. comes back." The Paladin was probably more at ease with a sword in his hand than accepting a simple thank you.

As Barak returned to the lab, his steps were lighter than they had been all day.

"You look like hell."

Ben looked up from his sandwich and glared at his superior. "Thanks, that's just what I needed to hear. My boss has already been riding my ass because of some screwups this morning. I can't very well tell him that I was lurking in that Other's parking lot until the wee hours of the morning to see how long Penn Sebastian's younger sister stayed."

He shuddered as he took another bite of his lunch. After swallowing, he gulped down some of his soft drink to wash away the taste that last night had left in his mouth. "Can you imagine a human girl like her shagging that animal?"

"You saw them?"

Ben rolled his eyes. "No, but judging by the lights that were on, they didn't just stay in the living room."

The other man's laugh was nasty. "What's the matter, Ben? Jealous?"

The remark made Ben choke on his sandwich. "Hell, no! Even before, she wouldn't have given me a second look. Okay, fine. I'm too old, too bald, too fat. But that she'd stoop to spreading her legs for the likes of him—that's sick."

"Maybe you should tell your buddy Penn about what you saw."

The suggestion sounded so reasonable that Ben actually considered the idea. But from what he knew of Penn Sebastian, he was the type to kill the messenger. "No, not yet. I can't prove anything, and he's more likely to believe his sister than me. And I can't imagine her admitting that she'd had a roll in the hay with her brother's enemy."

"And maybe it was all innocent, too."

Ben didn't appreciate the sarcasm, but there wasn't much about the man he *did* like. Once he collected the next payment, Ben was going to finally pay off his debts with his bookie and that would be it. No more midnight spying, no more blue stones, no more anything that could get him killed.

His companion reached for the bill. "Well, I had better be going. Lunch is on me."

Ben hid his surprise with another drink. "Thanks."

He'd never paid for lunch before, which probably meant he needed Ben to do something dangerous.

"Our benefactors are pressing hard for more information on how much the Paladins know. You've got the best chance of any of us to find out."

"And just how am I supposed to do that?" Ben didn't care if he sounded pissed. He was.

"Bug their computers, their phones. Put a trace on Bane's or Barak's calls. Figure out something, and damn quick. It isn't just your ass on the line; it's mine, too. And if I go down, you're going with me."

Then he was gone.

Ben shoved the rest of his lunch away, too unsettled to eat. Maybe he'd call in sick for the rest of the day and go home. After a long nap, maybe he'd come up with some idea of how to save his ass.

But somehow he doubted it.

Chapter 13

Something has happened to one of the boxes we set up in the tunnels. It's no longer transmitting data."

Lacey plunked her toolkit down on the counter near Barak. The lab was full of other places where she could have set it down, but she couldn't stand his continued silence much longer without doing something about it.

"So call Devlin and request an escort to go check on it. Maybe Trahern would go. He seemed to like helping you last time." Barak spun away from her on his stool before walking over to check the latest readings from Mount St. Helens. She glanced at his clipboard. His last numbers were timed only five minutes ago.

She smiled. He wasn't as immune to her presence as he'd like her to think. It was time to crowd him a bit. Moving quickly, she situated herself between Barak and the stool and waited for him to turn around. It didn't take long.

With his usual grace, he moved smoothly around her and reclaimed his seat. "I thought you were going to call your friend Trahern."

Of all the possible answers she could have used, she settled for the truth. "I don't want Trahern. I want you." She risked a hand on his shoulder, liking the play of his muscles under his shirt right where she'd left nail marks on his skin last night as she'd urged him on. And on.

His posture stiffened, and he set his pencil down with deliberate slowness. Playing with fire might get her burned, but she missed the heat they'd generated when they'd been skin to skin. He looked at her hand on his shoulder before meeting her gaze.

"It doesn't matter what you want, Lacey."

At first she thought he was talking about the two of them, but then she realized he was referring to the restrictions Devlin had placed on her venturing down into the tunnels. At least she hoped that was what he meant.

"I'll call Devlin, but I still want you to go with me."

He reached up to cover her hand with his. "Spending time alone together isn't wise." Then he gently removed her hand from his shoulder. The regret in his eyes didn't make the small rejection hurt less.

"Barak . . ."

The sound of the lab door opening had her stumbling back, putting more distance between the two of them. Barak shot her a burning look before turning away, leaving it up to Lacey to face the newcomer. She didn't want to get caught too close to him, and he didn't like it.

Just her luck; Penn stood outside her office, his arms crossed over his chest. Bracing herself for whatever argument he wanted to start, she headed straight for him.

"Yes, big brother. What brings you in here today?" She pushed past him into her office, wanting to put the safety of her desk between them.

"Can't I take my favorite sister out for lunch once in a while?"

He hadn't picked up the tab for a meal in months; even when he did, he firmly believed that the best food came from a drive-up window. She leaned back in her chair and considered her options. They could drive somewhere, get some food, and he could unload whatever words of wisdom he had for her in the privacy of her car. Or he'd stand right there in her office and let her have it.

With Barak out in the lab, she really had no choice. She pulled her purse out of her desk drawer and asked, "What lecture do you plan to deliver over greasy hamburgers and fries?"

He laughed, for once acting more like his old self. It was worth loading up on cholesterol to spend time with the old Penn.

She pulled out her car keys. "Where to?"

"I'll drive," Penn said, snatching her keys out of her hand.

"Okay, but where are we going?"

He pulled out the big guns. "I thought we'd try Dick's. I'm in the mood for one of their burgers."

She couldn't fault his taste. Dick's was a well-known drive-in restaurant, a favorite among natives and tourists both. She could always eat salad for dinner to make up for the big burger, fries, and chocolate shake she planned on enjoying. "Okay, bro, lead on. Let me see what plans Barak has for lunch."

Before they reached the lab door, Penn surprised her again. "You can ask him along if you have to, but I won't like it much."

She froze. Barak had been avoiding her all morning, and maybe he had every right to. Her heart pounded in her ears as she called out, "Barak, Penn and I are going to grab a burger. Would you like to come?" She kept her fingers crossed that he'd refuse. The thought of being shut up in her truck with both men was more than she could handle right then.

As usual, he seemed to read her mood with unerring accuracy. "You've already had enough of me. I'd better pass."

She'd definitely had plenty of Barak last night. "We can bring you back something, if you'd like. Maybe a chocolate shake or some fries?"

"Nothing," he answered without looking up. Then almost as an afterthought he added, "Thank you anyway."

Was that sarcasm she heard in his voice? His guttural accent wasn't as heavy as it used to be, but sometimes it made it difficult to interpret what emotions he was feeling. But if she couldn't read him, it was doubtful that Penn could either.

"Ready, sis?" Penn stood beside her jingling her car keys, impatient to be underway.

"Yeah, I'm ready." She didn't look back.

When the hallway door clicked shut, Barak threw his pen down and dropped his clipboard on the counter. Pinching the bridge of his nose, he prayed for patience and an end to the headache he'd been battling all morning.

His lack of sleep was catching up with him, but if Lacey could make it through the day after the night they'd shared, so could he. It didn't help that the air around him carried her scent or that anytime he looked up, she was there. Even if his mind knew she was off limits again, other parts of him weren't convinced.

How could they share such perfect communication in his bed and be so at odds when they had to depend on words to express themselves? One night of passion had reminded him how much he needed someone to share his life with, but Lacey clearly wasn't yet ready to make that commitment, and maybe never would be.

He didn't blame her, really. After all, he was the enemy, the alien, the freak, the Other. And he was no better. How could he ask her to trust him with her life when he held so much of his own back in

secrecy? He hadn't even answered her the one time
she'd asked what his people called themselves.

Without Lacey, even the lab felt empty and cold.
He needed to get out for a while. Maybe he'd go see
Devlin again, to see about taking Lacey back down
to fix her beloved machinery. The readings had been
stable the past two days, so maybe they could go
early in the morning. At least he could offer Lacey
that much to make her happy.

On the way out, he locked the door. He didn't
like the idea of anyone in the organization having access to the lab, especially that Ben fellow. A warrior
looked after his woman, no matter what world he
was from.

"Sis, you look like hell." Penn reached over and
dunked one of his fries in her catsup.

Leave it to her brother to make her feel even
worse. "I didn't get much sleep last night." Please,
Lord, don't let him ask why.

"Are you and that Other getting along? 'Cause
if he's making trouble for you, all you have to do is
tell me."

Penn finished off his hamburger, throwing the
last bit of the bun to some hungry seagulls. He and
Lacey had gotten their food to go, and they'd found
a picnic table in a nearby park. The warmth of the
sun felt great, even though Lacey needed her sunglasses to cut down on the glare.

"No, he's a hard worker and has caught onto

our technology more quickly than I would have expected." She took a long drink of her pop, hoping that Penn would drop the subject.

He stared down at the table for a few seconds before looking up at her, his eyes worried. "I'm not sure we should be teaching him anything, but I know I'm in the minority. What's to stop him from crossing back into his world and taking everything he's learned with him?"

"How would knowledge of how a seismograph or a microwave oven worked help their cause?" She smiled and snatched her fries out of reach when Penn made another grab for them.

Penn gave her a disgusted look, wadded up the rest of his lunch, and stuffed it back in the bag. "That's not what I meant. He's not only learning our technology but also how we do things, how we think and act when we're not swinging a sword. It's always easier to defeat an enemy you understand."

"Well, that works both ways. Wouldn't we use anything we learn about his people, too?"

"My point exactly. I know how he fights but that's about all I've learned. What have you learned about Barak?"

Casting around for something safe to say, she settled on a couple of small things. "I think his eyes are sensitive to light and maybe his sense of smell is better than ours."

Penn succeeded in snatching one of her last remaining fries. "Not exactly earth-shattering news,

Lacey. I've got a good sense of smell, too, and the eyesight thing was pretty much a given. As far as we can tell, his world is pretty dark."

Okay, so what else could she tell him? Certainly not anything that would reveal how up close and personal she knew Barak's physical attributes. Or how much she'd admired them. A giggle threatened to bubble up; she fought to keep it under control.

"He's pretty much a vegetarian. He didn't eat any meat at Laurel's last night."

Penn's good mood was gone in a flash. "You had dinner with Barak last night?"

"No, not specifically. I told you Dr. Young was having a dinner party. He happened to be another guest." She glanced at her watch and stood up. "Now, if you're done with your inquisition, I need to get back to work."

He clearly wanted to argue some more, but she didn't give him a chance. "Do you want a ride or not?"

"Damn it, Lacey, I don't want you around him one minute more than you have to be!" Penn stomped after her. "He's not human! Hell, you know better than most the way his kind affects our world—their filthy natures cause all kinds of problems."

Several other people in the park looked up from their own lunches to stare at the ruckus Penn was raising. Lacey wondered what they thought about what he'd said, but she decided she didn't care what Penn thought, much less some total strangers.

"Shut up, Penn, and get in. You're drawing too much attention to yourself."

He lowered his voice as he got in the truck, but he didn't back off. "I mean it, Lacey. Something's going on, and he might be involved. I don't want you getting caught in the cross fire if it all blows up."

"If what blows up? Do you really think Devlin Bane would have let Barak live this long if he didn't trust him? For Pete's sake, Barak worked with Laurel." She caught a break in the traffic and pulled out of the parking lot.

Penn made a disgusted grunt. "You'll note that Devlin managed to get him transferred out of there the first chance he got."

When she coasted to a stop at a red light, she looked at her brother. "Don't go all paranoid on me, Penn. Devlin watched me grow up. If Barak was that dangerous, you know darn well Devlin wouldn't risk me any more than he would Laurel. And even if he did, the rest of the local Paladins would come down on him. You know that. They're your friends, too."

"They used to be." He stared down at his hand as he flexed it a few times. "Since I got hurt, I have to wonder. Most of them don't know how to act around me."

A show of pity would only make it worse for him. "Maybe these new workouts with Devlin and Barak will help you regain your ability to fight."

"You think Barak's not dangerous? You should see him with a sword! He may seem quiet and calm, but then he explodes." Penn looked at her as if daring her to dispute him.

She put the truck in gear and started forward again. "You forget, Penn. I did see Barak use his sword, and it was scary. I can't deny that I've had a few nightmares over the sight of him carving up those two men in the tunnels. But you know what? He did that to keep me safe. Remember that."

They rode in silence the rest of the way back to the Center.

"I still don't know how you talked him into it." Lacey shifted her toolkit to her other hand and keyed in the code.

Barak was pretty pleased with himself. It had taken some powerful persuasion to get Devlin's permission for a quick foray into the tunnels to fix or replace Lacey's equipment, and he'd savored the expression on Lacey's face when he'd told her.

Not to mention the fact that she'd thrown her arms around him in a big hug. There'd been nothing sexual in the embrace, but it had felt great to hold her close again for those few seconds. It was one more step in getting her accustomed to his continued presence in her life.

He checked his sword as they stepped into the elevator, making sure it moved easily in its new scabbard. Even though the barrier had been quiet, their last expedition had proven that there was no guarantee they'd be the only ones prowling the tunnels below the city. At Devlin's insistence, Lacey was again armed with a pistol.

Barak reminded her that their time below was limited. "I promised Devlin that we'd just run a diagnostic on the equipment. If it can't be fixed in only a few minutes, we bring it back to the lab."

"Yes, Mother," Lacey teased with a laugh.

She was cute in this playful mood, her eyes bright with excitement. He didn't want to dampen her spirits, but they needed to be alert and cautious.

"I'm serious, Lacey. At the first sign that someone's down there besides us, we're right back in the elevator, hollering for help. Devlin planned on having a couple of the Paladins nearby if we need them."

They stepped out of the elevators at the same spot where he'd killed two humans on their last trip.

Her eyes went straight to the brown stains on the rock floor, her smile fading.

"They attacked first," he said. He normally wouldn't defend his actions, but seeing him kill had frightened her.

"I know." Then with a small smile, she grabbed his arm. "Come on, slowpoke. We don't have long before Devlin will send in the troops."

He let himself be pulled along, liking the feel of her hand on his arm, but it made it difficult to concentrate. Trusting her to keep him from running into any walls, he closed his eyes and reached out with his senses.

The tunnels were devoid of heartbeats other than his and Lacey's. But a faint taste in the air brought him to an abrupt halt.

"What's wrong?" Lacey asked, wisely dropping her voice down into a soft whisper.

He held up a hand in a silent signal for her to wait. Turning slowly in each direction, he drew a series of shallow breaths, trying to catch the scent again. He found it in the direction in which they were headed.

Ben from IT had been in the tunnels, and recently, since his cologne was still discernable. What business did he have down here? Nothing legitimate, that was for certain.

Barak drew his sword. "Someone has been here. I don't think it was recently, but I want us out of here as fast as possible."

"Who?"

"Someone who shouldn't have been. Now let's get moving."

Lacey wanted to press for details, but she took his worry seriously. The first box she'd set up was functioning properly, but the second one wasn't only down—it had been brutalized to the point that the pieces probably weren't worth salvaging.

Lacey kicked one of the broken pieces across the floor in frustration. "These things aren't cheap. Why would anyone do this?" She picked up one of the dials and frowned at the crack in its cover. "Would your people do this?"

"Maybe, if they ran across it, but that's unlikely. We don't usually cross in this area. It's more likely one of your people, upset because we killed some of their men." He sheathed his sword and helped gather up the scattered fragments.

"I'm sorry, Barak. I shouldn't have pointed fingers that way. It's just that it will be months before I have enough money in the budget to replace this. Paladins are the only ones who are supposed to patrol this area, and they'd have no reason to destroy my equipment. They all know I'm trying to learn how to predict earthquakes and things that affect the barrier."

Barak avoided looking at her, for fear she'd see his regret over not sharing his gift for predicting earthquakes long before equipment like Lacey's could pick them up. With such foreknowledge, the Paladins would be better prepared when the barrier collapsed, which meant more from his world would die.

He'd turned his back on his world, but not the people in it. Maybe that was splitting hairs, but it was the only way he could live with himself.

He shoved the pieces back into the machine's casing and picked it up. "Maybe we can salvage part of this, enough to reset some of the sensors."

She looked doubtful but gamely picked up another few items that Barak had missed. When she stuffed them in with the others, she surprised him by raising up on her toes to plant a quick kiss on his cheek.

"I appreciate your doing all of this with me."

Her scent filled his senses, sending a surge of white-hot desire burning through him. "Careful, Lacey. It's not all I would like to do with you." He let the heat show in the way he looked at her from head to toe, lingering in his favorite places along the way.

To give her credit, she didn't back away. Instead, she held out her hands for the broken casing. When he surrendered it, she set it down and stepped right into his arms.

The chill of the tunnels disappeared in the sweet heat of her kiss. He closed his eyes, using his hands to trace the curves of her body from memory, his ragged breath drawing in her scent and taste and making them part of his soul.

Her jeans put too much distance between them. He made enough room between them for his hand to reach for her zipper, but she beat him to it. Murmuring his approval, he slid his hands down the curve of her waist, easing both her jeans and panties off her hips and down to the ground.

As he slowly stood up, she smiled against his mouth. "Your turn."

This was madness, and they both knew it. He didn't care, and apparently neither did she. Maybe he wasn't the only one who'd been dying of frustration the past two days.

Not trusting himself, he reached for his wallet

and got out the condom he carried with him—just in case.

"Smart man." Lacey showed her approval by tugging off her T-shirt and bra.

He maintained enough control to strip off his shirt before unzipping his pants, managing to sheath himself before dragging his lover back into his arms. The press of her naked skin against his felt like coming home.

"This floor won't be comfortable."

She laughed, her voice husky with desire. "That'll be your problem. I plan on being on top."

He didn't argue. It didn't matter which position they chose, as long as he was inside her soon. The two of them tumbled to the ground. If the rock was cold or uncomfortable, he quit noticing the second she presented her full breasts to him, demanding his attention.

As soon as he suckled one ripe, plump nipple, she straddled his body, squirming and rocking her damp core against his cock. He splayed his hand on her ass, encouraging her to move faster and harder.

A few seconds later, she stopped. She stared down at him, her gaze hot and needy, her hair wild. "Barak, I want you inside me. Deep and hard."

"Gladly." He lifted her up enough for her to position herself so that he rested right at the entrance to her body. Then working together, she eased down until her body gloved him completely.

This time, when she rocked forward, they both moaned. He drew up his knees to support her as she put her hands flat on his chest and began a long, slow slide up and then down.

She was killing him. But he'd die happy.

He let her set the pace, enjoying the look of sensual power in her eyes. Her pretty breasts bounced with each motion, tempting him again. He cupped them with his hands, squeezing and kneading, loving the way they filled his hands.

"Harder," she demanded.

He did as ordered, flicking his tongue over one nipple until he caught it with his teeth and lips. Lacey threw her head back, giving herself over to the rising tide of passion between them.

He was so big, filling and stretching her, fitting her so perfectly, unlike any other lover she'd ever had. She loved the way he looked at her with those pale eyes, as if she was the one woman in this world or his that could make him feel this way.

Neither of them showed a lick of sense by giving in to the urge to make love down here in the tunnels, but the need had been building between them since the moment she'd left his bed. But now wasn't for thinking, feeling was enough. And the feel of him was perfect. Hard, hot, demanding, and so careful of her.

Barak's watch beeped, startling a curse out of him.

"What's wrong?"

His laugh sounded frustrated. "I set the alarm so we didn't run out of time and trigger a rescue mission."

"How much time do we have?"

He surprised her by flipping them so that he was on top. With a grin that was positively wicked, he leaned down and kissed her. "Just enough."

Then he showed her how much could be accomplished by a very determined man in a short amount of time.

Devlin was waiting for them in the records room. "You cut it pretty close."

"Someone destroyed some of the equipment. It took a while to salvage the pieces." Barak held them out for Devlin to inspect.

"Son of a bitch!" he said in a burst of temper. Then, remembering Lacey was there, he apologized. "Sorry, Lacey."

She looked at him as if he'd sprouted a second head. "Boy, Laurel's going to civilize you yet. Maybe she can work on Penn next."

Barak watched in amazement as Devlin actually flushed. "No, she just reminded me that you deserve to be treated with more respect. Even though you grew up surrounded by Paladins, it's time we realize that you're not just one of the boys."

Barak could offer firsthand testimony to that, but wisely kept that information to himself. If they'd been too blind to notice that they had a beautiful woman in their midst, that was their problem, not his.

Lacey shifted from foot to foot, Devlin's comment clearly making her uncomfortable. Barak understood. He'd had to redefine who he was the past few months, and it wasn't easy.

Devlin turned his attention back to the spider. "When did this quit working?"

"About two days ago. I'd have to look at my records back in the lab to give you an exact date and time if you need it." Lacey stuck her hands in her back pockets, clearly unaware how that stance emphasized the generous curve of her breasts.

Devlin noticed, then glared at Barak for doing the same. "Call me as soon as you know. Then maybe I can do some checking of my own to see if anyone else was scheduled to be down there at that time."

"Will do."

Lacey started for the door on the far side of the records room. Barak dropped back a couple of steps, signaling Devlin to slow down a bit. When they were a few feet behind Lacey, he whispered, "That same Ben was in the tunnels recently. I can't tell you when, but his scent was near where we found the damage."

Devlin nodded as the two of them hurried to catch up with Lacey before she reached the door. Barak moved past her to open it, taking the casing from her to carry up the stairs.

She gave him a look that warned him that his

efforts to pass information to Devlin had not gone unnoticed. Too bad. The more she knew, the more likely she'd be at risk. Until they had some idea what Ben was up to and who he was working with, Devlin was right to keep things secret.

No doubt Barak was going to hear about it from Lacey, but maybe he could distract her—and he knew just how to do it. He couldn't wait.

Penn prowled the hallways, killing time until Barak showed up for their next lesson. He hated—*hated*—waiting at the best of times. Waiting for Barak only pissed him off more. At least the Other had called to let him know that he was running late.

And why?

Because Barak had taken Lacey back down in the tunnels again. Alone, just the two of them. Was Devlin crazy? At the very least, he should have sent a Paladin or two along as escort. But no, Bane trusted Barak to keep Lacey safe from both the humans and the Others.

Where did that make any sense?

And besides, who was going to protect Lacey from Barak? The whole situation made him sick. It was bad enough that she spent all her working hours hanging around with the bastard. Again, alone. What if that pale-eyed freak decided he wanted a human lover? Penn liked to think his sister had better sense than to trust the bastard, but from what he could tell, the women treated Barak like a stray they'd brought home, instead of the vicious killer he was under that thin veneer of civilized behavior.

Penn's hand strayed to the hilt of his sword, the need to fight riding him more than usual. He forced his hand back down to his side, doing his best to look calm and in control. Here, where he could run into a Handler or Regent, it was imperative that he not let his jitters show. No one was more aware than he that he was being observed, weighed, and judged.

As far as he knew, the jury was still out. He might still have a career with the Regents. The alternatives were unacceptable. Either they would ship him off to some cornfield somewhere away from the barrier to vegetate his life away, or they would execute him.

And that wouldn't kill just him but Lacey, too.

The sound of footsteps caught his attention, and his hand reaching for the hilt of his sword again. His opponent at last.

"You said a *little* late, Other. I don't like to be kept waiting."

Barak sneered. "Like you have anything else to do. I was helping your sister piece together one of her machines."

Damn, Penn hated the vision these words put in his head of the Other and Lacey, heads together, working on some fucking scrap of metal. "She did fine working on her own before you showed up."

Barak ignored the comment, shoving open the

door to the gym. "We're here to spar. Let's get to it."

"Gladly, Other."

Inside, Barak stripped off his shirt and kicked his shoes into the corner. Penn followed his example, then assumed a position close to Barak, but slightly behind him. The stretching routine that the Other used felt surprisingly good once he'd gotten the initial moves down. Slowly, he was mastering more and more of the dance, as Barak called it.

When they'd both worked up a good sweat, it was time for blades. Already, after only a few workouts, Penn's proficiency with his left hand had greatly improved. His right, though, had made little progress. Only time would tell if becoming a left-handed fighter would be a help or a hindrance to those who fought along beside him to defend the barrier.

Barak swung his practice sword a few times, its blade catching the light like an arc of lightning cutting through the air. Rather than wait for formalities, Penn charged in from the side, giving the Other no warning.

The dance began.

Chapter 14

An hour later the two of them sat against the gym wall, panting and exhausted. Barak had won the match, but it had taken more effort this time.

That's where Devlin found them. "How did it go?" he asked as he tossed each of them a towel. "I don't see any blood. A few pretty spectacular bruises, though."

"Go to hell, Bane." Penn pushed himself up from the floor. "Even my bruises have bruises. I'm out of here."

Before speaking, Barak waited until Penn had gathered up his stuff and left. Devlin would expect Barak's honest opinion, but Barak didn't want Penn to hear what he had to say. "His left hand is adequate; there was definite improvement. The right is better."

"But not good."

Barak might not like Penn, but he respected the

man's desire to be the warrior he was born to be. "No, not good."

"Son of a bitch, I was afraid of that. Laurel had warned me, but I was hoping you'd see something she didn't."

"I am willing to continue his training. He may surprise us both." Barak carefully cleaned his practice blade before returning it to the rack. "So if you don't need me, I think a long hot bath is in order."

"I'll drive you home. We need to talk."

The Paladin leader obviously still had something he wanted to say. Barak didn't particularly want to hear it, but he knew it would do no good to try to avoid him.

"Fine, but you're buying the pizza and beer."

"I've already ordered an extra-large veggie for you and a real pizza for myself. Trahern will be meeting us at your place with the beer." Devlin shot him a wry look. "He gets to share your pizza."

Barak doubted that Blake Trahern ever ate anything purely veggie in his life, the man had carnivore written all over him. But even more interesting, it would be Trahern's first time inside Barak's home. Devlin hadn't bothered to ask if Barak had plans or if it was all right if Trahern joined them. It was just as well that Lacey had another commitment, or else he would've had to find a way to warn her away from his place.

Barak picked up his jacket. "Let's get this over with."

The drive to his apartment was a quiet one. He was still recuperating from his day spent with the two Sebastians, each of whom had given him quite a workout. His Lacey was an energetic lover, one of many things he liked about her. Penn lacked his sister's charm, but he'd also contributed to Barak's current good mood.

Which would last only until Devlin finally spilled whatever had him holding the steering wheel with a death grip.

"You're tense," Barak decided to say. "Whatever you have to say, just spit it out. I have no choice but to be at your command." And he hated that and let it show in his voice.

"This time you have a choice." All hint of teasing was gone. "Going in, you have a choice. Once you're in, though, there's no going back."

Barak stared out the car window, wondering if the death he'd escaped was about to catch up with him.

Trahern came out of the shadows as soon as Devlin pulled into the parking lot. Another Paladin stood farther back, making it difficult for Barak to identify him, but judging by his height it had to be Cullen. Each of them carried a twelve-pack of beer.

As Barak climbed out of the truck, he nodded in

the others' direction. "It looks as if you should have ordered more pizza."

Devlin was already reaching for his phone to order a second delivery. When he flipped it shut a couple of minutes later, he met Barak's gaze over the roof of the truck. "I apologize for having a party at your place without clearing it with you first. I thought it was the safest place to meet."

"Because I rarely have guests." Except on the few occasions when Devlin dropped by or the one night that Lacey had shared his bed.

"It sucks, I know. But yeah, that's why."

Barak led the parade up to his apartment. Inside, he turned the lights on and returned his sword to its place of honor over the fireplace. Normally his living room felt spacious, but not with three Paladins sprawled on the sofa and chairs.

At least they'd left his favorite chair free for him. Just as he sat down, there was a knock at the door. He checked through the peephole. Seeing it was D.J., Barak arched an eyebrow in Devlin's direction. "Did you forget how many invitations you sent out?"

D.J. came cruising in, balancing two large pizza cartons on his hand. "Who owes me for these?"

Trahern snickered. "D.J., do you really think we're going to fork out the money when you've already generously paid for them?"

"Hell, I knew I should've let that kid deliver

them himself." The disgruntled Paladin set the boxes on the coffee table and dropped down to sit on the carpet within arm's reach of the pizza. "So where are the plates and napkins?"

Every eye turned toward Barak. "Fine, I'll get them," he shot back. "Forks, too, for those of you who aren't complete barbarians."

That remark earned him a laugh from all but Trahern, but even he was smiling. Despite the inconvenience, it felt good to have these guests, unexpected and uninvited as they were.

As Barak set out plates, forks, and napkins, he noticed the light blinking on his answering machine. The only people who routinely called him were Devlin and Laurel. Was Laurel trying to reach Devlin? No, she would have tried his cell phone.

His hand hesitated over the play button. He didn't want to listen to the message where Devlin and the others could overhear. But the thought that it might be Lacey warmed him. He'd listen to the call when he was alone to savor the sound of her voice.

"Hey, Barak, the pizza is getting cold!"

"Keep your fingers out of my veggie pizza. I'm sure Devlin will be delighted to share his real pizza with you."

"Like hell I will! Trahern can have a piece, but you other two will have to wait for the second delivery."

D.J. looked much abused. "Fine, but I'm not paying for that bunch, too."

Devlin took a big bite out of a slice, exaggerating his enjoyment of it. When he swallowed he said, "You're right, D.J., that wouldn't be fair. Cullen can pay for yours."

The good-natured bantering continued as they ate. After D.J. and Trahern divided the last piece of Barak's pizza, the mood changed, with Devlin looking especially tense. If Barak was reading him correctly, the Paladin leader was feeling both determination and regret.

Both were aimed directly at him.

He started clearing away the empty beer cans and gathering up the trash. "Now that you've plied me with beer and pizza, Bane, it's time to tell me whatever has you looking so grim."

"He always looks grim. It's just a matter of degree." Cullen's small joke did little to lighten the dark shadows that had settled over the group.

Devlin wiped his mouth with a napkin, then tossed the wadded-up paper into an empty pizza box. "We're not getting anywhere in our efforts to stop the blue stones crossing over from your world."

Trahern joined in the conversation. "I've been following Ben Jackson from IT, and D.J. has been monitoring his computer contacts. So far, there's nothing concrete we can pin on him."

Barak dumped a load of trash into a bag. "But I knew he'd been in the geology lab and down in the tunnels."

Devlin's head snapped up. "I believed you, Barak. We all did."

Surprise warred with the pleasure of being trusted. "But then why are you here?"

"The trail on our side of the barrier is cold. We need to know if someone on the other side has any information we can use to track the bastards down."

Suddenly he knew what they were asking. To give himself a few more seconds before answering, he sat down and reached for another beer. It did little to wash away the sour taste of fear in his mouth.

"When are you sending me back? Or is that the part where I have some say in the matter?" Please not tonight. If he was going to die, he needed a chance to say good-bye to Lacey. And to Laurel. Or would it be kinder to simply disappear from their lives? He wished he knew the hearts of women in this world.

Devlin leaned forward. "Barak, none of us know what drives your people to leave your world for ours, and you haven't chosen to share that bit of information with us. We didn't ask, because in the long run, it doesn't matter. They invade. We fight. It's that simple."

It wasn't simple, and they all knew it.

"What exactly are you asking me to do, Devlin? Even if I go back, that won't do you any good, because I'll be there and you'll still be on this side." The irony was that he'd expected to die on this side of the barrier, but not in his home.

"We're not asking you to stay there, Barak. I need to know if you can make contact with someone on their side without getting trapped over there. If you can't, then say so and we'll think of something else." Devlin sat back in his chair and waited.

They weren't sending him back to stay?

"There is someone. She may be able to help." If she would. Knowing his sister, she wasn't about to lift a finger to help him or the humans, but she hated the insanity that drove their kind to cross the barrier. If stopping the illegal trade of the blue light would slow the exodus, her conscience would force her to help.

"She?" Cullen asked, his attention now focused solely on Barak. "What does this woman look like?"

Why would he care? "She's about Lacey's size, long hair similar in color to mine, and she could dance circles around you with a sword."

D.J. snorted in disbelief, but Cullen only nodded as if Barak had just confirmed something he already knew. Had the Paladin encountered his sister? She policed the barrier on the other side; there was no logical way these men had actually seen her. But judging from the odd looks he was getting from both Cullen and Devlin, he might just be wrong about that.

"How can you get in touch with her?"

Barak gave the matter some thought. "When the barrier goes down again, I'll slip across long enough to transmit a message to her to set up a meeting."

"How will you know if it will stay down long enough for you to send the message and get back?"

This from Trahern, his eyes narrow slits, his mouth a grim lash.

"It's a risk I'll have to take. I know some Paladins can repair the barrier. Tell them not to hurry."

"Son of a bitch, that's a helluva plan, Barak. The longer the barrier is down, the more on both sides die."

"You asked, Devlin. That's the best I can do."

"What are you going to do? Stand down in the tunnels and wait for the barrier to collapse? It could take hours, or even weeks."

"So give me alternatives."

The silence dragged on for an eternity. Finally, Barak tossed out one last suggestion. "If I were to send a letter across, just toss it when the barrier blinks, there's a good chance she would get it. Her men patrol certain areas regularly. If I made several copies, more of us could wait for a chance to throw the message across. No one gets trapped, no one person has to stand at the barrier for days on end."

After a bit Devlin nodded. "All right. It's getting late. Why don't you draft a note, then run it by me in the morning?"

"Don't trust me to write a simple letter?" Anger seethed in his stomach. They'd come to his home uninvited, asking him for the impossible, and then wouldn't accept his word that he'd do the job.

Cullen, always the calm one, answered. "When we work as a team, Barak, we work as a team. We don't leave one of our own hanging in the wind." He stood up and stretched. "It's been a long one, gentlemen. I'm going home. Come on, D.J., I'll give you a ride."

D.J. jumped to his feet, the only one of the group who didn't look as if he was overdue for a good night's sleep. "Okay, we're out of here. Nice place, Barak."

"Thank you." Did D.J. ever run out of energy? Just watching him made Barak tired.

As D.J. charged out the door after Cullen, Devlin said, "You need a ride, Blake?"

"No, I'll walk. 'Night, Barak. Thanks for sharing the veggie." The tall Paladin disappeared, leaving just Barak and Devlin.

"I'll draft a letter and drop it off in your office first thing in the morning," Barak said. He had no idea what he could say that would breach the rift between him and those he'd left behind, but he couldn't live with himself if he didn't try. "If the letter works, we can set up a place to meet even if we can't specify a time."

Devlin clapped him on the shoulder. "Thanks."

The phone wasn't broken. Lacey knew because she'd checked three times in the last hour. She had to get to bed, or tomorrow would be tough. It was going to be bad enough to face Dr. Louis in the morning over her latest budget requests without having big circles under her eyes.

Maybe she could squeeze in an extra few minutes of sleep by making her lunch before going to bed and setting the coffeepot to start perking before she had to get up. She'd already picked out an outfit to wear, one she normally didn't wear to work. But the way the dress draped emphasized her good points and played down a few that weren't quite so perfect.

But if Penn saw her, he'd want an explanation, and she doubted he'd believe she was wearing it to impress her boss. No, she'd just have to wait for a better opportunity to show it off in front of Barak.

The phone remained silent. She knew she'd left her message on the right phone number, because she'd recognized Barak's deep voice on the answering machine. God, she felt like she was back in high school with a big crush on the captain of the track team. Was Barak having second thoughts about what they'd done down in the tunnels? Was she a fool for hoping she could entice him to come over for a repeat performance?

No, it had been good for him, for both of them. She might not have much experience, but she'd definitely put a smile on his face. And a great big one on hers.

But the phone sat there, silent and worrisome. To keep busy, she made a second sandwich and stuck in an extra apple for Barak in case they worked through lunch. As she smeared a double-thick layer of peanut butter on the bread, she stared at the phone, willing it to ring.

When it did, she almost didn't believe it was real.

And if it was Barak, why had he waited until almost midnight to call? He had no right to think she'd wait up to all hours for him to find time in his busy schedule to call.

"Hello," she answered. Short and not so sweet.

Barak's deep voice came through the wire. "Lacey, I hope it isn't too late to be calling. Something came up, and I just now heard your message."

"Oh?" She leaned against the counter and crossed her legs. Was he going to explain himself?

He caught her unspoken hint. "Some friends dropped by. The last one just left."

"I didn't know you had any friends." Oh, God, that was a horrible thing to say! "Oh, Barak, I didn't mean that the way it came out. Please put it off to me being extra tired."

"No apology necessary when you are speaking the truth." There was laughter in his voice. "Pizza and beer with four Paladins is not a common occurrence for me."

A strong sense of relief had her relaxing again, until she realized that what she'd been feeling had been that green-eyed monster, jealousy. How could she have thought that he might have been with another woman? Her brother might think she was crazy, but she knew right down to her soul that Barak valued his honor.

"I would guess not. Was it some kind of guy thing? Pizza, beer, and baseball?" Penn and some of the others were ardent Mariner fans, but she couldn't picture Barak yelling at the television every time an umpire made a call he didn't like.

"Uh, yes, I'm learning the rules of the game from Devlin and Cullen."

She looked down at the receiver as if she could see Barak's expression through the wire. What was with that slight hesitation in his voice? Maybe she was mistaken, but it sounded as if he'd latched onto the baseball comment even though it wasn't true.

"It's late. I should let you go."

"Okay." She'd hoped for another long, late-night conversation, but clearly that wasn't going to happen. What had changed since they'd parted ways earlier?

"Good night, Lacey. Sleep well."

"Good night, Barak." She tried one more time to find that special intimacy they'd shared earlier in the tunnels. "Today was, well, pretty wonderful."

Again the short silence. "Yes, it was. I shall have to keep more beer on hand, though, if the guys are going to keep dropping in unexpectedly. Well, I'll let you go."

The click as he hung up echoed in her heart. She blinked rapidly, telling herself that the burning in her eyes was due to the lateness of the hour. After all, though she and Barak had done the horizontal tango down in the tunnels, that didn't mean they had a real relationship. Not that that's what she wanted. Life around the Paladins was enough of an adventure without complicating things by taking an Other for a lover.

After all, she had a purpose in her life. If she could solve the puzzle of predicting earthquakes and volcanic eruptions, her work would save Paladin lives. She hated the life they were forced to live for the sake of humanity. They didn't complain—well, yes they did—but they still picked up their swords and stood on the line.

And she was lying to herself. Yes, her job was important to her, but so was Barak, far more than he should be. Had he deliberately misunderstood her? And if so, why?

A huge yawn surprised her, a reminder of how late it was. She turned out the kitchen lights and padded down the hallway to her lonely bed. There was no use in beating herself up trying to figure out what was up with Barak. He'd be in the lab tomorrow. Time enough to find out what was going on.

"Here's your letter." Barak dropped it on Devlin's desk.

Devlin set aside the report he'd been reading to pick up the short note. "It's in English. Can this woman read our language?"

Barak hated revealing even a small bit of information about his sister. Anything the Paladins learned could be used as a weapon against his world. He avoided answering the question by saying, "I assumed you'd want to be able to read the letter.

Since we don't know when she'll get the message, I thought it made sense for her to have to respond before we try to set up a meeting."

Devlin gave him a measuring look but didn't press the matter. "Okay, I'll need you to show me on the map the best spots to try to get the letter across. This is probably a fool's mission, but we're not getting anywhere on this side. Go down the hall and make half a dozen more of these on the copy machine. If you don't know how to use it, get Cullen or D.J. to show you."

"I need to do the copies by hand. She won't trust anything but something in my own handwriting. It will only take a few minutes to write out the other copies."

Barak had a favor to ask of Devlin, one he wasn't sure Devlin would like. "Would you please call Lacey and tell her that you have need of me for a while?"

"Trouble in paradise?" Devlin's expression shifted into what Barak thought of as a Paladin warrior face, making it impossible to guess what he was thinking.

"No, we've made some real progress in refining the machines she uses to study the mountains. Her work is very important to her. Deep down, she hopes that it will save Penn and the rest of you."

Devlin winced at that. "It's hard on the women around us. Like Laurel, Lacey has it especially hard because she cares about you, too. It gets complicated."

Barak met his gaze head-on, doing his best not to

reveal the powerful emotions that Lacey stirred in him. Devlin might have his suspicions, but he didn't know for certain, and Barak wanted to keep it that way.

"Yes, well, you call her. She won't like it."

"But she'll take it better coming from you." That was a lie. Lacey wouldn't like it no matter which one of them made the call.

Devlin reached for the phone, but before he dialed Lacey's extension, he asked, "And just how long do I desperately need you?"

"I suppose all day would be too much to ask?"

"Not without an explanation." Devlin hung up the phone and leaned back in his chair. "What's going on between you two?"

Now there was a question Barak didn't want to answer. Maybe another truth would suffice. "My life here remains precarious, especially if I end up crossing back to my former world. It wouldn't do for me to get too attached to the people in this one."

"And just how attached have you been to the delectable Lacey Sebastian?" Devlin stared at him with his best "I can smell a lie a hundred feet away" look.

Barak stared right back. "Are you going to call her or not?"

"Son of a bitch, Barak, you do like living recklessly. You know Penn will gut you with a rusty sword for touching his little sister."

"He can't gut me if I'm already dead, Devlin. Now make the call. I'm going to write your notes."

He walked out without looking back. Devlin saw far too much; he didn't need to see how much it hurt to separate himself from Lacey's warmth.

D.J. looked up from his computer. "Hey, Other, what are you doing on our side of the building?"

Last night must have changed the Paladin's hostile attitude toward Barak. "I need paper, a pen, and a place to work for a few minutes." Barak looked around the cluttered office.

"Use Cullen's desk. He's not due in for a couple of hours. He's got paper and pens in the top right drawer."

"Thanks." Barak began the laborious job of copying the letter he'd drafted over into his own language.

It wouldn't translate word for word, but the meaning would be close. He added a private message to his sister, knowing only she would recognize the reference to a game they used to play. Maybe it would convince her to meet with him. He would've set the contact up for both cultures regardless, but the chance to see his sister again was a bonus. He hoped that she'd see it that way.

When he was finishing the tenth copy of the note, he felt someone standing behind his shoulder. Whoever it was had walked up without Barak's hearing a sound. Being that careless was a good way to get himself killed. He slowly looked up and grimaced.

"So what's so all-fired important that you can't

do your job?" Lacey didn't bother to keep her voice down. "I have some important data coming in that needs attention. What's Devlin got you doing? Writing invitations to his birthday party?"

Her blue eyes were shooting the same sparks they had the day before when she'd walked into his arms down in the tunnels. Right now he doubted that she would appreciate the comparison. He turned the last piece of paper over—not that Lacey would have been able to read the message anyway.

"Lacey, I will return to your department as soon as circumstances allow." Provided he didn't end up dead or captured on the other side of the barrier. "I'm sure Devlin explained things."

She crossed her arms over her chest and pursed her mouth. "Like hell he did! All I got was a voice mail that you'd been reassigned to his office for an indefinite amount of time."

She was clearly furious and ready for a fight. Aware of D.J. frowning as he watched them, Barak decided to take this discussion somewhere more private. The closest possibility was Devlin's office.

"Come with me." He automatically reached for Lacey's arm, but she jerked free of his touch.

"I can walk, Barak. I'm a big girl, which you already know." Her anger was affecting her common sense. Neither of them needed rumors flying around about the nature of their relationship.

He whispered near her ear. "You can yell all you want, Lacey, but not here."

"Fine, but brace yourself. I plan on doing quite a bit of it." She followed on his heels straight into Devlin's office.

The Paladin leader looked up from his computer screen at the unexpected interruption. As soon as he saw Lacey, he looked up at the ceiling, as if praying for patience or wisdom.

"Sure, come on in, Barak, and bring Lacey with you. Despite my reputation for shooting first and asking questions later, I don't actually expect people to knock." Sarcasm dripped from every word.

"Shut up, Devlin. You're part of this problem, so don't act all innocent and put upon." Lacey plopped down in one of the chairs that faced his desk. "Now tell me again why Barak is over here writing grocery lists or whatever you're having him do, instead of reporting to the lab?"

She glared at each man in turn. "And don't lie to me."

Barak took the other chair. "Devlin, I left those grocery lists out on Cullen's desk. I'm not sure where you wanted them filed."

Devlin stood up. "In other words, you want me to get lost for a few minutes."

"That's exactly what I mean."

Barak was aware of the big Paladin walking out, then the soft click of the door locking. "Devlin did need me for a special project. That much is true."

"And the rest of it? About you needing to be gone indefinitely? Was that true, too?"

He'd put that hurt look in her eyes, and he hated himself for it. "It is also true that he will need me to further assist him on this project, but I don't know how long it will take or when he'll actually need me."

A little of her anger faded away, to be replaced by her disappointment in him. "For some reason, you don't want to be around me. I didn't hear any complaints yesterday."

It would be so much easier for them both if he let her believe that lie, but he couldn't do that. He reached out to put his hand on hers, but she jerked her hand back where he couldn't reach it.

"The problem," he responded quietly, "is quite the opposite: I want to be around you too much. I told you before that I wouldn't be your guilty secret. How many people have you told about me—that you want me to be an important part of your life?" He knew the answer even before her eyes shifted away.

"That's what I thought." He sighed, wishing all of this was easier. "I don't even blame you, Lacey, but it's only going to get worse, the more we work together."

"You know what I don't like, Barak? I don't like people making decisions about what's right for me. I may not be ready to go dancing down the streets screaming that I'm dating an Other, but at least I'm not slamming the door on the possibility." She stood up. "I hope you and Devlin are happy together, although I suspect Laurel is the jealous type. She's not going to like being part of a threesome."

Lacey walked away, her back ramrod straight.

The weapons on Devlin's wall rattled on their hooks when she slammed the door. He wanted to charge after her and drag her back to convert her anger to another, more palatable, form of passion. The image was so real that when the door opened, he was half convinced that she'd had a change of heart.

But it was only Devlin returning to reclaim his office. He wasn't even trying to hide his grin. "I don't know what you did to get on that woman's shit list, but for Pete's sake, don't let me do it."

"Shut up, Devlin. We haven't been fair to her."

"How so?"

"We forced my presence on her. All she wants to do is make your world safer for her brother. She shouldn't have to sleep with the enemy to get enough money to do the job." A poor choice of words, but that didn't make it less true.

Devlin's hand snaked out to grab Barak by the shirtfront. "And did she sleep with the enemy, Barak? I sent you over there to learn a job, not to seduce your boss."

The Paladin's touch triggered all of Barak's frustration and anger. Devlin's superior size made little difference to a man who had lost everything—home, family, lover. Barak brought his fist up, connecting with Devlin's jaw with a satisfying crack. When

Devlin's head snapped back, Barak broke loose from his grasp, following up with a kick aimed right at Devlin's groin.

The Paladin hadn't spent his life fighting without learning a few dirty tricks. He blocked Barak's kick with one of his own, sending Barak stumbling back to land on a chair with a crash. Barak ignored the pain in his back and surged to his feet, intent on doing Devlin some serious harm.

Neither of them noticed the door opening again as they each jockeyed for position, looking for a weakness in their opponent's defenses. As they circled the room, a female stepped between them. It took Barak two more steps before he recognized it as Lacey.

"Lacey, out!" He knew she didn't much like taking orders, but now was not the time for polite conversation.

"I'm not going anywhere." She kept moving, doing her best to stay between the two men.

"Damn it, woman, get out of the way!" Devlin barked.

"No." She planted her feet and stood her ground. With her hands on her hips and meeting them glare for glare, it was easy to see that the blood of warriors ran true in her family. She was irresistible: a woman at her strongest, ready to do battle to protect those she cared about.

The two men had no choice but to surrender. Neither would risk accidentally hurting her, and she knew it, too. When they each backed up a step and dropped their hands at their sides, she smiled.

"Now, care to explain this exhibition of stupidity?" She tapped her foot and waited for a reply.

"We had a slight disagreement."

She eyed the broken chair and the scattered trash from the wastebasket they'd knocked over. "Oh? I'd hate to see what would happen if you two decided to actually *fight* about something."

Devlin dabbed at the blood dripping from a split lip. "So, Lacey, did you forget something?"

"Yes, I did. I got halfway back to my office and realized I'd left something in your office that belongs to me."

Barak looked around the room but saw nothing. "I don't see anything."

"That's because you're not looking in a mirror." Then she gave him a gentle shove toward the door. "Come on. You've got work to do."

"I'll still need him." Devlin followed them out of his office. "We've got a special project that requires his expertise."

"Yeah, and I can see how well the two of you work together. Call me and we'll negotiate."

Trahern loomed up from down the hallway. As usual he saw way too much. "So, Devlin, you back to having hands-on discussions again? Last time you damn near broke my jaw, and both Cullen and D.J. were moving slowly for two days."

Barak and Devlin told Trahern to go to hell at the

same time, setting off a round of laughter. Doing his best to ignore both Paladins, Barak marshaled his dignity and followed Lacey down the hall.

But he couldn't be too angry. Right in front of the biggest, baddest Paladins around, she'd admitted that Barak belonged to her.

Chapter 15

$\mathcal{H}$ey, Penn, what's happening?"

Penn kept his eyes on his beer, debating whether he wanted to drink another one. If he left now, he'd be able to catch the beginning of a preseason football game.

Ben Jackson's unexpected arrival pretty much made the decision for him. The last thing he wanted right now was to sit and listen to the man bitch about his job some more. It was ironic that Ben had a job he hated but could walk away from anytime he wanted to. Penn had a job he loved, and he was going to be shoved out the door any day now.

The last couple of sparring matches with Barak had not gone well. He didn't need the Other's sympathy, but he could see it in Barak's expression every time Penn made a poor showing with his right hand. His left hand was definitely getting stronger, but there was no way he was ever going to be as comfortable fighting from that side.

Barak kept telling him to give himself time, but Devlin had made it clear that Penn's time was limited. Barak's claim that he could see some improvement might buy Penn some leeway, but being indebted to an Other stuck in Penn's craw big-time.

At least he wasn't so drunk that he didn't realize that there was something wrong about Ben's unexpected appearance. This wasn't the bar close to the Center. It was a good distance away from where they both worked, and not particularly close to where Penn lived. Penn could hold his own among the bar's rough clientele, but Ben was clearly out of his element.

Keeping his expression neutral, Penn glanced at his unwanted companion. Ben was nervous and doing a piss-poor job of hiding it. Something had the man by the ass, but what? Or who? Either way, it shouldn't have anything to do with Penn, but it did. Otherwise Ben wouldn't keep hunting him down and inflicting his sweaty, nervous self on Penn's downtime.

"What do you want, Ben?" Penn didn't bother sounding polite or interested.

Ben winced, his smile slipping for only a second before he managed to shore up its edges. "I want a cold beer. I haven't thought much beyond that part."

"Well, have a nice time." Penn slid off his stool and signaled the bartender he wanted to pay up.

"What's your hurry, Penn? I just got here and

wouldn't mind some company." The older man started to reach for Penn's arm to prevent him from leaving. When Penn shot him an angry look, he thought better of it. "At least have one for the road."

"Sorry, no can do." Penn gave up waiting on his bill and walked down the bar to toss a five down on the counter.

"Got big plans?" Ben trailed right along behind him.

"No, this place has suddenly lost its appeal." Maybe the truth would get through to the idiot.

His shot scored a bull's-eye, judging by the way Ben flushed red hot. "What's the matter, Penn? Too good to hang out with a mere mortal?"

Great. All he needed was for word to get back to Devlin that he'd pushed this sweating pig into outing the Paladins. Already they were drawing too much attention to themselves. He made a grab for Ben, planning on dragging him outside. In a move surprisingly quick for his size, Ben danced back out of reach.

"Go on home, Penn, and drink alone. See if I give a rip." He lumbered back up on his barstool and reached for the beer the bartender had set there.

Before turning to leave, Penn waited a second or two to make sure that Ben was going to behave. He'd gone no more than a step or two before Ben launched a final attack of his own.

"Of course, I'd be drinking, too, if my pretty little sister was doing the dirty with a fucking Other." He laughed as if he'd told a great joke. "I guess in your sister's case, he really *is* a fucking Other."

Penn wanted to kill the bastard on the spot, but his Paladin loyalties kicked in, reminding him that the priority was to maintain secrecy above all else, even defending Lacey's honor. That time would come. Luckily, this wasn't the kind of bar that objected to settling an argument with your fists as long as you took it somewhere else.

"Come on, Ben, I'll make sure you get home. You're spoiling for a fight, but I'm not going to give you one." With a nod to the bartender, assuring the man that any further discussion would take place outside, Penn strong-armed Ben toward the door.

Ben, however, had just realized that he'd opened his big mouth once too often—and that he'd forgotten just how strong a Paladin was, especially one who was in fight mode.

He tried to pull away from Penn. "I'm sorry, Penn. It was the beer talking, I swear." He stumbled along, pleading for mercy. "How was I to know you approved of your sister's new boy toy?"

That was the last thing Ben had to say on the matter. Penn made sure of it with a good left hook before shoving Ben into the backseat of his own car. Penn had caught a ride to the bar with another Paladin, so at least he didn't have to worry about getting two vehicles home. He fished out Ben's keys and started the car.

After driving a couple of blocks, Penn pulled over

to the curb and hit Devlin's number on the speed dial of his cell phone.

Bane answered on the second ring. He didn't sound happy, but then he never did. "What now, Penn?"

"I've got one question for you, Bane. Did you promise that Other my sister if he'd leave your woman alone? Because if you did, I'll *kill* you." He hated that his hands were shaking.

"NO, I SURE AS HELL DIDN'T!" Bane yelled so loud that Penn had to hold the phone away from his ear. "I have more respect for your sister than that, even if she does have an idiot for a brother. Where the hell did you get that stupid idea?"

Penn wasn't sure if he believed the older Paladin or just wanted to. "Ben Jackson followed me to an out-of-the-way bar, trying to get all friendly again. When I made it clear I wasn't interested, he told me that Barak was fucking my sister."

"Son of a bitch, where are you now? Do I need to come bail you out?" His voice made it clear that he wasn't kidding.

"No, I got him out of the bar before I cold-cocked him. Right now he's throwing up in the back-seat of his own car."

"I'll call Trahern and we'll meet you at Jackson's place. Maybe if we get him into his own apartment and pour more liquor in him, he'll wake up thinking it was all a bad dream."

"Except for the bruises after I finish beating the

crap out of him." Penn rolled down the windows to diffuse the sour smell of the drunk in the backseat.

"Penn!" The warning was clear.

"I was just kidding. Sort of. I got his address off his license." He read it off as he started the car again.

"Thanks. Give us fifteen minutes to meet you there."

"Will do."

Of course he couldn't help it if Ben picked up a few more injuries stumbling out of the car and into his apartment. No, he'd wait until after he found out for certain if Barak had been hitting on Lacey. If not, then Ben deserved to be beaten within an inch of his miserable life. If he was telling the truth, Penn would end Barak's existence once and for all.

After glancing back at his disgusting passenger, Penn decided he'd kill the messenger for good measure.

Barak looked up when the lab door opened to reveal Devlin Bane, a grim expression on his face. His arrival so soon after Lacey's leaving for a meeting with Dr. Louis seemed a little too convenient to be a coincidence. What was wrong now?

Then Devlin tossed an envelope on the counter and waited for Barak to pick it up. One look was enough to know it had come from the other side of the barrier. Barak let his fingers trace the letters on the outside as he recognized the anger in his sister's handwriting.

He smiled, picturing the frown on her face as she'd responded to his request. She alone of their family had resisted his banishment, begging him to choose differently. And when his honor had made that impossible, she had turned her back and closed her eyes so that he no longer existed in her world. Or any other.

Well aware of the impatient Paladin hovering over his shoulder, he gently peeled back the flap on the envelope and opened it. The paper inside was definitely of his world and no matter what his sister had written in her role of commander, he cherished the small connection with her.

"She makes it clear that she is unwilling to trust anyone from this world. However, she will meet with me. I'm to cross at the same point where I entered your world." He looked at Devlin. "I will be allowed to stay only until the next time the barrier flickers long enough for me to cross back."

Devlin smacked his hand down on the counter. "No, she comes here. I won't ask you to risk your life that way."

"She will keep me safe." At least she'd try, but there was no sense in letting Devlin know he doubted her ability to protect him from the rabid factions among their people.

Running his fingers through his hair in frustration, Devlin paced the room and back. "And what makes you think we can trust her to keep her word? Who is this woman, anyway?"

"Her name is Lusahn." Barak once again traced her name with his fingers. "She is a leader among my people . . . and she is my sister."

Devlin clearly hadn't expected that. He pulled up a stool and sat down next to Barak. "We've never talked about why you left your world."

"No, and we're not going to. My reasons are my own. I won't betray my people." He'd die first, even though this world had given him new reasons to live.

"I guess I can deal with that. I know you're willing to go back for this, Barak, but I won't ask it of you until you've had a chance to think about it. As unstable as the barrier has been, the chances are you'd only be there for a short time, maybe even only a couple of hours . . ."

Barak took over. "But it could be days or weeks, and the longer I'm over there, the higher the risk. I know all of that."

"Let's contact her again. Tell her that it's imperative that we meet here or it's no dice."

"She won't come. I will go to her. She will take us more seriously if there is risk involved on our side." He pushed the letter back in front of Devlin. "I will do this for my people, Devlin."

"We'll meet in my office after you're finished here today. Maybe some of the other guys can come up with some ideas."

"All right. I'll be there."

Devlin picked up the letter and stuffed it in his pocket. "One more thing, Barak. Ben Jackson got a little drunk last night and told Penn that you and Lacey were sleeping together. Any reason he should think that?"

A sense of foreboding settled in Barak's chest. "No, I don't know why he would say that." Unless he'd been right about someone watching his apartment the night that Lacey had stayed over.

"What did Penn say?"

"He didn't kill the stupid bastard, which he would have if he'd actually believed Ben was telling the truth." Devlin's green eyes took on a definite chill. "Whatever you and Lacey have been doing is none of my business, but—"

Barak rose to his feet, meeting Devlin's rock-hard gaze head-on. "That's exactly right. And Lacey doesn't deserve to be the subject of gossip."

"No, she doesn't. But if her name is linked with yours, it will make her life miserable, not to mention yours. People are just now getting used to having you around."

Devlin wasn't saying anything Barak didn't already know. He'd only hoped that this day would have come later rather than sooner. "People cannot fault us for the time here at work. She gave me a ride home from your place, and we've been to the mountains on business. That, and the two trips down into the tunnels, are the extent of our relationship."

Devlin wasn't buying it. "I'm not your judge or

jury, Barak. At least use some discretion. Ben had to have seen something or he wouldn't have felt so confident in shooting his mouth off to Penn. We've been suspicious that this guy was trying to get something from Penn, only we don't know what. He sure didn't win any points by making these accusations to Lacey's brother."

The two of them were so intent on their discussion that neither of them heard Lacey walk in. "What accusations to my brother?"

Devlin muttered a vicious curse before turning to face her. It was the second time in two days that the two of them were on opposite sides of a discussion.

"If you can tell Barak about it, you can tell me. He's not my protector."

"No, the question is whether or not he's your lover."

Barak might have been able to fool Devlin, but the stricken look on Lacey's face had the truth written all over it. The Paladin immediately let loose with a tirade of obscenities.

"Bane, shut your mouth. Regardless of what you know or think you know, you do NOT speak that way in front of Lacey." If it took another fight to convince him of that truth, Barak was prepared to start swinging.

Lacey stepped past Devlin to stand next to Barak, seeking his support. "Who's been making accusations, Barak? Who knew?"

Devlin answered. "Ben Jackson from IT tried to

convince Penn that you two were having an affair. Penn didn't take him too seriously, although it probably wouldn't take much to convince him that Ben wasn't just blowing smoke."

Barak waited for Lacey to deny it, and he would have supported her lie. Instead, she turned to him, her blue eyes filling with tears. "Why couldn't that bastard leave us alone?"

"Because he's a desperate man. By pointing his finger at us, he diverts attention away from himself." The more Barak thought about it, the more that idea rang true. "He doesn't strike me as the kind who would lead such an operation. Perhaps his superiors are concerned about how much we learned from those disks Trahern got from Judge Nichols."

Devlin's cell phone rang. "Bane here . . . Okay, tell Colonel Kincade I'll meet him in his office in fifteen minutes."

He disconnected the call and stared at Barak in cold silence. "I do NOT need this complication, Other. I told Laurel she could keep you as long as you didn't make waves."

Lacey bristled. "He is not some pet to keep in a cage, Devlin! Besides, I don't see you following the rules yourself. Everybody knows Handlers aren't supposed to sleep with their patients. Where does that leave you and Laurel? Or Trahern and Brenna? Was he really supposed to bring in a civilian? I don't think so."

Barak watched his woman with admiration. This

was the second time she'd stood up to Devlin Bane, something most men would have been leery of.

Bane shook his head. "We all know that Penn's never going to think anyone is good enough for you, but in this case, I have some sympathy for his point of view." Before Lacey could explode again, Devlin held up his hand. "Don't get me wrong. Once I got past *what* Barak is, I respected *who* he is. But you're going to be fighting an uphill battle if you think you can convince folks around here that a human woman belongs with an Other."

That was enough. "Devlin, you go too far. Leave," Barak ordered.

Devlin stood his ground. "I'll leave when I damn well want to, Other."

"You'll leave now, or we'll take this discussion to a whole other level." Barak was sick and tired of these Paladins' overblown sense of importance. "Either way, you have no say in what goes on between Lacey and me. You might not like it, but I don't care." He shoved his stool back out of his way and stepped in front of Lacey, clearing the floor for whatever came next.

Then he heard her sniff, trying to hold back tears. She was a strong woman, but he and Devlin were putting her through hell. Turning his back to the angry Paladin, Barak reached out to offer his woman the comfort of his touch. He didn't like it much when she refused, but he didn't blame her.

"Devlin, you've caused enough trouble for one

afternoon, so leave. Barak, I'll be in my office if you have any questions about the data I left for you." She walked away, her pride the only thing holding her together.

"It's going to get worse," Devlin warned.

He wasn't telling Barak anything he didn't already know, even if he didn't like hearing it. "What would you have me do? Could you walk away from Laurel if the Regents ordered you to?"

The big man's hand came down on Barak's shoulder. "Do me a favor: at least be careful."

"We will." Barak picked up the letter from his sister. "I'll tell Lacey that my expertise is going to be needed soon. Until then, I'll make sure no one sees us together outside of the lab."

Devlin checked his watch again. "Shit! I'm going to be late. Let me know when you want to try to cross."

"It'll be a couple of days at least." The barrier would remain stable that long unless something offshore triggered a problem. He hadn't been near all the tectonic plates long enough to learn their habits, but the volcano was going to be quiet.

"Okay. By the way, Laurel wants you to come to dinner again soon. She's been looking at recipes again." Devlin's mouth quirked up, sharing his slight dread of his lover's experiments in cooking.

Barak took the comment as the peace offering it was. "Thank you for the warning. And as you said, the vegetables were edible."

Once Devlin disappeared, Barak considered how best to approach Lacey. He moved closer to her door and was relieved to see her at work on her computer. For the moment, it was probably best that he leave her alone. But before he could retreat to his work area, she looked up and saw him.

"Don't hover out there. I won't bite. Or cry." She managed to smile, although her eyes looked a bit red.

"I promised Devlin we'd make sure no one sees us together outside of work."

"I won't have my life dictated by anyone, not even you, Barak. If I want to see you, I will."

Part of him was selfish enough to appreciate her determination, but he didn't want her hurt. "You might be willing to risk it, but I'm not."

It hurt to turn his back on her and walk away, as if he'd jabbed a knife in his own chest. Out in the lab, he picked up his clipboard and pretended to work.

Damn men, all of them and all kinds. Paladins, Others, brothers, bosses. From the time she'd been a little girl, Lacey had remained focused on one goal: finding some way to make Penn's life better, safer. Luckily, she'd developed a real love for geology and vulcanology. If she hadn't liked them, she'd have found some other discipline that would have allowed her to serve the Regents in some capacity.

But right now, she was about to chuck it all and find some sane people to work with. And maybe some eligible men who didn't know which end of a sword to hold, much less how to wield one.

She had tried dating outside of the organization, but that meant watching every word to make sure she didn't reveal something she shouldn't. The few men she'd dated among the guards had been too afraid of Penn to do little more than show her to her front door. Paladins rarely had siblings, yet they seemed to have an unspoken agreement to stay away from each other's sisters.

And when she finally found someone whose touch set her aflame, he had to be an Other! Right now she wasn't sure whom she was maddest at: Penn, Barak, or Devlin. Not that it mattered. Ever since Devlin had walked out, Barak had been pretending she didn't exist.

Well, that was going to change right now. She paused to check her appearance, wishing she had worn her sexy dress rather than her usual jeans and T-shirt. If Barak wouldn't come near her, she'd go to him.

He flinched when he heard her approach. Good, he wasn't immune to her, no matter how hard he tried to act that way. Time to go for broke. She slipped her arms around his shoulders and leaned in close, pressing her breasts against the rock-hard planes of his back. He kept working, but his pulse sped up.

She kissed his neck and then worked her way up to breathe next to his ear, sending a visible shiver through Barak. Sliding her hands around to his chest, she whispered, "I make a mean veggie lasagna. How about dinner at my place?"

He froze. "Didn't you hear what Devlin said, Lacey? We can't be seen together."

"I heard; I just don't care. Now, either you come to my place for dinner tonight, or I'm going to show up at your apartment. Your choice." She held her breath, hoping he wouldn't refuse her.

He slowly turned to face her. Although he wasn't smiling, she thought she saw the smallest bit of humor in his eyes. "You are one stubborn woman."

"Are you surprised? If I hadn't learned to stand up for myself, Penn and his friends would have walked all over me. Either that or they would have wrapped me up in bubble wrap to keep me safe."

"Can you blame them?"

She laughed. "No, probably not, but hiding is no way to live. Which brings me back to tonight. My place or yours?"

He looked at her long and hard before making his decision. "Yours. I'll come after dark."

"But it stays light until ten o'clock this time of year." She trailed her fingers along the strong line of his jaw. "I don't want to wait that long."

"Then eat dinner without me." He caught her wayward hand and held it still over his chest.

She still had one hand free to wander. "I wasn't talking about dinner."

He grabbed that hand, too. "Stop that, woman!

What if someone came walking in here right now?" Despite his stern words, his touch was gentle. "I'll be there as soon as I think it is safe."

"I'll keep everything warm and ready for you." She ran the tip of her tongue across her upper lip.

"Fine, but right now I have to go spend some time with your brother in the gym."

"Tell him hi for me," she said as he got up and walked to the door. "And, Barak, you might want to bring your toothbrush. We need to go out to the mountains tomorrow, and it will save time if you don't have to stop by your place on the way."

He started to say something but realized that he was fighting a losing battle, one that he probably didn't want to win anyway. After he was gone, she realized that she was staring at a closed door with a big, stupid grin on her face. Tonight would be special. More than special.

If she hurried, she could get her work done in time to make a quick stop at the mall on the way home. Most of the time she slept in one of Penn's old T-shirts, but suddenly she felt like wearing something a whole lot sexier. Maybe something black and slinky.

Yeah, that was the ticket.

The scent of lasagna filled the kitchen; the table was set; the candles were lit; and the bed was turned down. Everything was ready, especially her. But so far, no sign of Barak. He'd promised to be there as soon as he knew it was safe, so maybe that was delaying his arrival. Or had something happened at practice? No, Barak would have called, or he would have had Devlin do it.

She looked out the front window, glad to see the sunshine fading into the west. Soon her lover would arrive and the evening's festivities could get started.

An older couple who lived up the street strolled by, taking their dog for its walk, holding hands as they enjoyed the late-evening air. Lacey smiled. Every time she saw them, obviously still in love after so many years together, she felt a small pang of envy.

A woman dreamed of finding a man to love her, to hold her hand year after year. But what if it was the wrong man? One her family and friends could never accept? Was love worth giving up everything and everyone for? It was too soon to know how strong her feelings for Barak would become. Maybe it was only a momentary infatuation.

No, she wouldn't risk her job, her brother's respect, and everything else for some guy she just had the hots for. She'd already gone way past mere lust. She wasn't ready to think about how far past; it was scary enough to know that she was headed down an unknown path and maybe a lonely one.

A soft knock at the back door jarred her out of her reverie. She hadn't left the outside light on for obvious reasons, but she recognized the dark outline of a man standing on her small porch. She opened the door and walked straight into her lover's arms.

Barak's kiss had her curling her toes in the carpet and her bones melting. He didn't rush the moment. They were headed for her bed, but they were in no hurry to get there. His hands stroked the length of her back from her neck to her bottom, stoking the fire already burning hot between them.

Finally, he stepped back slightly, leaving no more than a hand's breadth between them. "What is this that you are wearing?" He traced the curve of her breast through the black satin and lace.

"It's a negligee. I bought it for tonight, so I hope you like it." She was fishing for compliments but didn't really need to. His clear approval was putting a pretty big strain on the front of his slacks. She did a slow turn to show off a bit.

He caught her and pulled her backward against his chest. "I like it very much."

She arched her head back to nuzzle his neck and tugged his hands up to cup her breasts. How did he know the exact amount of pressure to have her moaning for more? She slipped a hand back between them to caress the hard length of him.

"Keep that up, woman, and we won't make it as far as your bed."

She gently squeezed him and laughed softly at his immediate response.

He swept her up in his arms and carried her down the short hallway to her room. He slowly lowered her to the bed, then stepped back to strip off his clothes. The soft glow of the candles she'd left burning cast his warrior's body in a warm light for her to admire.

Then he was beside her, then in her, and everything was perfect.

"Don't think so hard, Barak." Lacey looked up from where she cuddled against his chest. "Or maybe I should give you something to think about that won't have you frowning so much."

She trailed her hand down his chest to his stomach and beyond. Barak closed his eyes and smiled as she cupped his sac and gently squeezed. "Like that, do you?"

"Yes, I do."

"How about this?" she teased, giving his cock several gentle strokes.

"That as well." Then he turned the tables on her, doing a little exploring of his own.

She giggled and surrendered to his superior forces. "Take me, Barak. Take me again."

He rose above her, settling in between the welcoming cradle of her legs. "You are so beautiful."

She knew that wasn't true, but she accepted that he believed the words to be true. Every move he made, every touch he gave her, made her feel cherished. He leaned down to kiss her, his tongue and taste driving her up and up until all that existed was him.

"You honor me with your welcome, Lacey," he murmured near her ear. Passion made his accent more pronounced, sending shivers of pleasure through her.

As he took her, she wrapped her ankles around his waist and held on for dear life as the two of them rode out the cresting waves of passion. "Yes, that's it, like that," she gasped as he filled her with his strength.

"Come for me, Lacey," he demanded, their bodies sliding against each other, sweat-slick and hot.

"Only if you come with me," she said, straining up to take more of him, more, and yet more.

Then the night shattered around them in light and heat and joy.

Chapter 16

I can't! He won't let me near him."

Ben pulled at his collar, trying to loosen its chokehold. Those further up the food chain had ordered him to find a weak spot among the Paladins for them and he'd done his best, but none of those scary killers were about to get chummy with the likes of him.

Not even that bastard Penn Sebastian, which pissed him off. Who was he to look down his nose at Ben? It was one thing to act all superior when you carried a sword and skewered those freaky Others for kicks. But Penn was out of the game, which made him no better than anyone else—worse, because at least Ben could *do* the job the Regents paid him to do. It wasn't their fault that he didn't make enough to support his gambling habit.

But the voice on the other end of the line clearly didn't care about any of that. One guard and one Regent had already died for not getting the job done. He needed to keep that in mind.

"All right. I'll see what I can do."

Obviously that wasn't good enough. He held the phone away from his ear and let the man rant some more. More money didn't matter. No amount was worth losing his life for, but the cold fear in his gut screamed that it was too late to worry about that. Either he roped Penn into spying for them or Ben would die. Trouble was, if Penn wasn't the weak link they thought he was, Ben would die anyway. It was all a matter of who would make him suffer the most.

He shuddered, knowing he'd done this to himself. "Yes, sir, I understand, sir. I'll bring him into the fold. I promise. I may need some muscle, though."

Judging by the immediate offer of names and numbers to call, he'd finally managed to get something right. After a few more last-minute instructions, he hung up. Asking for muscle had been a stroke of genius. Now he just needed a plan for how to use his new assistants.

He couldn't risk another fiasco like last night. The events of the evening were pretty hazy, but he'd woken up sporting a few bruises he hadn't had when he'd left work. Memories of the first three bars he'd checked while looking for Penn were crystal clear. It was the fourth one, where he'd finally found the Paladin, where things went to hell.

Sebastian had not been happy to see him; that was certain. If memory served correctly, Penn had gotten up to leave as soon as Ben had arrived. Fear mixed with too many beers had been a bad combination, and Ben suspected he'd shot his mouth off about Lacey Sebastian.

Even if she *was* boinking the Other, her brother hadn't wanted to hear about it. If Ben had really said it. He shifted his jaw from one side to the other, wincing at the dull pain. If he really *had* been stupid enough to say that, he was lucky he was alive.

What he really didn't remember was driving home or how he'd gotten upstairs into his apartment. A couple of empty bottles by his bed might account for that—not that it mattered. Right now, he needed to formulate a plan to force Penn Sebastian to betray his fellow Paladins.

If he succeeded, it would be one for the history books; there'd never been a breath of scandal connected to the Paladins. But the scam ripping off the blue stones from the Other world could stay hidden for only so long. Eventually, Devlin Bane or one of those other bastards would figure out what was going on and decide to put a stop to it.

And God help them all when that happened.

But for now, Ben needed to figure out how best to use Penn Sebastian's weak point. As far as Ben knew, the only person Penn cared about was his sister.

If someone were to threaten her, Penn would do anything to keep her safe. Anything. Now Ben just had to find a way to use that bit of information. Maybe he wasn't a dead man quite yet.

• • •

Lacey sighed and leaned into Barak. They seemed incapable of going more than a few minutes without touching, kissing, breathing each other's air. Out on the edge of the wilderness, they were free to be just another couple. The few people they'd encountered on the way up the mountain had smiled or waved, each intent on their own enjoyment of a beautiful day.

"Kiss me." She smiled up at him, her eyes full of promised heat.

He tucked a stray lock of hair back behind her ear, basking in her warmth. His lover was a wonderfully demanding woman. As their lips came together, he sought out the sweetness of her mouth with his tongue, pleased with her murmured encouragement as he took on a new energy from his head to his toes. Then the ground rolled under his feet, almost sending him to his knees. He froze, hoping against hope that the sudden surge came from the strength of their shared passion.

But a wise man never lied to himself, especially about something that could get them both killed. He gently broke off the embrace, wishing he could trust Lacey with his secrets. Once she found out, she'd expect him to use his sensitivity to the moods of the mountain to help the Paladins, at the expense of his own kind and his honor.

The dilemma made him sicker than the shifting of stone beneath his feet.

"We'd better be going, don't you think?" He gave Lacey a gentle push in the right direction: down and away from the mountain's anger.

"What's your hurry?" She tried to step right back into his arms.

Desperate times. "The sooner we get back to your place, the sooner we can have some of that left-over lasagna."

She giggled. "Are you sure that's all you're interested in?"

This was no time for teasing, but he couldn't resist. "Fishing for compliments, Lacey?"

"Yeah, maybe." Her eyes twinkled with good humor and the satisfaction of a woman who knew her man wanted her.

"All right. If I give you one, will you get moving down the mountain?"

"Yes." She planted her feet to wait him out.

He pretended to give the matter grave consideration. "Fine. You make great lasagna. Best I've ever had."

Her laughter rang out in the summer air. "Ooooh, you sweet talker. That kind of sweet talk will get you a piece of cold lasagna and not much else." Then she kissed his cheek and dutifully set off down the path ahead of him, adding a little extra swing to her walk for good measure.

Barak waited until Lacey turned the corner ahead of him before reaching out to touch a nearby boulder, hoping that he was wrong. The connection was always stronger with his eyes closed; the stone immediately told him its truth.

The mountain thrummed with dark energy; it was about to unleash some of its fury by tossing bits of itself down toward the valley below. Barak muttered under his breath, wishing the ground below his feet could be soothed with his words.

But right now, wishes weren't going to be much help.

He withdrew his contact from the stone and picked up his share of the lab equipment. For the sake of speed, he considered leaving it behind, but that would involve questions he couldn't answer. By the time he caught up with Lacey, his senses were reeling with the increasing pressure building below his feet.

They weren't going to make it all the way down in time unless they started running. Did he risk their safety for the sake of his secrets? The question wasn't even worth considering.

He set down the cooler and toolbox. "Lacey, drop the equipment and start running!"

She looked at him with understandable confusion. "Why would I do that?"

He latched onto the kit in her hand and yanked it away from her. "Drop it and run. I'll explain later."

Not that he'd need to. If they didn't get moving right then, it would be too late for explanations. "Run!"

They'd only gone a short distance when the first

surge of energy rolled down from above them, sending a shower of loose gravel skittering past them on the path. "What's happening?" Lacey cried, but she knew because she finally started running as much as the steep path allowed.

The second wave hit when the trail hit a switchback turn, almost sending the two of them sliding down a steep drop-off. Barak kept to his feet, but Lacey wasn't so lucky. She fell hard, landing with her ankle twisted underneath her. Barak grabbed her arm and pulled her back from the edge.

It was too late to get away; the next best choice was to get to some cover, away from loose rock and trees that could be uprooted. He hauled Lacey up off the ground, wrapping her arm across his shoulders, and supported her as they stumbled down the path toward a small overhang just ahead. He quickly lowered her back down to shield her body with his. They hugged the rock wall and waited the mountain out.

The next rumble was smaller, pelting them with a stinging spray of small gravel. It quickly faded away. When the mountain remained silent for several minutes, Barak closed his eyes once again and reached out to test the mood of the rock and stone. It was a relief to feel nothing but a faint echo of the last few rocks settling in their new homes.

He slowly sat up and lifted Lacey's booted foot onto his lap. "Let me check your ankle. Does it feel broken?"

She winced when he moved it gently from side to side. "No, I think it's just sprained. I should be fine as long as we go slowly."

She started to stand up, but he stopped her. "Wait here while I go back up for our equipment."

Maybe if they kept moving, she wouldn't start to wonder how he'd known when they'd needed to start running to get out of the way of the rockslide. He trudged up the path, knowing each minute he was away from Lacey was time for her to start thinking, but there wasn't anything he could do about that but hurry.

Their cooler had fallen over but was otherwise unharmed. The toolbox had been knocked open, and a few tools had spilled out. The more fragile equipment that Lacey had been carrying hadn't fared as well. Two of the meters were now bits of broken plastic and bent wire, having been in the direct path of a rather large boulder. Lacey wouldn't be pleased about losing two such valuable pieces of equipment, but at least the monitor they'd been carrying was intact.

There was no way he could carry it all and help Lacey walk. He'd have to get her down the trail to her truck and then come back for their gear. She wouldn't like leaving anything behind, but too bad. Well, the madder she was, the less likely she was to ask too many questions.

His skin itched from a combination of sweat, dust, and fear for what was about to happen. As soon as he made the last turn back to Lacey, he knew that luck wasn't with him. She had spent the short time he'd been gone adding up details and coming to only one conclusion.

She pushed herself up off the ground. Bracing herself against the overhang, she turned angry blue eyes on him. "You knew, didn't you? Somehow you felt the earthquake coming long before it hit. That's why you were trying to hustle me off the mountain."

The betrayal in her eyes dared him to deny it. He could pretend not to understand, but why bother? "Yes, I knew."

"How?"

He set the equipment down on the side of the trail. "I won't answer that. Now, let's get you out of here." When he reached out to take her arm again, she jerked away from him even though the sudden movement hurt her.

She fought for balance. "Don't . . . touch . . . me."

"Lacey, use your head. You can't make it down from here without help. The rangers won't appreciate having to come get you just because you're mad at me."

"Mad is *way* too weak a term for what I'm feeling." She hobbled a few steps away to pick up a tree branch to use as a cane.

"Lacey—"

"*No!* Damn it, Barak, what goes on out here is my life's work, not some little hobby. I've spent years trying to figure out how to predict earthquakes and eruptions. You've been working beside me every day in the lab, watching me beg for enough money to figure out how to make my equipment even one percent more sensitive. And that whole time, you've already known the answers to those questions."

She stumbled on, rage coming off her in waves. "Year upon year, my brothers and his friends have lived on the edge of battle, dying over and over to defend my world. You must think it was a riot watching foolish me trying to keep them safe."

When a tear trickled down her face, she scrubbed it off with the heel of her hand. "God, I slept with you! My brother's enemy, and I slept with you! And the sad part is, I thought you were worth the cost."

Her eyes burned with rage. "And do you know the funny part? I thought you were honorable! Can you imagine?"

Lacey's pain ripped his heart right out of his chest. Did she think he didn't understand the cost of sacrifice?

He caught up with his woman and blocked her stumbling rush downhill. "Yes, Lacey, I can feel the rock moving. Yes, I know when the volcano is going to erupt. And yes, before you ask, I sometimes know when and where the barrier is going to fail. And do you know what that knowledge cost me? *Everything,* Lacey. It cost me everything."

She flinched, but right now all he wanted was her hatred, because he hated himself as much as she did. "I've never told you why I abandoned my home, where my talent was coveted because it helped those who wanted to leave. Fools thought they stood a chance of making it into this world of yours." He looked around them. "Do you have any idea how it feels to walk in the warmth of this world after living a lifetime in the cold darkness of my own?

"Imagine how proud I was as a young man, knowing I carried this gift, this burden. I was insufferable." His lungs hurt with the need to lance this festering wound deep inside of him. "But imagine, too, how I felt when I found out that all they faced was certain death. I chose disgrace and refused to use my gift.

"I understand your pain, watching the way your brother's life must play itself out. But if I would not use my gift for my people, how could I possibly use it for yours?" Then he stepped out of her way and let her pass. Since she wouldn't allow him to touch her, he picked up her precious equipment and followed her slowly down the mountain.

Lacey put the truck in park and let it idle. The gridlock on the interstate was the perfect ending to the day. All she wanted was to get Barak out of her truck and out of her life. Instead, they'd been trapped together for an extra hour as traffic had crawled along a few feet at a time.

His betrayal had clawed huge holes inside her that she wasn't sure would ever heal. She'd given him her body, her heart, and, worst of all, her trust.

He knew, he *knew,* what her work meant to her.

Sure, his secret had cost him, but whatever price he'd paid for withholding his gift from his world had at least been a choice he'd made for himself based on all the facts. That he had also withheld that same information from her, preventing her from making real progress toward saving the Paladins, had been cruel and unfair. If she was being selfish, too bad.

The cars ahead of her started moving again. She waited until they'd moved forward enough to make it worth her time to shift gears. As the highway curved ahead she could see where the tangle of traffic broke free at last. Unless there'd been another accident farther up, they should be on their way at last.

"Drop me at the Center, and I'll put the equipment away." Barak made the offer without looking in her direction. "I can walk from there."

"I don't want you in my lab again. I can put it away tomorrow."

"You can hardly walk. This much I will do for you." His accent was more noticeable, warning her that he was still fighting some pretty strong emotions.

"Fine. Leave the key on the counter on your way out." She whipped the truck off the highway at the next exit and drove the rest of the way on surface streets. "I'll see that Ruthie mails you your last check."

The silence between them felt as if it were sucking the last bit of air out of the truck. The ache in her chest only got worse when they reached the end of their journey together. Barak quietly got out of the truck and unloaded the equipment. Before she could pull away, he approached the driver's side window.

Refusing to roll it down would be childish and immature, but right now she couldn't bear the pain of talking to him, of trying to make plans for tomorrow without him, of trying to explain to everybody why he was no longer welcome in her lab.

There were bound to be questions, ones neither of them would want to answer. She drove home, thinking no further ahead than a hot shower and crying herself to sleep.

"Meet me at the gym. Now."

Barak immediately disconnected the call, not giving Devlin any choice but to do as he asked. The phone immediately began ringing, but Barak ignored it as he picked up the last of his equipment and walked out the door.

If he didn't find a handy target for all of this rage, he was going to do something stupid. Like crawl back to Lacey's house and promise her anything if she would only find it in her heart to let him back into her life. He'd been holding onto his honor for so long because it was all he had left. But without her, his honor was cold company.

He could not regret the time they had spent in

each other's arms, but how was he to go on knowing exactly what he had lost?

He would do one last favor for Devlin, crossing back into the darkness, but there would be one small change in the plans. Once he convinced his sister that she needed to cooperate with the Paladins in this one matter, he would surrender himself to the authorities of his world. With luck, the standing order for his execution would be carried out swiftly.

He was relieved to see Devlin waiting for him in the gym. In other times and places, he would have deemed himself fortunate to count Devlin Bane as a friend. And if a man could be judged by the strength and honor of his enemy, then Barak was indeed fortunate.

He walked up to the Paladin, wishing things could have turned out differently. "One last match before I carry out my mission for you?"

Bane stared at him for several long seconds, probably seeing far too much. At least he didn't ask any questions.

"Sure. I could use a good workout."

Inside, the two of them stripped down to their sweatpants and drew their swords, this time using the real thing. Barak offered a salute, then charged with no warning, no warm-up, no caution. Bane danced back out of reach long enough to find his balance, then went on the attack. Barak was dimly aware of several other Paladins lining up along the walls, careful to remain out of the way as they called out words of encouragement. Most spoke for Devlin, but one or two cheered when Barak scored a good hit.

The scent of so many of his enemies in one room filled Barak's head, overwhelming his usual caution in a practice bout. He caught a glimpse of the two of them in a mirror along the wall and realized that they were both grinning as they pulled out the stops and fought full out.

Bane finally got in a lucky parry and wrenched Barak's sword out of his hand, sending it clattering across the floor. Barak charged forward, ready to take on his opponent with his bare hands.

Devlin retreated, giving Trahern and D.J. a chance to wrestle Barak to the ground. He fought them both, succeeding in flinging D.J. off to the side, but Trahern managed to pin him to the floor, his heavy knee on Barak's chest.

Devlin gasped out orders to the rest of the spectators. "You all have something better to do than watch us. This is between me and him."

When the gym emptied out, Trahern slowly let off the pressure. "I'm going to stand up now, Other. Don't make me show you which of us is gonna win this."

Barak nodded, knowing his fight wasn't with Trahern or even Devlin Bane. He closed his eyes and waited for his lungs to catch up with his need to breathe. Devlin gave him all the time he needed.

When Barak slowly sat up, Bane tossed him a bottle of water.

"Now, you want to tell me what the hell that was all about?"

"No." He gulped down half the bottle of water. As long as he was drinking, he couldn't answer questions.

Devlin hunkered down beside him. "When are you going down to the tunnels to wait for the barrier to blink?"

"When I leave here."

"That's sooner than I expected." Devlin allowed a few seconds to pass. "What happened to change your plans?"

Barak kept his eyes on the far wall, avoiding direct eye contact. Devlin was far too talented at reading those around him.

"I don't see the need to delay. The longer I wait, the more of my people die on your swords." And he felt the weight of each and every one of those lost souls. That was his burden to bear, and he had no right to ask Devlin to share it.

"I got a call from Lacey right after your invitation to meet you here." Devlin shifted so that he could look Barak right in the eyes. "She says I can borrow you indefinitely. In fact, permanently."

Damn. He'd hoped she would wait until at least morning when she would have better control of her emotions. Devlin had obviously not appreciated either phone call.

"I think I will do well working in the laundry,

don't you?" Barak managed a small smile. "Do you like your socks folded or rolled?"

"Damn it, Barak, that's not funny! You know that as soon as Laurel finds out that Lacey has cut you loose, she's going to start pushing to get you back in her lab." Devlin shoved his fingers through his shaggy hair. "Neither of us wants that to happen."

"It won't be a problem." That was true, but it was also the wrong thing to say.

"Barak, what aren't you telling me? I'd bet my last dollar that Lacey had been crying, and you look like you died two days ago. What the hell happened between the two of you? I can't fix the problem if I don't know what it is."

"This can't be fixed, Devlin, so don't try. Lacey doesn't deserve to have my name linked with hers. You said so yourself." He choked down the rest of his water.

"What the hell do I know? I didn't think Laurel needed me in her life either, and look how far I got with that." He chuckled. "I keep waiting for her to realize I was right, but I'm sure not going to be the one to tell her."

"Laurel is an intelligent woman, Devlin. She knows she is destined to be your mate. You make her happy."

"I drive her crazy."

"That, too." Barak pushed himself up off the floor. "Don't push Lacey on this, Devlin."

Devlin took Barak's empty bottled and crushed

it. "I don't take orders very well, Other. Especially from you."

"Then pretend I'm a friend and asking a favor." Barak picked up his father's sword and held it up to catch the light. He had no male heir to pass it along to, but his sister would use it with the honor it deserved. The idea felt right.

Bane's big hand came down on Barak's sword arm. "As a favor for a friend, then, I won't press Lacey. Let's hit the showers, and over dinner we'll make final plans for your crossing back to the other side."

The Paladin's words lessened the darkness surrounding Barak. "Sounds good. I'll even buy."

Lacey felt like death warmed over. Her head hurt to the point of nausea, and her eyes were swollen shut from crying. She considered drinking herself into a complete stupor, but nothing was more pathetic than a weepy drunk, unless it was a weepy drunk throwing up. Now *there* was a pitiful image.

She wrapped a towel around her hair and pulled on her favorite faded sweats. They were ragged in places and deserved to be retired, but they were too comfortable to give up. And right now, comfort was what she needed.

Barak. Even his name was enough to send pain tearing through her, almost crippling in its intensity. She'd made it through three hours now without him; that just left the rest of her life. Maybe she should make herself a chart and cross off each hour until they blurred.

When would his loss and betrayal stop hurting? A week? A year? An eternity?

She grabbed a tissue to mop up another bout of tears. This was so stupid. She hadn't known him all that long. But she had known him well—or at least fooled herself into thinking so, right up until she'd found out that he already knew the answers to all of her questions about the nature of the barrier and the things that triggered its periodic failures.

Maybe with a night's rest she'd be better equipped to figure out where they would go from here. Not that *they* were going anywhere, at least together. Her boss might not appreciate her unilateral decision, but she was willing to go to the mat on this one.

Budget or no budget, Barak was history. Gone. Finished. Missed.

She wadded up the tissue and tossed it in the direction of the wastebasket, then headed for bed.

One step inside her bedroom made her spin around and head for the couch in the living room. No way she was going to sleep in the tangle of sheets that still carried Barak's scent.

She stuck in a random DVD and turned on the television. The local anchorman was talking about the earthquake, saying it had been felt as far away as Spokane but that no injuries had been reported. Evidently broken hearts didn't count.

The movie finally started. As the credits began to roll, she realized she'd picked *Beauty and the Beast*. Now there was a nice touch of irony. She doubted she was much of a beauty right now, but Barak definitely was a beast. She'd reached out to him, accepted him as both friend and lover, and he'd betrayed that trust.

He had good reasons for keeping his secrets, and she could understand his torn loyalties, but how could they share any kind of relationship if she couldn't trust him to tell her the simple truth about who and what he was?

She drew a shuddering breath. To give him some credit, he had tried to warn her off, but she'd refused to listen. Why hadn't she pressed him harder for information about his world and why he'd left it?

She nursed her anger. If she let herself waver for an instant, she'd start siding with him. Granted, she'd never been involved in such an intense relationship before, but he was in a strange world with strange customs. There had to be so much about his new life that he found bewildering.

But values like trust and honesty had to cross boundaries, and if she couldn't have that with the man she loved, then all they had left was a relationship built on hormones. Her eyes wandered toward her bedroom door. Those had been some pretty powerful hormones, but they weren't enough, not by a long shot.

She tucked the afghan around her feet, feeling chilled through to her soul. It was going to be a long, lonely night, and tomorrow wasn't looking any better. Resolutely closing her eyes, she concentrated on unknotting the tangle of nerves twitching in her stomach.

Why had she never noticed how uncomfortable this couch was? No matter which way she turned, she couldn't find a position that allowed her any comfort. Maybe she'd be better off sleeping on the twin bed in the guestroom. She'd have to clear off the boxes of Christmas decorations she'd never gotten around to putting in the attic, but that wouldn't take long.

Before she could get that far, though, the phone rang, shrill and piercing. With her heart in her throat, she counted off the rings until her answering machine would pick up. If it was Penn calling, she'd answer. Her throat felt like ten miles of bad road, but she'd convince him she was catching a cold so he wouldn't come charging over to check on her. If it was Devlin calling her back, she'd tell him to back off and leave her alone before disconnecting.

But no, of course it wasn't either of them. Barak's voice echoed in the hollow emptiness of her heart. The rough sound of his words built up pressure inside of her until she thought her head would explode. It was such a temptation to pick up the phone, to let him explain, to grasp at whatever excuses he might offer up to soothe her pain.

But even though she was not a Paladin, she found her own warrior's strength and held back. Or maybe she was a coward for not answering. She heard his words and then the sound of his ragged breath as he waited for her to respond.

When she didn't, he sighed, a wealth of regret and pain in the sound. "Lacey, I am sorry. I wish it could have been different—that I could have been different."

Another pause stretched on until her resolve threatened to snap before he finally said, "I hope that someday you will look back at . . . at what we . . . and remember some of it without regret. Good-bye."

Then he hung up and she cried.

Chapter 17

*T*hat's her."

Ben pointed at the Sebastian woman before ducking back out of sight. "When will you make the grab?"

His two companions looked thoroughly disgusted. The taller of the two answered, "We can snatch her right now if you want. Save having to follow her around."

The muscle he'd been provided with weren't at all impressed with him, but Ben didn't care, as long as they did their job. At the end of the day, he was the one with the money. Either they did what he wanted or they didn't get paid.

Although considering the number of prison tattoos they sported, he doubted he'd have the balls to not fork over the money. Their eyes were dead, almost reptilian in appearance. If he weren't so desperate, he might have felt sorry for Lacey Sebastian.

"Give me thirty minutes before you do the job,

and take her to where I showed you on the map. I'll join you there after I get off work. It's important that I follow my usual routine."

One of his new buddies snickered. "Yeah, wouldn't want anyone to think you got your hands dirty, would we? That's okay. Jack and me, we'll take care of it."

Jack nodded. "Mind if we entertain ourselves a little once we've got her stashed?"

When Ben realized what the man was really asking, he said, "No! That's not all right. She's not to be harmed, you understand me?"

Not that there was much he could do to stop them. A cold wind blew through him, chilling him to the bone. It was bad enough he was plotting against a Paladin by threatening the man's sister. But these thugs wanting to hurt Lacey Sebastian just because they could . . . It didn't bear thinking about. He swallowed heavily, trying to soothe the churning in his stomach.

"You pick her up, take her to the tunnel, and wait for me. That's it. Nothing more."

Jack shrugged. "Fine. Nothing more." Shifting his toothpick to the other side of his mouth, he smiled. "But it's going to cost you more. I hate to be bored."

"Fine." Ben peeled off five more twenties from the stack in his hip pocket. "I'll sweeten the pot some more once I see that Dr. Sebastian is unharmed."

There, he'd done all he could to keep the woman safe. Good thing his conscience had atrophied after years of lying and cheating to keep up with the mountain of debts piled up from his gambling. But you didn't have to have self-respect to have a strong sense of self-protection. If it came down to Lacey Sebastian or his own skin, there was no contest.

Too bad about her, though.

Barak stared at the blank wall in front of him.

Lacey obviously regretted their involvement. He was sorry that she'd been hurt, but he couldn't regret one minute that he'd spent in her company. Maybe he could have trusted her with his secrets, but then both of them would have had the stress of living with that knowledge. It would have ripped her apart, torn between her love for Barak and her love for her brother and the others like him.

A knock at the door dragged him back to the present.

He picked up his sword and turned off the lights, knowing it had to be one of the Paladins. The barrier was weakening again. The energy had been humming along with the occasional touch of cacophony, a sure sign that it was about to go down.

Cullen Finley was raising his hand to knock again when Barak opened the door. He stepped back, allowing Barak room to step outside and pull the door closed behind him.

"Devlin asked me to pick you up. It's my turn to stand guard at the weak spot."

"I appreciate the ride."

Barak followed Cullen down the steps and out to a bright red sports car. He paused to study the vehicle, liking its design and the way it screamed power and speed. Glancing at Cullen, he tried to align what he knew of the Paladin with the image the car created.

They didn't exactly fit together. Cullen had a reputation for being the quiet, thoughtful Paladin. He was the one everyone turned to when they needed a level-headed opinion. Yet he was a warrior, too. Perhaps the car wasn't such a surprise.

Cullen shuffled his feet a bit. "I just bought it. What do you think?"

Barak walked around the car, nodding at what he saw. "I envy you the joy of it, Cullen."

Cullen's mouth quirked up in a sneaky smile. "Devlin said I should pick you up and bring you to the barrier. He didn't say what route I had to take. What do you say we go the long way?"

"That would be an honor," Barak said, meaning it.

If this was to be his last day in Seattle, he would like the chance to say good-bye in style. He sat in the passenger seat and leaned back, ready to enjoy the ride.

The tunnel was crowded. He'd expected Devlin and Trahern, maybe, but Cullen had walked down with him, along with D.J. and Lonzo.

When they heard him coming, Devlin and Trahern stopped talking and watched his approach. Did they think he'd change his mind about this mission? No, if his limited knowledge of human emotions was right, that was regret he was seeing in their expressions.

Devlin immediately took charge. "I still don't like this idea, Barak. There has to be a way to get her to come here."

Even if there was, Barak wouldn't risk his sister in this world. The transition had been difficult enough for him, and he'd left his home willingly. She would hate being trapped here.

"It is simpler this way." He would deliver the message and surrender to whatever fate awaited him.

Trahern loomed closer. "Don't do anything heroic or stupid." His tone clearly said that the two were interchangeable.

"Yes, sir." Barak allowed himself a small smile.

The others stood around, waiting for something to happen. Barak wished they would all just leave. If his sister was waiting for him, she wouldn't take it well to see him surrounded by her enemies.

Devlin held out an envelope. "I wrote out what we know, assuming someone over there will be able to translate it into your language. If the barrier doesn't seem like it's going to stay down long enough for you to explain in person, leave the envelope and haul your ass back home."

Home. The word burned warmly in Barak's heart.

"Thank you, Devlin. For everything. Now get out of here and let me do my job."

The big Paladin frowned, then held out his hand. Barak accepted the gesture from Devlin. Trahern met his gaze and nodded. D.J. gave Barak a friendly whack on the shoulder as he and Lonzo followed them out, leaving only Cullen. The two of them watched in silence until the others were out of sight.

"You don't need to wait with me." Barak leaned against the tunnel wall in a futile attempt to look relaxed. His guts were in knots over what was to come and what he would lose, and what he'd already lost.

He used to watch the barrier from his world for hours on end, loving the play of color and light. But here, it was different, perhaps because in his world the barrier was viewed as the threshold to a better place. Going back, he would be facing the same pain that had driven him away in the first place.

Cullen sank down on the floor, clearly not interested in leaving. "Devlin didn't want you to be alone. He's not happy that this is happening."

"And you?"

The quiet Paladin shrugged. "From what I can tell, we've always been at war with each other. Until you, we never doubted that was the way it should be. It's unsettling."

"I'm no different than those who die on your swords." He might as well sit, too. Hours, even days, might pass before the barrier failed. Closing his eyes, he reached with his senses, delving deep into the stone surrounding them. No, it wouldn't be long.

Cullen shook his head. "I don't buy that, Barak. You might see it that way, but there's no way we would. We've seen too many crazy bastards come charging across with murder in their eyes."

"But according to your own scientists, you and I have common genes. In the history of your world, some of your people must have accepted my kind among them." He'd hoped to be one more example of that.

Conversation coasted to a stop, neither of them in the mood for idle chitchat while they waited. After a bit, Cullen pulled out a deck of cards and started shuffling them time after time. The soft whirring noise the cards made seemed to echo up and down the tunnel.

"So this female that you're to meet. Tell me more about her." Cullen kept his eyes firmly on the cards, his tone of voice carefully neutral.

All of which made Barak suspicious. "Why? What would you know about her?"

Shuffle, shuffle. Then the Paladin laid the cards out in a pattern that only made sense to him. When Cullen had them arranged to his liking, he finally looked up.

"I think I may have seen her once." His hand strayed up to touch a small scar on the side of his face. "Not too long before you came across, there was heavy fighting farther south from here. Lonzo was injured to the point we almost lost him. Anyway, cleanup was underway when a female and some males came charging down the tunnel. Devlin took on the males, but the female challenged me." He glanced at Barak. "Damn near killed me, too. Whoever she was, she's a helluva fighter."

"I didn't know she'd ever crossed over. Did you drive her back?" Gods above, as good as his sister was, these Paladins were even better. She could have died!

"Actually, no. I think she and her companions were caught out on this side and were trying to get back. As soon as the barrier blinked off again, they charged back home. I only saw her that one time."

He actually sounded disappointed. Barak fought the urge to tell the Paladin that his sister was off limits to the likes of him. Who was he to talk? Penn Sebastian felt the same way about Barak's interest in Lacey, but Barak hadn't been inclined to listen.

The sound of the elevator opening down the tunnel brought both of them back up to their feet, swords drawn. Chances were that one of the Paladins had forgotten something, but neither Cullen nor Barak was about to risk being too complacent. Or maybe Devlin had sent someone down with food for them. It was the sort of thing he might do.

But no. Barak jerked his head in Cullen's direction. "Were you expecting Penn?"

Cullen looked as puzzled by the wounded Paladin's appearance as Barak. "He's still on restricted duty—no tunnels. He looks pissed about something, but that's normal for him these days."

Barak had a bad feeling about this. Over the course of their workouts, Penn had become more civil to him. Judging by the expression on his face now, they were back to their old roles of hated enemies. He braced himself for the imminent attack and waited, his hand on the pommel of his sword.

Penn aimed straight for him, his hands clenched in white-knuckled fists. "You bastard Other! What have you done with Lacey?"

Barak froze, allowing Penn to get within inches of him before he could think of anything to say. There were a lot of things he'd done with Lacey, but none of them were anything he was willing to discuss with Penn.

Cullen intervened, pushing his shoulder between Barak and Penn. "Back off, Penn. Barak's here under Bane's orders, which is more than I can say about you."

"Fuck off, Finley. I want to know what this bastard has done with my sister." Penn gave Cullen a hard shove, but the Paladin came boiling right back at him.

"Damn it, Sebastian! Get out of here and quit being such an asshole! Even if you've got a beef with Barak, take it up with Devlin. You keep screwing around down here, you'll be lucky if you don't get an armload of toxins shoved in your arm." There was little to be seen of Cullen's normally calm demeanor.

Penn shoved Cullen again. "*You* go take it up with Devlin. And while you're at it, ask him about how he foisted this bastard Other off on my sister to keep him away from his precious Handler! And now Lacey's missing. Somebody's kidnapped her, and all they'll tell me is some bullshit about blue stones from across the barrier."

He lunged again, knocking Cullen to the ground on his way to get Barak in a chokehold. Barak was too stunned by Penn's ranting to put up any resistance.

Despite the pressure on his throat, he managed to gasp, "Who has Lacey, Penn? And what does that have to do with the blue stones?"

"You tell me! Judging by the shape her kitchen is in, she put up a fight, but she's gone. All they left was a note telling me that if I didn't find out who was trying to interfere with the flow of blue stones from across the barrier, they'll kill Lacey."

His eyes glittered with hatred. "Since you're the only bastard I know from across the barrier, I figure you're involved up to your freaky eyeballs. Now, *where is my sister?*"

"Damn it, Penn, he can't answer you when he can't breathe!" Cullen managed to peel one of Penn's hands off Barak's throat.

Barak took a desperate gasp of air and choked out, "I would never harm your sister. I love her too much."

He realized his mistake as soon as the words left

his mouth. Penn's reaction wasn't long in coming. The Paladin's fist came swinging up from the side to knock Barak's head backwards into the rock wall behind him.

"Shut the fuck up about my sister, you freak. Just tell me where you have her stashed before I gut you right here, right now."

All the blood rushed out of Barak's head, making it difficult to breathe or even think. Someone had taken Lacey? For what purpose? She had nothing to do with the blue stones.

He shook his head to clear it. Neither of them was going to do Lacey any good until they could think things through. Penn wasn't going to listen to reason unless Barak forced him to. Ignoring Cullen's efforts to calm Penn down, Barak attacked, taking the furious Paladin straight to the rock-hard floor. The impact rattled Barak's spine, but he managed to trap Penn beneath him.

"Get off me!" Penn tried to heave Barak off to the side.

"Not until you listen." Barak shifted his weight, getting a knee firmly planted on Penn's chest. "I did not take Lacey. I wouldn't hurt her!" Not like that anyway.

"Go to hell! I'm going to find her and then I'm going to kill you!"

"I'll let you try, if that's what it takes to make you listen to reason. I did *not* kidnap Lacey. We have to figure out who did and where she is before they kill her." The idea that she might be hurt and frightened enraged him.

The two of them glared into each other's eyes, taking full measure of their mutual hatred and their need to protect Lacey. Some of the tension slowly ebbed from Penn's body as he fought for control.

"Who else would have taken her?" His voice was rough with pain and fear for his sister.

"If I let you up, we can think this through." Barak waited for Penn to nod before standing up. He offered his hand to help Penn up but wasn't surprised when the offer was rejected.

Penn wiped a small trickle of blood off his lip as he glared at both Barak and Cullen. "If you're not involved in this, why are you two hanging out down here?"

Barak looked at Cullen, who shrugged, leaving it up to Barak how much to tell Penn. Now wasn't the time for secrets. Not with Lacey's life on the line.

"Someone has been telling my people that they can buy their way across the barrier with blue stones from my world. That guard who kidnapped Laurel Young was involved; so was the Regent who killed Judge Nichols with a car bomb. Devlin has been trying to trace the corruption to put a stop to it, but with only limited success."

He paused to see if Penn was following or if Cullen wanted to add anything. When neither of them said anything, he continued, "I'm going to cross back to my world to make contact with someone who may be able to help from that side. Cullen was waiting with me until the barrier goes down."

Penn didn't bother to hide his shock. "You're going home? Does Lacey know that?"

"No one did, as far as we knew. We hoped I could cross and get back without being missed." Well, that's what Devlin had hoped. Barak hadn't planned on even trying.

"So why are they going after my sister? Her only connection to this is her association with you." Penn ran his fingers through his hair as he paced a short distance away and back. "There has to be more."

Cullen stooped down to pick up his scattered playing cards. "Devlin has had me monitoring Ben Jackson's computer activity. Could be he has something to do with it."

Penn jerked back around. "He's been following me around lately, but I couldn't pin him down on his sudden desire to be my new best friend."

"If Ben Jackson is involved in this mess, someone must have been crushing his nuts for information on what the Paladins know and don't know," Cullen said.

Barak grimaced at that image. "Everyone knows how close-knit the Paladins are. Only a fool would think one of them would betray the rest."

Penn's face went ashen. "Unless one of the Paladins was no longer able to function as a Paladin—like me, for instance. Jackson and whoever is jerking his chain might think I was vulnerable. And when I wouldn't buy into Ben's buddy-buddy crap, they went after my sister."

Barak thought about what little he knew of Ben Jackson. "He wouldn't have done this on his own. He's greedy, but Lacey was raised around warriors. She is proud of the fighting skills Penn taught her. I am betting she would've bested Ben easily."

Penn went back to pacing. "So he had help. But that doesn't tell us much. They could be anybody, and they could have taken her anywhere."

A thought popped into Barak's head. "Jackson will have been careful to make sure we couldn't prove he was involved, which means he's still at work. If we go now, we can follow him."

Just then the barrier wavered, streaks of sick colors flickering up and down its length. Barak froze. What about his mission? If he missed the appointment, he didn't know if his sister would agree to another meeting. She definitely wouldn't understand his need to choose a human female over the needs of their world.

Cullen studied him with those calm eyes, knowing his dilemma and waiting to see what he would do. But there was no choice. Penn was about to charge off to rescue his sister, and he would need help. When the barrier failed—as it was going to shortly—Devlin and the other Paladins couldn't abandon their posts.

"I've got to go with Penn."

Barak pulled out the envelope with Devlin's message to his sister and scribbled a few lines of his own to her and handed it to Cullen. "When the barrier fails, throw this across and then do what you have to do to defend your world. Either Lusahn will listen to reason or she won't. When Lacey is safe, I'll return and try again."

Cullen nodded. "I'll take care of it. And give D.J. a call. He'll be able to hook you up with a nifty little piece of electronics that will let you trail Jackson."

Penn knew which car was Ben's. They attached the small device underneath the chassis, which would allow them to follow Ben from a distance. If he was behind the abduction, he was going to be jumpy enough without them making it worse by following too close. As long as he thought he was above suspicion, they stood a better chance of trailing him.

Penn's car felt cramped and uncomfortable. The seconds ticked past, each one marking that much more time that Lacey was scared and maybe hurt, perhaps even dying. No, he couldn't think that way, not and function. But what kind of low-life bastards threatened a female? Soon to be dead ones, if Barak and Penn had their way.

Penn hadn't spoken more than half a dozen words in the hour they'd been watching for their quarry to leave the building. The Paladin sat low in his seat, his angry eyes scanning the street incessantly, as if he could will Ben Jackson to magically appear. The silence between them was all sharp edges.

Barak shifted a bit, the inaction stretching his nerves to the breaking point. Keeping his hand on the pommel of his sword helped, knowing as he did that it would soon drink the blood of his enemies. The thought heated his need to fight. Penn had offered him the use of a gun, but Barak had only a nodding acquaintance with that weapon. He'd be of more use with his blade.

He closed his eyes, imagining the sweet feel of his sword slicing through the bastards' guts, spilling out their lives on the ground in wet splashes and screams. Nothing less would do to avenge his woman—even if she was his no longer.

A movement between two parked cars caught his attention. Penn slowly sat up taller, staring at the man who had just walked out of the building. Ben Jackson had finally put in an appearance. Judging by the way his head swiveled back and forth nonstop, they'd been right. He was guilty and worried, a bad combination.

"That son of a bitch is mine to kill," Penn growled.

"Devlin might have something to say about that, because Jackson is the first solid lead we've had." Barak turned to face Penn. "But I'll hold the bastard down while you gut him. Fair enough?"

Penn's answering grin would have made a brave man shake in his boots. "Works for me."

Jackson edged his car out into traffic, checking his mirrors every few seconds. If the situation hadn't been so grim, it would have been funny to watch the man twitch with nerves. He *should* have been worried. And the more distracted he was, the more likely he'd make a mistake, preferably a fatal one.

Penn waited until Jackson turned the corner three blocks ahead before starting the car. Once he was out of sight, they checked the readout on their tracking device. So far, so good. They'd have a solid signal as long as they stayed within two miles of Ben's car.

Traffic on the interstate traveling south was heavy enough to give them good cover while allowing both cars to make good time toward their unknown destination. Penn had been worried that Jackson would head home, leaving them sitting outside of his apartment complex for hours and not knowing if he was really their man.

All of a sudden, Ben's car shot across two lanes to exit with no signal, no warning. Penn cursed and slowed down. Either the IT man had a sudden urge to shop at the large mall right off the highway, or he wanted to flush out anyone following him. Luckily, several cars in a row moved into the turn lane behind him, giving Penn enough cover for them to follow.

"Wily bastard almost caught me out." Penn slipped on some sunglasses. "Check the backseat and see if there aren't a couple of ball caps on the floor."

Barak managed to snag them. He handed one to Penn, then tucked his own hair up on top of his head before putting on his own. "Good idea. He might not notice you, but my hair is pretty distinctive."

"There's a jacket back there, too. We should vary our appearance as much as we can. Later you can sink down low enough that it will look like I'm by myself."

"Another good idea." Barak pulled the jacket on and buttoned it up. "This is the route your sister takes to Mount Rainier."

"Yeah. I'm thinking they're using one of the old tunnels near the mountain. The barrier has been stable along that area for years, so we don't patrol it much. I'll tell Bane that we should add surveillance in these remote spots."

As traffic thinned out, Penn fell farther back, not wanting to spook Jackson.

"Think he's in contact with them?"

"I'd say yes, because he wouldn't trust anyone enough not to ride herd on them. But if they're underground near the barrier, his cell phone will be of limited use. We'll have the same problem if we need to call for reinforcements."

A wave of energy washed over Barak, churning his stomach. He grabbed onto the front edge of his seat to keep from swaying. "The barrier is weakening. Help won't be coming."

Penn shot him a questioning look. "How do you know that?"

Barak didn't bother to lie. "It's either my gift or my curse. I can feel it, especially when the barrier fluctuates and thins out. And right now, it's weak. It will fail soon." He closed his eyes to control his rising nausea.

Penn muttered an obscenity. "Lacey know you can feel it? Because that's what she's been searching for all this time—a way to predict when the barrier is going to fail."

The first wave passed. Good, the barrier would have blinked off for only a few seconds. Barak considered his answer.

"She found out."

For the first time, Penn's laughter sounded genuine. "Bet she wanted to kick your ass two weeks from Sunday for keeping that little tidbit from her. The woman's got a temper that won't quit. Of course, that's nothing like what Bane will say when he finds out that you've been keeping that particular secret."

"I won't use it for the Paladins." And he meant that, even if it meant his death. "I left my home for this world, but that doesn't mean I no longer care for my own people."

He kept his eyes firmly on the small screen tracking Ben Jackson's movements. "He changed directions again. Go about another of your miles and then watch for a left turn."

They both sat up taller, knowing the time until they would face their enemies was growing short. Mount Rainier loomed up ahead, its snow-covered sides gleaming in the setting sun. The road stretched out before them, each mile bringing them closer to Lacey.

Barak's fingers traced the inlays on his sword as he prayed to any and all gods who would listen for the safety of his woman. Lacey deserved better than to die in the cold darkness of the tunnels under the mountain.

He closed his eyes and pictured her sunshine hair and sky blue eyes, a woman of the light who, for a short time, had warmed his dark, cold soul.

Chapter 18

*F*ear had a bitter taste that made her shiver in the dank chill. Ignoring the discomfort, Lacey concentrated on the pain in her wrists as she tried to work free of her restraints. Anything was better than worrying about how she'd ended up bruised, bound, and abandoned in the darkness.

If she lay perfectly still, she could hear the muted voices of her captors. The two of them had burst into her kitchen door when she'd been carrying in groceries. One of them was now sporting a nasty bruise from where she'd bashed him with a can of green beans. He'd gotten off lightly. The other bastard walked with a decided limp because she'd racked him but good.

She hoped she lived long enough to thank her big brother for teaching her that particular nasty little trick. She'd paid for it with a few extra bruises, but it had been worth it. What was of more concern was the fact that the two thugs hadn't bothered to hide their faces when they'd kidnaped her. She'd watched enough television to know what that meant: they were going to kill her. The only questions were when and why?

What did she have or what did she know that was worth her life? A tear burned down her face. She'd spent so much of her life focused on finding a way to save her brother's that she hadn't had much time left over for adventure. Unless she counted Barak.

Even thinking his name hurt. He'd lied to her, betraying everything she stood for, and it didn't matter. She'd loved him before she'd found out, and she loved him still. Her only regret was realizing it too late. Short of writing him a message in the blood dripping from her wrists, Barak would never know.

And that was a damn shame. Melodramatic romantic that she was, she wanted him to know that at least one person loved him. From the moment she'd met him, he'd worn his innate loneliness with dignity, as much a part of him as his silver and black hair and pale eyes. He had good reason not to trust easily, and he'd gradually let her past all of his barriers, except the one that mattered the most.

She felt, rather than heard, approaching footsteps. Her struggles with her bonds had left her laying on her side, but she didn't want to face anyone from a position of weakness. Sitting up wasn't much of an improvement, but it was the best she could do at the moment.

When the sudden glare of a flashlight blinded her, she turned away, giving her eyes time to adjust. When she looked back to snarl at her tormentor, her jaw dropped. The man who stood staring down at her was new to the party. For a millisecond she thought she'd been saved, but then she saw the gun in his other hand.

"Ben? Ben Jackson?"

She blinked a few times, sure she was imagining things. Of all people, he was the last one she could picture holding her hostage at gunpoint. She didn't know him all that well, just to nod and say hello to when she passed him in the hallway. Certainly not well enough to have done anything that warranted the hatred glittering in his beady eyes.

"I'd say I'm sorry about all of this, Lacey, but when it comes to protecting my own hide I'm afraid that your welfare comes in a poor second." The gun didn't sit steady in his hand, making her worry he'd shoot her by accident before he had a chance to explain what was going on.

"What *is* all of this, Ben?" She thought she sounded remarkably calm considering the fact that she was talking into the end of a gun barrel.

"This was the only way I could get your brother's cooperation. I need his help."

Sweat ran down his face despite the cold air that surrounded them. Was it fear or excitement that had him so on edge? What possible help did he need from Penn? The answers wouldn't change the situation, but as long as he was talking, maybe he wouldn't pull the trigger.

"What kind of help?"

Ben shifted the flashlight under his gun arm, freeing up his hand to delve into his pants pocket. "I need to know what Bane and the Paladins know about these." He tossed a blue stone about the size of a large marble into her lap. "Did he ever mention anything about them to you? Or maybe that Other you've been spreading your legs for?"

He had been watching them! The idea made her sick and furious. Her temper took control of her mouth. "Jealous, Ben? I know Barak's not human, but he's all man, I can assure you."

"Shut up, bitch!" The gun moved closer to her face.

"Make me!"

She regretted the words the second they left her mouth. With his hands full, he had to content himself with kicking at her. His foot caught the side of her knee with enough force to render her breathless with shards of pain. Despite the new addition to her collection of injuries, she took pride in immediately sitting back up, meeting him glare for glare.

She swallowed her pain and snarled, "You'll die for this, you know. You'll be lucky if Penn leaves enough of you for the coroner to mop up with a sponge. And it won't be an easy death. I'm thinking it may take hours or even days. Unless, of course, Barak finds out what you've done. Then there's not a place on Earth—or in his world—that will keep you from choking on your own blood as he whittles you to pieces. I've seen him kill. It wasn't pretty, and his victims died begging for their lives." That was a lie. The speed of Barak's blade hadn't allowed time for conversation.

Ben's foot swung back for another kick. "And to think I ordered my two associates to leave you unharmed. Maybe I should call them back in for a little playtime before I kill you. Personally, I wouldn't want the leavings of an Other. Who knows what kind of contamination he's left behind?" He jerked his head in the direction of the other two men. "But I suspect they aren't quite so fastidious."

Her muscles clenched in new fear. The threat of rape had been in the back of her mind since they'd manhandled her out of her kitchen and into the back of their van. But some of that fear had faded as the hours had ticked by with her captors all but ignoring her. Had they really only been waiting for Ben's approval before . . .

No! She wouldn't let him panic her with his threats! They might control her fate, but she controlled how she reacted to it. Jerking her chin up, she met Ben's gaze head-on. He stumbled back a step, rewarding her efforts.

She smiled. "Oh, yeah, Barak and Penn are going to have fun with you. Maybe they'll have Trahern with them, too. They say he's mellowed some lately, but I wouldn't count on it if I were you. In fact, I'd save one of those bullets to blow your own brains out before any of them get within sword range of you."

Ben glanced back over his shoulder, as if he could already feel the Paladins breathing down his neck. Lacey hadn't known that fear had a smell, but Ben Jackson was ripe with it. She chewed on her lower lip, trying to decide what to say or do next. Baiting him might not be the smartest tactic to use, but her pride wouldn't let her cower.

"Seriously, Ben," she said, using his name as a reminder that she wasn't just a random person but someone he knew and worked with. "There's no reason to panic. We can work something out if we try."

He considered her offer for all of two seconds before rejecting it. "You and that jackass brother of yours wouldn't spit on me if I were on fire, but I'm holding all the cards this time. He will help me find out what I need to know or you'll die."

Then he tilted his head to one side. "Actually you'll die anyway, but he won't know that until it's too late." Then he walked away, leaving her alone in the dark.

"He stopped moving." Barak studied the small screen for another minute or two before setting it aside. "His car must be a short distance ahead."

Penn steered their car over to the shoulder of the narrow gravel road and stopped. "It would be better to go on foot from here. We can't risk him seeing the car and panicking."

Barak nodded as he reached for the door handle. He had a bad feeling about this. Ben Jackson was a weak man, which meant he was more likely to panic and lash out. If they cornered him at the wrong moment, Lacey would die.

Penn walked around to the front of the car and waited for Barak to join him. He checked his guns and the slide of his sword in its scabbard. "Sure you don't want a gun?"

Barak shook his head. "I'm better with my blades."

As they started up the road, keeping just inside the tree line, a rolling surge of energy sent Barak stumbling to his knees. He grabbed onto the trunk of a small fir and held on for dear life. Penn, who was oblivious to the power moving through the rocks, turned and frowned at Barak.

"Quit dicking around. We don't have time for this."

Barak managed to regain his footing on the second try. "It's not me. It's the mountain. Same thing happened the other day when Lacey and I were out here. We've got thirty minutes, forty-five tops before things really start rocking and rolling."

He put his hand in direct contact with a stone. With luck he might be able to draw off some of the power building up below their feet, releasing the strain before it reached critical level. If it worked, he could buy them another handful of precious minutes.

But it was too late. He could feel rock grating on

rock, each pushing and shoving in opposite directions. Right now, it hadn't built up enough force to break free, but it would, and then no one would be safe.

"We need to run. There is no time for caution," Barak told Penn.

"It's been a while since I've been up here, but if I remember correctly, there are two entrances to the tunnels. One is directly ahead. The other about a quarter of a mile that way." Penn nodded to the east.

Barak picked up his sword and fell in beside Penn as together they loped up the road with little regard for secrecy. "Show me the front entrance and then you cover the second one. I'll give you ten minutes to get into place before I challenge them."

Penn cursed. "Hell, Other, we have no idea how many of them are there. You're going to get yourself shot. At least I'd come back from the dead. Do you have that particular talent?"

"Doesn't matter. While I've got them occupied, you come in from behind and get Lacey out. She'll need you to show her the way out. I'd be going in blind."

Penn slowed and moved off the road again as it bent around a corner. They eased forward, this time with more care. Ben's car was pulled off under some trees next to a van. The side door of the van was open, showing it was empty. There was a jacket hanging half in and half out, trailing onto the ground.

It was Lacey's. Worry warred with relief over the sight. It meant they'd followed the right man, but why wasn't she wearing the jacket? If she was inside the tunnels, she would need it. Barak closed his eyes and prayed to the gods that the men had been thoughtless about her welfare, not that she was dead and had no need of the jacket at all.

Penn spotted it at the same time, his mouth set in a grim line. "If she's even broken a nail, they're going to die begging for mercy."

"She will be avenged, by their blood and by mine if necessary. This I promise you, Penn Sebastian." Barak held out his hand to seal his pledge.

Penn didn't hesitate. "I'll get her out, but then I'm coming back. Save some of the fun for me."

"I'll try." Before Penn could move away, Barak latched onto his arm. "If I do not make it out, tell her that I . . ."

His throat choked closed before he could finish. There was so much he would tell her and no time left for the words to be said.

Penn nodded anyway. "I'll make sure she knows, Barak. And I will come back for you."

Barak accepted that Penn meant what he said, but neither of them knew what they were walking into. Ben Jackson wasn't alone in this, and enough money would have hired him the kind of men who killed without remorse. Properly situated, it wouldn't take many defenders to hold Barak at bay.

The only hope for their meager rescue plan was

that neither Ben nor the others knew of the second entrance. If Barak could keep them occupied for a short time, Penn should be able to free his sister. Even so, Barak feared they'd never make it down the mountain before the pressure reached critical mass and all hell would come raining down.

He stared at Penn's watch, counting the minutes until the Paladin would be in place. Another three to go before Barak would make his own move. Despite his distaste for guns, he'd accepted one from Penn. Even if his aim was off, it was one more weapon to use against their enemies.

Two more minutes.

He shifted his weight from side to side, trying to keep himself limber and ready to move. Thirty seconds ticked by as he checked his sword one last time. Twenty seconds. He tested the weight of Penn's pistol in his hand. Ten seconds. He stared up at the sun, enjoying its warmth on his face this one last time.

His people lived in darkness and craved the light. But for him, the sun's heat and light paled by comparison to the woman who waited inside that tunnel. Lacey's golden hair and gentle blue eyes had burned the last bit of chill from his soul.

For her, he would walk back into the darkness and fight for her life. And if the gods decreed that he should die, at least he would die for a cause he understood and accepted. He would die for the woman he loved and count himself a lucky man.

He'd only gone a handful of steps when he heard someone coming in his direction at a dead run. Dropping to the ground behind a cluster of rocks, he drew the gun and waited. A few seconds later, Penn came into sight. The Paladin looked pissed.

Barak stood up slowly to give the hair-trigged warrior a chance to recognize him. "What's wrong?"

Penn looked relieved to see him. "That end of the tunnel has already collapsed. We have to go in from the front, and they'll be watching the entrance."

"Then they'll see Death coming."

With grim smiles they walked into the darkness, shoulder to shoulder.

"What do you mean, there's been no contact? You left Sebastian the note with the cell phone number on it, didn't you?" Ben Jackson's voice cracked like an adolescent boy's. "I gave you very explicit directions that even a fool could follow."

Lacey winced. She didn't want him to provoke his hired guns into killing him, leaving her alone with them. Despite his threats, Ben hadn't allowed the two thugs to get close to her since his arrival.

The argument continued, although she could only catch a few words now and then: something about the strange blue stones, money, Others crossing the barrier, and money. Evidently lots of money.

And whoever had control of the money had Ben Jackson running scared, because he was a sniveling coward, one who would strike out if he felt threatened. If she wanted to last long enough to either escape or be rescued, she would need to watch her every move. Judging by Ben's increasing hysteria, it wouldn't take much more to push him over the edge.

Finally, the whiny jerk ran out of steam and the three of them settled down in a sullen silence. She waited until no one had stirred or spoken for several minutes before she renewed her attempts to break free from her bonds.

With one last surge of energy, she managed to work her hands free. It felt damned good to have accomplished that, and ignoring the pain in her wrists, she worked at the knots holding her feet together. Her fingers had stiffened with cold, but after two broken nails and a few muttered curses, she managed to get the ropes off. All of which accomplished nothing. She was still trapped between the darkness and the dim light where her captors were.

She leaned back against the wall and let her eyes drift shut as exhaustion and the chilly darkness surrounding her sapped her strength. A few minutes' rest would go a long way toward restoring her equilibrium. She would need it to deal with Ben and his two thugs.

Her head nodded forward, the movement startling her awake. She shifted to the side in an attempt to better support her head. Before she settled in to doze again, a small rock bounced off the side of her face. She froze. Where had that come from? She glared around in the darkness, unable to see more than vague details of her surroundings.

Another pebble bounced toward her, this time landing in her lap. Judging by its trajectory, it had come from in front of her, close to where her captors lay stretched out on the tunnel floor. She studied the deep darkness, looking for some kind of movement. Finally, a shape detached itself from the shadows and slowly moved toward her.

She automatically tried to back up, only to remember that she had nowhere to go. If she made any noise at all, her captors would come running, shooting anything that moved.

A hushed whisper floated out of the darkness. "Lacey."

Was she dreaming, or was Penn really there? "Penn?"

He came closer, materializing out of the darkness into something solid and comforting. Leaning down close to her ear, he whispered, "Can you walk?"

She nodded and struggled up to her feet. That's when she saw the second shadow beyond Penn, one she recognized immediately. Only two men in this world loved her enough to risk their lives to rescue her. Her big brother, Penn, and his sworn enemy, Barak.

She walked right into their arms. Penn gave her an awkward pat on the back, a typical brother reaction. But Barak pulled her close to his chest, sharing his strength with her. They couldn't waste time, but for the moment she reveled in the powerful comfort of her menfolk.

Then Barak stripped off his jacket and put it around her shoulders, surrounding her with his scent and his warmth. She raised up long enough to kiss him, not caring if Penn approved or not. She'd had a long time to think about Barak and knew the man mattered more than his secrets.

Penn tugged her back and whispered, "We need to go before they notice something's up."

Before they'd gone two steps, a deep noise rumbled through the tunnel, and the floor rolled and pitched beneath their feet, startling a scream out of Lacey before she could help herself. Barak shoved her toward Penn, who managed to keep them both upright through sheer cussedness alone.

Ben Jackson and the other two men hollered in fright as bits and pieces of rock cracked and rained down from the ceiling above them. When the shaking slowed, Jack turned to say something and looked right at Penn and Barak. He immediately went for his weapon.

Barak already had a gun in one hand. "Get her out of here before this place collapses completely. I can slow it down and deal with them," Barak told Penn. Then he put his free hand on the wall with a grim expression on his face.

"No, Barak!" Lacey tried to fight free of her brother's grasp, but he was too strong.

"Keep moving, sis! He won't be able to hold their attention for long. We need to be gone."

"But he's one against three." Fear tore through her, ripping her heart to shreds. "They'll kill him."

Penn muttered a vile curse and something about stubborn women. "Damn it, he's a warrior and knew the risks going in. Now let me get you out of here, so that he doesn't die for nothing. Once you're safe, I'll come back to help him."

She hated that Penn's words made the only sense. As gunshots rang out behind them, she looked back one last time. They turned the last corner just as Ben Jackson spotted them.

"Stop her! She's getting away!" Ben Jackson shrieked, pointing at her and Penn as they bolted into the shadows.

"Fuck that, Jackson! I'm not taking a bullet for any amount of money!" The rest of their argument was drowned out by another eruption of gunfire and the rumble of the mountain.

Penn picked up speed, forcing Lacey to concentrate more on where they were headed than what they'd left behind. Tears streamed down her face, burning her cold skin.

Then the gunfire stopped just as quickly as it had started, the silence in its wake more ominous than the shooting had been. Her heart skipped. Was Barak dead? Please, God, no! She fought the compulsion to turn back, to run to her lover's side, knowing she would only play into Ben Jackson's hands. All she would be was either a target or a hostage; so she ran on and on, praying for Barak each step of the way.

There was light ahead. The rumbling grew louder and more violent as it chased them out of the mountain. When they reached the warmth of the sunlight, the tunnel entrance collapsed behind them in a belch of dust and debris. Lacey fell to her knees, wrapping her arms around herself as bone-deep grief and fear racked her body.

"He can't be dead, Penn. He can't be." She wouldn't stand for it. Not even the mountain in all of its terrible power would dare take him from her. *Please, God, let that be true.*

Penn pulled out his cell phone, punched the buttons, then stuffed it back in his pocket. He lifted her to her feet with more care than her big, tough brother had ever shown her. "Come on, sis. We've got to get down to where I can get reception so I can call headquarters for help."

Her mind was telling her what her heart wouldn't—couldn't—believe. "I won't leave him here, Penn. No matter what Bane says, I want to bring him home."

"I know. We'll bring him home."

"Hurry."

"We will." He started the engine and began the grim journey down the mountainside.

When the shooting stopped, Barak was surprised to find he still lived. That was far more than he'd counted on when he'd ordered Penn to get Lacey to safety. At the most, he'd hoped to give them a few minutes' head start. But here he was, pinned down but breathing.

Why? He doubted they were out of ammunition, which meant they were up to something. He closed his eyes and reached out with his other senses, listening for clues. Three hearts still beat, but he could taste the tang of blood in the air. Good. He'd managed to hit one of the bastards.

He smiled, grimly pleased with the strength of English curse words. They were bastards and sons of bitches, and every other foul thing he could think of. They had threatened his woman and would die for that mistake. If not by his hand, than by the mountain's power. The pressure was building beyond his ability to hold it back.

They were whispering now, their words too faint to hear over the screech of stone against stone as the mountain prepared to show these puny men what true power was. Too bad that none of them would live long enough to benefit from that knowledge.

His strength faded with each second that ticked by. He could absorb and diffuse only so much of the mountain's pain before the backlash would crush him. But each heartbeat's worth of effort bought that much more time for Penn and Lacey.

Finally, he gave up the weapon of this world, laying the gun down as he took up his father's sword. Drawing comfort and a quick flare of renewed en-

ergy from its familiar feel, he let go of the cold wall
of the tunnel. The mountain would do what it would
do. He had enemies to kill, his woman's honor to
avenge.

As he stepped forward, ignoring the pitch and
roll of the floor beneath his feet, he marched toward
his enemies. And when they saw him coming, fear
filled their eyes at the promise of death written in
the edge of his blade and the hatred in his smile.

A warrior caught between two worlds, he rejoiced
as their blood ran red and hot. Then the mountain
joined in the chorus of his fury, and the rocks came
tumbling down.

Lacey walked from man to man, handing out bottled
water and smiles she hoped were encouraging.
Nothing registered inside of her; the pain and loss
had burned away anything but the most basic of
thoughts. She breathed because her body forced
her to. She ate because her brother wouldn't have
it otherwise. And her heart beat even though it was
shattered in a million pieces.

Hope had all but died, too. She knew because
of the pity in the Paladins' eyes whenever they
glanced her way. They'd all come charging up the
mountain as soon as the barrier had stabilized. It
was a tribute to their friendship that they kept digging anyway. Despite hours of backbreaking work,
they'd cleared only a small part of the rubble that
used to be a tunnel.

Still, they worked through the last hours of the daylight and into the thick darkness of the night. Even the strong glare of man-made light could barely hold back the shadows that haunted her mind. If only they would let her do more than watch, maybe the hours wouldn't crawl by so slowly.

Devlin Bane loomed up out of the night. "Lacey, why don't you go stretch out in the backseat of my car and get some rest."

"Maybe in a few minutes."

He studied her for a minute before patting her on the shoulder, the same rough comfort that several of the others had offered her. He meant well, but she would stand vigil until they broke through to where Barak waited for them to come. No doubt they all believed that they would be carrying a corpse down the mountain, an enemy hero to be laid to rest with honor among the Paladins who had gone before him.

But even as hope faded, that didn't mean it was gone completely. Each stone they lifted away, each inch of progress brought her that much closer to the man she loved, the man she needed in her life. He might be hurt and bleeding, but she had to believe that he was as willing to live for her as he had been to die for her.

Trahern came trudging past with another wheelbarrow of rocks and dust. He paused to accept another bottle of water from her.

"We're guessing we have another ten feet to

reach the cavern where you last saw him." He
glanced back to where Devlin and Penn stood talking. "Devlin sent for Laurel in case Barak is injured.
She and Brenna should be here any minute."

It was more likely that the Paladin leader had
sent for the women for Lacey's sake, but she appreciated the small lie. Who would ever have thought
that Trahern had it in him?

"Thanks, Blake."

He picked up the wheelbarrow handles and
headed over toward the slope where they'd been
dumping their loads. She wished they'd let her do
more.

The sound of a car caught Lacey's attention.
As soon as Laurel parked, she and Brenna made a
beeline straight for Lacey and enfolded her in their
arms. Both of them lived with the constant threat of
losing the strong warriors they loved. They shared
her pain because they shared her fear.

"Have they gotten through to him yet?" Laurel
looked as if she'd taken the news especially hard.

"No. Trahern says they have about ten more feet
to dig out. They have to go slowly because they don't
know how stable the mountain is right now." If she
had her equipment with her, maybe she could have
told them whether it was safe to hurry or not. At
least she would have been doing something other
than watching and waiting.

"We brought sandwiches and more drinks. Tell us
where it would be best to set up."

Lacey let them lead her back to their car. Anything was better than staring at the dark mouth of the tunnel with only her own fear for company.

A little before dawn, Penn came to her. His face was streaked with dust and dirt, making it impossible to read his expression. "We're breaking through, Lacey."

She shrugged off the blanket that someone had wrapped around her shoulders. "I'm coming in."

"I think you should wait until we know. He wouldn't want you to see—"

"No, Penn. I'm exactly who he needs to see when they clear the way. And I need to tell him exactly how I feel about him." She drew a deep breath. "I love him, Penn. And if he'll have me, I want to spend the rest of my life making sure he never forgets that."

"You know it won't be easy, sis. There will always be some who only see him as the enemy. But if it means anything, you'll have my blessing."

"It means everything." She let him wrap her in his arms. "It means everything. Now let's go find him."

Trahern was waiting at the entrance with a hard hat in his hands. "You shouldn't be coming in here."

"If it were you trapped in there, Brenna would claw her way through to you." It was nothing less than the truth.

"Yeah, I know. That doesn't mean I'd like her putting herself in danger for me." He thrust the hat into her hands. "If you're coming in, put this on and watch your step."

He led the way through the narrow passageway they'd cleared to where Devlin and a couple of Paladins were gingerly lifting rocks and passing them bucket-brigade style out of the way. When they'd created a hole big enough to shine a light through, Devlin blocked her view until he could see what lay beyond.

He turned toward them, his face set in grim lines. "Get some stretchers. I can only see Ben Jackson, or what's left of him, and a couple of men I don't recognize."

The terror that threatened to overwhelm her eased off. Devlin went back to lifting rocks. When he had an opening wide enough to accommodate his broad shoulders, he crawled through and disappeared. Lacey could only watch and pray.

Barak breathed. Again, and again. That was more than he'd expected after the mountain had quit dancing around him. His enemies had died long before then; their fear of the earthquake had kept them from staging much of a defense against the stroke of his sword.

But maybe they had been the lucky ones. The way out of the tunnel was blocked by several tons of rock. He would die of thirst and hunger long before he could dig his way out. His only regret was never knowing the sweetness of Lacey Sebastian in his arms again.

He closed his eyes, too weary to hold on to consciousness. At least in his dreams, he could still hold his lover and know her warmth. Gradually pain faded away, and sleep came to gently carry him away from the hard rocks beneath his back and the dust settling over him like a blanket.

"Devlin, I'm coming through." She didn't wait for permission but followed right on his heels into the opening beyond.

She bit back a scream when she came face-to-face with one very dead Ben Jackson. His two accomplices were sprawled in a bloody heap just beyond him. The horror in their final expressions didn't speak of an easy death.

"Take this flashlight, Lacey."

Trahern handed one through to her before he started working his broad shoulders through the opening behind her. Devlin was already crawling farther back into the tunnel where the roof hadn't collapsed. She could see his light making sweeping arcs as he looked for some clue to Barak's fate.

She worked in the opposite direction, taking the left side along the wall as Devlin turned and came back toward her. If he'd found Barak, he gave no sign of it. Rather than assume the worst, she kept walking, her eyes firmly on the ground ahead of her.

Something sticking out from under a pile of rocks caught her attention. A shoe or a boot? It was hard to tell from a distance.

"Devlin! Blake! Back here."

The two men started toward her as she made her way over piles of rocks and debris. Oh, Lord. The shoe was still attached to a leg. Barak's leg.

"Barak!"

No answer. She tried again as she clambered closer to her target. On her knees, she began shoveling handfuls of dust and rock out of her way. Devlin joined her as Trahern held his light up high so they could see what they were doing.

"Is he? . . ." She put her hand on his leg and almost collapsed in relief when she realized his skin was warm. "He's warm, Devlin!"

It didn't take long to clear off the thin layer of rock and dust that covered Barak from head to foot. He stirred briefly and mumbled something about dreams when she touched his face. It was the sweetest sound she'd ever heard.

"He's alive!"

Devlin grinned. "I'll get Laurel."

Lacey cupped the side of his face and called his name.

"Barak, honey, can you wake up? We need to know how badly you're hurt." She picked up his hand and rubbed it between her own. Trahern handed her his jacket to cover him with.

Finally, Barak blinked, then squinted up at her. His smile chased the chills out of her heart. "Lacey. I knew I'd dream of you until I died."

"You're not dreaming, big guy. I'm really here."

"Are you sure?" He struggled to raise his head.

Trahern leaned down into Barak's line of vision. "She's real, all right. Besides, if you were dreaming, would I be in it?"

Barak slowly shook his head, his eyes wide with wonder. The tears she'd been fighting all night broke loose as she clutched Barak's hand in hers. "I know it's not comfortable, but try to rest easy until we can get you out of here."

"I need to tell you . . ." His voice trailed off, sounding dry and rough.

She fumbled for the bottle of water in her pack and held it to his lips. "Sip it slowly. There'll be plenty of time to talk later."

"No, now."

To keep him calm, she leaned down close to speak a few words of her own. "I'm so sorry I blew up over your gifts. They are yours to use as you see fit. That doesn't make me love you any less."

His beautiful silver eyes met hers. "I cannot imagine a world without you in it, Lacey."

Trahern cleared his throat. "Uh, look, could you hold off on the mushy stuff long enough for us to get out of this place?"

Laurel came through the opening, followed by Devlin, who was carrying a stretcher. She completed a quick check of Barak's injuries before supervising the two men as they lifted him onto the stretcher. Lacey reluctantly let go of his hand as they began the delicate process of passing the stretcher out into the narrow confines of the tunnel.

Paladins lined the way, each man taking his turn in bearing the burden of her wounded lover. When they finally had him outside in the morning light, each and every one of them insisted on shaking his hand or patting his shoulder before finally loading him into the back of a truck. A helicopter waited in a meadow below to evacuate him to the Regents' medical facilities.

Before they got Barak strapped in, Penn hugged Lacey, then offered his hand to Barak. "I owe you, for her life and my own." Then he stepped back. "Take good care of my future brother-in-law, Lacey. I still need a few more fighting lessons from him."

Leave it to her brother to jump the gun. "We never said we were getting married, Penn!"

"You'd be a fool to let a man who loves you that much slip away." Penn gave her a gentle shove toward the helicopter door. "Let me know when to rent the tux."

As she crawled into the helicopter, Barak said, "Tell him to rent one soon. That is, if you'll have me. I promise no more secrets."

It was definitely a day for tears mixed with smiles. "I'll take you any way I can, Barak. I love you, secrets and all."

Carefully, so as not to jar her wounded warrior, she bent down to press a kiss on his lips, a promise of many more to come.

Epilogue

*C*ullen stared at Barak's note in his hands, the light from the barrier making the letters appear to flicker and dance. Her name was Lusahn. He traced the form and shape of her name with his fingers and thought of the woman who waited on the other side. As her image filled his mind, his hand strayed to the small scar on his cheek.

She had marked him that day they'd fought, in ways that didn't show on the outside. Even now, weeks later, he could still see her, moving with the confident power of a true warrior combined with the grace of a beautiful woman. Would she be as passionate a lover as she was an enemy?

He grinned, figuring she'd carve him up for even thinking such a thing.

The barrier was weakening again. He hoped it held for a while longer, because the majority of the Paladins were still on their way back from rescuing Barak. Details were sketchy, but it sounded as if their enemy had risked everything to save Lacey Sebastian. He'd sustained minor injuries, but Laurel would see that he got the best care possible.

They owed it to Barak, for saving one of their own. No doubt he would no longer be Laurel's pet Other but an accepted member of their close-knit community. He wouldn't be crossing back into his own world anytime soon.

Which left Cullen standing at the barrier in his place, waiting to toss the note across to Barak's sister. But someone needed to tell her that her brother wouldn't be coming. He glanced up and down the length of empty tunnel stretching out in both directions.

He smiled and shook his head. He would cross the barrier to tell Lusahn that their two peoples needed to cooperate to end some of the bloodshed. He wondered if he'd live long enough to do more than hand her the note. He hoped so. He very much wanted to taste her passion.

The barrier flickered, flared, and failed.

She was there, just that short distance away, her pale, angry eyes focused solely on him. With a nod, he sheathed his sword and stepped forward. Her blade touched his throat as the barrier closed off his only avenue of retreat. He smiled, knowing he was either meeting his fate or his future. Holding out the envelope, he waited to find out which it would be.

POCKET BOOKS
PROUDLY PRESENTS

Redeemed in Darkness

Coming soon from
Pocket Star Books

Turn the page for a preview of
Redeemed in Darkness. . . .

Chapter 1

*T*he barrier shimmered and stretched thin, the beautiful cascade of color giving way to streaks of sickly light. Lusahn shared her brother Barak's ability to read the barrier's moods and knew it would fail soon. In fact, very soon.

She drew her sword. Its familiar weight grounded her against the emotions threatening to overwhelm her: anger, grief, and a sense of betrayal that ran so deep her blood boiled with it.

Barak was alive.

Not only alive, but living and thriving among the enemy. He stood convicted of treason, the evidence a note written by his own hand and tossed from the enemy world into hers. By the laws of her people, he was already condemned, only awaiting the swing of a sword to carry out the execution. *Her* sword, her duty.

She closed her eyes and imagined the smooth stroke of her blade biting into Barak's neck, the slight resistance of the skin and muscle and bone giving way before the razor-sharp metal. If she was lucky, or perhaps if Barak was, it would require but a single blow to take his head.

And then what?

The q'Arc clan numbered but two now. If she were to end her brother's life, she alone would carry on the burden of their family name and honor. The idea made her sick. She had already grieved over him when he'd sought out the light of the other world, even knowing that it meant certain death at the hands of the Earth's warrior clan.

As much as she'd mourned his passing, at least she'd understood it. Glaring at the note in her hand, she once again read the words written in Barak's angular scrawl, asking that she cooperate with the enemy for the sake of both of their worlds. At least he had not asked for mercy—only a brief meeting at an appointed time.

He had to know that she would be waiting for him, sword in hand. Her first duty as a Sworn Guardian was to protect their people, even from themselves. Secondly, with their parents both gone, defending the family honor was her burden to carry. As much as she missed them, at least they had not lived long enough to learn of their son's disloyalty. No matter what pressures had driven him into the light, she would not, could not, forgive a betrayal of this magnitude.

Barak had been considered truly blessed in their world because of his affinity with not just the blue jewels that gave them light, but for stone of all kinds. A gift as strong as his came along perhaps once in a generation.

How could he live among the enemy when his own world needed him so badly? When *she* needed him? The fact that he'd survived the crossing at all was unusual, but what had he found in that strange place of light that had ensnared him?

An image replaced Barak's in her mind: that of the warrior whom she'd fought on her single crossing into the light. The day remained sharp in her mind despite the passage of moon cycles. She and her Blade of three had followed the trail of stolen blue jewels across with the intent of dragging the thieves back to stand trial for their crimes. Unfortunately, the warrior Paladins had already executed the traitors.

She and her Blade had hoped to return to their world without incident, but they'd run into two of the enemy at the edge of the barrier. She'd signaled her Blade to occupy the green-eyed devil while she took on his companion. She hated Paladins, but had to admire their skill with swords.

Even now she could remember the powerful grace with which her opponent had fought. With his dark eyes blazing, he'd dazzled her with his power and sleek moves. His bigger friend fought her Blade with power and muscle, but this one had danced with lethal grace and beauty.

Her warrior heart had admired his skill; her woman's body had admired him on a whole different level. More often than she cared to admit, the human had revisited her in dreams.

She shook her head. Now was not the time for such thoughts.

The barrier flickered again, almost but not quite failing completely. She moved closer, ready to face her brother one last time. Her soul ached with the pain, but she would do her duty. It was all she had left.

Cullen Finley had a decision to make. Among his friends and fellow Paladins, he'd been nicknamed "the Professor" because of his calm demeanor and thoughtful ways. If he actually did what he was contemplating, he'd change his image forever.

He studied the envelope in his hand for the umpteenth time, unable to read more than one word—Lusahn. The rest was written in an alien language. But he knew the woman the name belonged to; not everything about her, but enough to whet his appetite for more.

He had to be out of his freakin' mind.

Sure, someone had to deliver Barak's message to his sister, asking if she'd be willing to call a truce long enough to solve the mystery of who was marketing the blue stones from her world in his. It wouldn't stop the killing for good, but it might reduce it. Ever since someone had told the Others that they could buy their way into this world with blue garnets, they'd been crossing in ever-increasing numbers.

Far too many Others had died, learning too late that the Paladins and their swords were all that awaited them. And the constant fighting had taken its toll on the Paladins. Even though their genetic makeup allowed them to come back from the dead, they did so at a terrible cost.

If things continued as they had, there wouldn't be enough Paladins left to mount a defense against the crazed Others. Someone had to stem the tide of invasion, or swarms of the bloodthirsty bastards would run free in the streets, out of their minds and killing anything that moved.

Barak had planned to meet with his sister himself, but he'd been faced with a nightmare of a choice: save the human woman he loved or wait at the barrier to confront his sister. It had taken Barak less than a heartbeat to choose. After scribbling a note to his sister, he'd asked Cullen to throw it across the barrier, the same way they'd delivered the first letter asking for a meeting. Then he'd charged off after Lacey Sebastian.

Which brought Cullen back to his own situation. The note felt heavier than a simple piece of paper should. Lusahn—he'd never forgotten their one encounter. She'd left him with a small scar on his face, a much bigger one on his ribs, and her image burned into his brain.

The barrier was weakening again, the vibrant colors fading away. He had hoped that it would hold long enough to give the Seattle Paladins a chance to rest. They'd spent the entire night digging Barak out from under tons of rock, after the Other sacrificed himself to give Lacey's brother time to get her out of danger.

Barak's injuries had been serious, and someone should let his sister know why her brother couldn't come. Not just anyone—Cullen. Just that quickly, he made his decision. He would hand-deliver Barak's message and tell Lusahn why her brother wasn't there. The only question was whether she would let him live long enough to explain.

He hoped so. She would probably carve him into little pieces for even thinking such a thing, but he burned to taste the depth of her passion.

The barrier disappeared with a flash of light, bringing the shadow world beyond into view, and there she was—her pale, angry eyes glancing around before finally focusing on Cullen. With a nod, he sheathed his own weapon and stepped forward. Her blade came up to rest against his throat just as the barrier flickered back to life, cutting off his avenue of retreat. He smiled and wondered if he was about to meet his fate or his future. Holding out the envelope, he waited to find out which it would be.

Her chin came up a notch and her eyes narrowed. "Where is he?"

Her words were heavily accented, but intelligible. He didn't know if she was disappointed or relieved to see Cullen instead of her brother.

"Last night, he was injured badly enough that he couldn't be here. Before that happened, he wrote you a message." Cullen slowly raised his hand with the envelope in it.

Lusahn glanced at it long enough to read the message Barak had scrawled on it, her mouth set in a grim line. "Open it."

He did as she ordered, careful not to make a sudden move that might startle her into ending the conversation permanently. From his position, he had a close-up view of her sword and knew it had been honed with a master's hand. One wrong slip that close to his carotid artery, and he'd bleed out before she could summon help, if she would even bother. More likely, she'd wait until the barrier flickered again and roll his dead body back across for his friends to find.

He eased the letter out of the envelope and slowly brought it up to eye level for her to read. Her eyes moved swiftly down the page. He didn't need a translator to read her body language. The woman was seriously pissed and getting more so by the moment, which didn't bode well for him. Even if he could draw his sword in time to defend himself, he was stuck in this world until the next time the barrier went down.

Her silver eyes, so like her brother's, studied the paper for several seconds before turning back in Cullen's direction.

He offered her a small smile. "I know I'm not who you expected, but that doesn't change anything: we need to stop the theft of the stones. Can we talk?"

He held his hands out to the side, palm up, trying his best to look harmless.

She kept the sword firmly against his neck. "I didn't come here to talk. I came to execute a traitor."

It had occurred to him that she might not be too pleased to find out that her brother had chosen to live with the enemy, but none of them had thought she would come after Barak with deadly intent. He felt obligated to speak in Barak's defense.

"Barak has told us nothing of your world, nor has he aided us in any way that would bring your people harm. He wants to stop the theft of blue stones as much as we do."

That much was true. Barak had managed to guard his secrets well, unless he'd let something slip to either Lacy Sebastian or Laurel Young. He was as much a mystery now as when he'd first crossed the barrier and risked his own life to save Laurel's.

"He has chosen the enemy over his own people." Bitterness and anger underscored her words.

"I can't argue that. I do know that your people are dying in bigger numbers, and so are my friends. You can kill me instead of your brother, but that will only add to the bloodshed."

She stared at him in silence, then finally eased the blade away. "Paladins have always killed my people. Why do you care how many die?"

It was an honest question that deserved an honest answer. He wished he had one. He settled for the truth as he knew it. "It is my job to defend my world with my sword and my blood, just as you defend the people of this one with yours. That doesn't mean I enjoy killing."

In fact, he'd killed until his muscles and soul ached from the pain of it all. As resilient as Paladins were, eventually they did die, usually with a shitload of toxins shoved in their veins by the very people they were born to protect. No one had ever questioned the constant cycle of fighting and death because the Others crossed the barrier out of their minds and with weapons drawn.

Until Barak, that is. The bastard could swing a sword with the best of them, but he was no crazed killer, any more than Cullen himself was. Lusahn might not see it that way, though, having once faced him in battle.

"Do you remember me?" The words slipped out.

Her hand touched the side of her face, where a small scar marred her otherwise perfect skin. "Is that why you came? You thought I would show mercy because we once danced in battle?"

No, he'd come because he wanted to dance with her horizontal and naked—but this wasn't the time to mention that.

"I thought if you recognized me, you'd let me live long enough to explain what we wanted."

"And if I don't care what you want?" The sword moved closer again, but clearly she did care. It was there in the pain in her beautiful eyes and in the fact she hadn't killed him.

Yet.

"We have to do something to fill the time until

the barrier goes down again. We can talk or . . . " He let his words trail off as he let his eyes journey down the length of her long, lean body, taking his time and enjoying the trip. When he got back to her face again, he smiled.

Her pale skin flushed pink, although that could have been temper rather than interest. Then she frowned.

"We would have to talk a long time, Paladin. The barrier will be up for most of the next moon cycle."

How long was a moon cycle? On Earth, it was a little more than four weeks. But here? He had no way of knowing.

"How do you know it won't go right back down? It's been unstable for weeks."

"I was born with the same ability as my brother to know such things."

The sneaky bastard had never mentioned *that* little fact. Hell, he'd even been working with Lacey Sebastian, who was trying to find a way to predict the earthquakes and volcanic eruptions that usually preceded the barrier failing. Devlin would find Barak's talent most interesting—providing Cullen lived long enough to tell him.

He turned his head to look back at the barrier. Its bright colors were back to full strength. Son of a bitch, she was probably telling the truth. And here he was without his toothbrush or even a change of underwear.

"So how long is a moon cycle? A month? A day? A week?"

She scrunched up her nose, looking adorable as she calculated the time, probably trying to convert it from her terms into something he would understand. "Two of your weeks. Maybe a little less or more."

He glanced around the shadowy passage they stood in. "I guess I'll make myself comfortable here and wait it out."

Lusahn rolled her eyes. "And live on what, Paladin? You would either starve to death or die at the hand of my Blade on their next patrol."

He crossed his arms over his chest and widened his stance. "I'm open to suggestions, Lusahn."

His use of her name startled her. She stepped back, letting her sword fall to her side, and stared at him as if really seeing him for the first time.

"Your name?"

"Cullen. Cullen Finley. It's nice to see you again, Lusahn." He held out his hand, wondering if she would respond to the overture.

She stared at his hand as if it were a snake ready to bite her. Finally, she shifted her sword to her left hand and reached out to let her fingers brush his, sending a flash of heat through to the core of him. She felt it, too, judging by the way she immediately jerked her hand back.

Good.

She glanced around the immediate vicinity as if looking for something. Finally, she turned back to him.

"You cannot remain here, Cullen Finley, but I

can't take you with me looking like that. Stay out of the light until I return." She looked at his cargoes and bright red T-shirt with disapproval. "I will bring you something else to put on."

"Where will you be taking me?"

"Does it matter?" she asked with the first hint of a smile. "You will live longer following me than you would wandering around by yourself." She sheathed her sword and walked away into the shadows, where the light of the barrier faded into darkness.

The energy that had been buzzing through him faded away and the air around him felt colder. He looked around for a spot to rest where he wouldn't be an easy target.

He spotted a place to sit where he could watch for Lusahn's return without being out in the open. After laying his sword within easy reach, he pulled out his deck of cards and started shuffling.

The repetitive motion was soothing, but unfortunately it left his mind free to drift.

How long would it take for anyone to notice that he'd disappeared? Would they guess where he'd gone? They'd worry, and he regretted that. He had no family, but the Paladins he fought and died with were like brothers to him. Laurel Young, the Handler who took care of them when they were injured, already worried too much about them. Her lover, Devlin Bane, would kick his ass from one end of Seattle to the other for adding to her burden.

Yet he couldn't regret his decision. His gut feeling

was that he'd done the right thing by coming here. Maybe, just maybe, he could make a difference.

He let loose a huge yawn, a reminder of how long it had been since he'd slept. As tired as he was, he wouldn't be fit to defend himself if he was discovered. Maybe it wouldn't hurt to close his eyes. For a few minutes he listened to the soothing buzz of the barrier, and then there was nothing.